HAUNTING VIOLET

ALYXANDRA HARVEY

BLOOMSBURY

LONDON · BERLIN · NEW YORK · SYDNEY

Bloomsbury Publishing, London, Berlin, New York and Sydney

First published in Great Britain in July 2011 by Bloomsbury Publishing Plc
36 Soho Square, London, W1D 3QY

First published in the USA in June 2011 by Walker Publishing Company, Inc.
175 Fifth Avenue, New York, NY 10010

Text copyright © Alyxandra Harvey 2011
The moral right of the author has been asserted

ISBN 978 1 4088 1131 3

MIX
Paper from
responsible sources
FSC® C018072
www.fsc.org

Typeset by Hewer Text UK Ltd, Edinburgh
Printed in Great Britain by Clays Ltd, St Ives Plc, Bungay, Suffolk

1 3 5 7 9 10 8 6 4 2

www.bloomsbury.com
www.alyxandraharvey.com

HAUNTING
VIOLET

HAUNTING
VIOLET

PROLOGUE

1865

I was nine years old when my mother decided it was time I took part in the family business. I was pretty enough now, she said, that I might be of use. I'd grown into my ears and my long neck and might be clever enough to handle myself. Besides which, she claimed, she had no other option.

So that December, full of Christmas cheer and mulled wine, she'd changed her mind. It wasn't until later that I realised it wasn't Christmas cheer that had prompted her but desperation.

Still, she'd promised me a visit to an actual bookshop, where I might even be able to purchase my very own book if I did well. Until then I had read only discarded magazines or books tossed out into the alleys behind the shops and fine houses because of unsightly stains of damp or smoke damage.

I wasn't entirely sure what was happening, only that it was vitally important. Even Colin, who was just two years older than me but fancied himself more mature, now looked grim. He'd come with his mother from Ireland and had been orphaned and survived as a crossing boy, sweeping the street clean for the gentry, when my mother found him. She brought him home a month earlier to live with us, also contingent on how well we did that night. Crossing boys who were growing tall enough and strong enough to muscle the fine folk of Mayfair didn't get many tips. Not to mention that he was a fair hand at pickpocketing and had to change corners every day so he wouldn't get caught.

The snow was gathering slowly in the muddy streets as we left Cheapside. It turned the grey stones and dirty gutters into a landscape made of gingerbread and buttercream icing. It made me hungry just to see it. My stomach growled loudly. Mother sent me a disapproving glance.

"Violet, a lady does not betray bodily needs."

I nodded, looking down at my feet.

"A lady gets to eat, don't she?" Colin murmured, but not so loud that she could hear him. He slipped me the end of a potato, wrapped in a rag, from his pocket. Usually it was insects he delighted in pulling out of his pockets, to see me squirm. Christmas cheer must be contagious. I wished it would last all the year long.

"But what will you eat?" I whispered back.

"I'm not hungry."

He was lying. We'd both had just one piece of toast for breakfast and nothing since. I took a bite and handed him the other half.

"We'll share," I said. And then I hurried ahead so he wouldn't be able to give it back.

Lanterns burned in grimy windows, turning them to fine crystal. Swirls danced around us, like bunnies made of snow. Ice hung from lamp posts and glittered on carriage wheels. I heard singing from a pub and weeping from the next doorway. When the sun finished its descent into the Thames, the frigid wind shattered the softness.

I was wearing my very best dress—the one with only a few tears and scorch marks along the hem—and layers of flannel petticoats against the cold. Best of all was the red capelet Colin gave me that morning. He didn't say much, just shoved it at me, mumbling something about the holidays. I'd never had my own capelet before and I fancied myself very grown-up and distinguished. It didn't matter a bit that it was ragged on one side and smelled damp, or that the tip of my chilled nose was currently the same shade of red.

"I'm going to get my very own copy of *Jane Eyre*," I said, changing my mind for the third time since we'd left home. I read the first chapter once, furtively, in a dark corner of a shop before one of the clerks chased me off.

"I'd rather read about pirates," Colin said disdainfully.

"Pirates! But they never bathe."

"But they carry blunderbusses and have adventures. They meet krakens." He'd sailed from Ireland when he was eight years old and, though he wouldn't talk about the details of it, he fancied himself an expert on pirates. "There are no krakens in *Jane Eyre*, I reckon."

I couldn't argue with that.

"I could get *The Goblin Market* by Christina Rossetti," I suggested. "It's bound to have goblins."

"I suppose," he grudgingly admitted.

I was secretly entranced with the idea of a lady novelist. I should dearly love to be one. Or maybe a goblin-fighting pirate queen. It was difficult to choose sometimes.

"I could teach you to read," I offered again. "I think you'd like it."

"I can read," he scowled, but I knew he was lying again.

"Enough, you two," Mother snapped, without even turning her head to look at us. Our mouths shut instantly, as if she were a mesmerist. "I've been preparing for tonight for nearly a month now. Be quiet and look smart."

We walked for nearly an hour in silence. It never occurred to me at the time that other folk would have hired a hackney from their front door, instead of flagging one a block away from their destination. Mother wanted to arrive in proper fashion and didn't want the widow to know we were poor. I wasn't sure what the number of coins to our name had to do with talking to the dead, but then, as Mother often said, I had a lot to learn. So I never asked.

Mother didn't like to be questioned.

So I never asked her about the flowers sewn into the hem of her dress or the vial of liquid she'd slipped into my pocket either.

The townhouse we were delivered to was very grand, even with the windows curtained in black and the knocker muffled.

The widow had recently acquired that status then. We went up the front steps, not going around back to the servants' entrance where we surely belonged. I knew that much of the world. My stomach gave a funny little hitch. I slipped my hand into Colin's. He didn't grimace at me like he sometimes did; he just squeezed back.

The door swung open and a rotund butler with a curling moustache greeted us in hushed tones after Mother introduced herself. He didn't shout at us or drive us around to the proper entrance. He only stepped aside to let us in.

"Mrs Gordon is expecting you. If you'll be so good as to follow me, please."

I'd never heard anyone speak half so well as he did and there wasn't a single mend in his fine pressed suit, not even near the seams or pockets. The hall was draped in black, paintings and mirrors decorously covered, gaslights burning low. Even the drawing room, which was the same size as our entire flat, was sombre despite the gilded furniture and seashell lamps. An elderly woman wearing a gown of bombazine, the dull black material all widows wore, sat placidly on a sofa larger than my bed. Another woman sat opposite her, napping.

"Mrs Willoughby, welcome."

"Mrs Gordon." My mother bowed her head in greeting. "Allow me to offer my most sincere condolences. And may I present my daughter, Violet."

"Aren't you a pretty thing." Her smile wobbled. "My daughter had hair just like that when she was little." My mother's insistence on wrapping my hair into perfect ringlets the previous night suddenly made sense. It wasn't a style that was currently popular. "Come closer, gel, I don't bite." Perhaps not, but she smelled like talc and too much perfume and lemon drops. But since she offered me one of those lemon drops, I was inclined to like her.

"Tell me, child, do you see spirits, like your mother does?"

I swallowed, glancing at my mother. Her eyes narrowed warningly. And her eyes never narrowed like that in public; she was afraid of looking as if she had wrinkles.

"No, ma'am," I said quietly.

"My gifts only came upon me after I lost my own dear husband," Mother added smoothly, her eyes now glistening prettily. "And so I understand your pain very well indeed, Mrs Gordon."

The other old lady gave such a loud snore that she woke herself up. I tried not to giggle.

"Eh? What's that now?"

Mrs Gordon poked her with her cane. "Wake up, Agatha. The Spiritualist medium has arrived."

"Horace is dead, you daft cow," Agatha said bluntly. "You're wasting your pennies."

Mrs Gordon sniffed. "They're mine to waste, so be quiet, you old fool." She reached out to pat my hand. She wasn't wearing gloves and her skin was dry and papery, marked with brown spots. "Never mind her," she said. "That's my sister, Miss Hartington. She's an old witch."

I was instantly burning with curiosity. "I've read about witches," I confessed. "Are you really one?"

"Violet! What a thing to say," Mother said.

But Miss Hartington only laughed. "I am, my girl. The very devil of one." She squinted at me. "You do look like my niece. We were sorry to lose her so young." She cleared her throat briskly, then frowned at my mother. "Come to rob my sister then, have you?"

"Certainly not," Mother replied, her smile brittle.

"This fashion for talking to the dead is pure poppycock, if you ask me. Dead is dead."

"Agatha, that's rude even for you," Mrs Gordon said. "Shall we begin, Mrs Willoughby, before my sister's abominable manners drive you away?"

"I am at your service, ma'am," Mother said to Mrs Gordon. Then, turning to Miss Hartington, she replied, "I assure you, there is considerable evidence to the contrary."

We moved to a round table draped in a lace cloth. I itched to stroke it. It looked like fairy wings all stitched together.

"Come sit next to me," Mrs Gordon said to me. Mother hid a smile of triumph. It made me queasy to see it. Colin was still standing by the door. I sat next to Mrs Gordon.

"Could we please have hot chocolate?" I asked as my mother had instructed, even though it was very rude of me.

"Violet, such rudeness," she said straight away.

I was confused. My smile started to slip. Mrs Gordon patted my hand again. Mother had suggested I ought to cry to get the hot chocolate, but I couldn't quite manage it.

"I'll ring for a pot," Mrs Gordon offered. "If it won't disturb your work, Mrs Willoughby?"

"Not at all," my mother assured her graciously. "I apologise for my daughter's manners. She is perhaps too young to be out in society this way, but she so likes to see the Christmas bows on the houses at this time of year. I couldn't bear to leave her behind. A mother, as you well know, would do anything for her child."

Mrs Gordon nodded while her sister rang for the tea cart. "My own Amelia loved Christmas."

The long-deceased Amelia was why my mother had decided to bring me along. I was meant to distract Mrs Gordon, to keep her off balance. It was a cruel thing to do to a sad old woman.

I stared at my mother mutinously. She pinched me under the table hard enough to leave a welt and make my eyes water.

The hot chocolate finally arrived and everyone except for Colin was offered a delicate porcelain teacup. The sweet aroma of chocolate and cream smelled so good, it nearly made the whole night worthwhile. I'd never tasted any before and I sincerely hoped to taste it again soon, and often. I drank greedily until my mother spoke.

"We'll start with a prayer."

That was my next cue. As everyone closed their eyes and bowed their heads, I slipped the small bottle of liquid out of my pocket and tipped a little into each of the ladies' cups. Mother said it was medicine, brewed from opium flowers, and that nothing made from flowers could ever be harmful. Hot chocolate was meant to mask the bitter taste, as the ladies mustn't find out they were drinking laudanum. She was very emphatic about that. I still didn't understand why it had to be a secret, if it was harmless flower juice. I hesitated for a fraction of a second until my mother opened one eye.

"We'll sing the traditional hymns now," she said. She made us sing three of the longest songs in her repertoire until all of our throats were dry. Meanwhile, Colin had smothered the fire, just enough to let a chill creep over us. The old women reached for their cups, taking several deep, restorative swallows.

Mother had us hold hands. "Horace Gordon, we call on you, beloved dead, to speak to us."

Mrs Gordon's fingers trembled. She looked eagerly around the room.

"Horace Gordon," Mother called again, louder. We all reflexively looked at her. Colin seized the moment to toss a handkerchief packed with Epsom salts and table salt into the dying fire. It flared high, tinged with green and yellow, then burned white when the Epsom salts in the centre of the bundle caught.

Mrs Gordon caught her breath. Even Miss Hartington looked impressed.

And then the laudanum took effect. Their pupils dilated so that they really did look like sinister old witches. I cringed.

"He's here!" Mrs Gordon exclaimed. "Oh, Horace!"

Mother tilted her head as if she were listening to ghostly voices. I peered into the shadows, looking for a transparent foot or ectoplasmic cloak. Disappointed, I saw only Colin and a small fluttering ball of dust under one of the sofa legs.

"Mr Gordon would like me to tell you that he is well,"

Mother said. "He is happy on the other side and is with your Amelia."

"I do smell his horrid cigars," Miss Hartington admitted, stunned. She blinked several times, then yawned.

"I see him!" Mrs Gordon wept. "I see him standing right there. Like he used to be, so handsome!"

She was looking over my shoulder. A chill crept over the back of my neck.

"And Amelia, dear Amelia." She wiped her eyes. "Might I speak to her?"

"I can try," Mother said, sounding exhausted. "I have a little strength left. Amelia? Amelia, dear?"

Mrs Gordon was practically on her feet, staring into the space over the table where my mother's gaze was focused.

"She's here." Mother's arm lifted slowly, her white glove pale as moonlight. She extended her elbow with such concentrated energy, such purpose, that we were all arrested. We couldn't look away.

She pointed right at me.

I stared back at her in horror, my dark ringlets bobbing at my temples.

Mrs Gordon looked down at me, laudanum, grief and desperation clouding her vision. "Oh, Amelia. My Amelia."

She reached for me but I cringed back in my chair. Miss Hartington was smiling as though she'd drunk too much gin. Their fingers were knobbly and crooked, grasping at my hair and the mended ruffle on my pinafore.

"I don't like this," I whimpered.

Colin threw another handful of salts into the fire and it flared so high and hot that the weird green light burned the colour from us all, until we were as pale as wilted celery. The ladies barely noticed. They wouldn't stop reaching for me, looking so hopeful and pleased even as they wept.

Mother suddenly pressed the back of her hand to her forehead and gave a heartbreaking little sigh. "Alas, Amelia has left us," she declared in a strong voice that was distinctly at odds with her drooping posture.

Mrs Gordon blinked at her, then at me, her arms dropping suddenly to her side. The diamond ring on her hand hit the table with a *crack*. She looked even older than before.

"Amelia?"

"I'm sorry," Mother said. "I am simply too tired to go on." She paused delicately.

"Perhaps next week?"

CHAPTER 1

1872

A lady does not dance more than two dances with the same gentleman.

The daughter of an earl precedes the wife of the youngest son of a marquis but not the wife of the youngest son of a duke.

And I was the daughter of a Spiritualist medium lately from Cheapside.

I was used to simple rules: *don't get caught.*

I went back to memorising the many intricate and involved rules of the British aristocracy, because as convoluted and boring as they were, it was still preferable to talking to my mother.

A lady eats what she is served at dinner without comment.

I was usually hungry enough to eat what I was given without comment, but if the earl served boiled tongue or calves' foot jelly, I fully intended to wrap it in my napkin and hide it in the nearest umbrella stand.

A well-bred lady always removes her gloves at dinner but never at a ball. She should also travel with two sets of silk gloves and one of kid.

Never mind that I had only two pairs of gloves to my name to begin with, I wasn't a well-bred lady. I might look the part in my secondhand dresses with the added silk ruchings and delicate embroidery, but I'd done all that work myself, sewing until my fingers bled, to have them ready for this journey.

It was all a pretence.

And it might work well enough in our London parlour for an hour or two, but this trip was a different matter altogether. I'd never dined with earls or dowager countesses or even wealthy tradesmen. Frankly, I'd rather walk alone on the outskirts of Whitechapel. At least I knew what I was about there; I knew what the dangers were and how to avoid them.

An earl's country estate might as well be deepest India.

When the train reached the next station, I slipped on to the platform before my mother could start another lecture on regal bearing under the cover of the noise of the crowds and the steam engine.

I knew I shouldn't venture out into the crowd unaccompanied, but I needed a few moments away from my mother and the starched and proper aristocrats with whom we shared the car. They knew we didn't belong there. *I* knew we didn't belong there. Only my mother seemed determined to ignore that fact with sniffs of disdain and complaints about the violent rocking of the train and what it was doing to her delicate sensibilities.

Mother was delicate the way badgers were delicate.

Since this was likely to be my last moment to myself until later in the evening when we reached Lord Jasper's estate in

Hampshire, I rushed out, accidentally bumping into a countess with a tiered bustle that took up the space of three people. I didn't even stop to apologise properly.

Because if I had to be shut up in that box for another minute, I'd run mad.

Mother would say it was frightfully ungrateful of me, but it was true nonetheless. She'd been hours without her glass of medicinal sherry and that alone was enough to make her cross, never mind the fine ladies looking down their noses at us.

We were situated in the first-class car, which was far and away the most luxurious place I'd ever seen. It was set with chandeliers hanging from the decorated ceiling, carved mahogany tables and blue silk cushions, and was better appointed than the parlour in our house. The movement might have rattled my teeth alarmingly, but I didn't care. I did, however, feel rather bad for Colin and Marjorie stuck in the last car, with no walls to shield them from the elements or the dust and no seats to speak of. At least it wasn't raining.

I'd never been on a train before, with the great roar of sound, the billows of steam like a dragon's breath, and the rapid blur of London tenement houses followed by fields of sheep and oak groves. I rather liked it; it made me feel as if I were leaving my old life behind me.

If only that were true.

I attached myself to a tired-looking woman and her five daughters, all dressed in browns, like plump, happy sparrows. I trailed behind them as if I were a member of the family, a sixth daughter in a black-and-white striped dress. It wasn't a travelling dress exactly since I'd never had occasion to travel, but it was dashing and hid the dirt well enough. My adopted family afforded me enough protection to see me to the ladies' necessity and then to a lounge set aside for ladies to procure tea and soup. I didn't have money for tea but I didn't care. I didn't even know what station we were at. I only knew it wasn't our narrow house near Wimpole Street and that was good enough for me.

Our house was far superior to any of our previous residences, but it felt tainted. We'd only been able to afford it after Miss Hartington died last year. She'd outlived Mrs Gordon, which was a surprise to us all. We'd been visiting once a month for years, facilitating conversations with her dead husband and daughter. She finally joined them, but Miss Hartington, though older and more cross, stubbornly lived on. More surprising still, when she eventually succumbed to a lung fever, her solicitor contacted us with a tidy and surprising sum of three hundred and fifty pounds, which she had willed to me, having no other children or close living relations of her own. Mother took every farthing and rented us a house within walking distance of a very fine neighbourhood.

Now we had the veneer of respectability, heaven help us, and doors opened to Mother all over London. When she wasn't drunk on sherry, she was drunk on fame.

But this was our trickiest demonstration yet. Lord Jasper wasn't just an earl; he was clever and kind and well versed in Spiritualist matters. Not to mention that we were travelling to him, instead of working in the comfort of our specially rigged parlour. There were so many pitfalls it hardly bore thinking about.

The crowd had thinned on the platform, with most passengers still in the lounges, lingering over their supper. The air was thick with steam and burning coal, the wind pushing the iron hinges of the wooden signs into constant creaking. I skirted a pile of trunks, taller than I was and teetering dangerously, and ran straight into three boys about my age.

They looked to be from the second-class compartments by the state of their suits and smart waistcoats. And they were smiling that certain kind of smile that sent an alarm through me, lifting the hairs on the back of my neck.

I should have preferred being crushed by the luggage.

"Well, what have we here, lads?"

I looked away, refusing to meet their eyes. Colin told me once that if I came upon an angry dog, I shouldn't meet his eyes as it would be interpreted as a challenge. I adjusted my grip on my parasol. It was plain, with no ruffles or silk roses, but pointy all the same.

"Travelling all alone, are you?" one of them asked with what could be described only as a leer worthy of any penny dreadful.

Blast.

"Let me pass," I demanded. Where the devil was everyone?

"There's a toll, love," he insisted. "Didn't you know?"

We were well hidden by the luggage and a shroud of steam, thick as London fog. The third boy looked uncomfortable, as if he wanted to stop his companions but didn't know how. Fat lot of good his squirming would do me.

"Give us a kiss, then."

When the ringleader reached for me, I jabbed my parasol at him. I was rather proud of my aim. It should have hit him painfully between the ribs. If I hadn't been wearing a corset and had a proper range of motion, that is. I wasn't used to wearing corsets, nor the way they restricted my movements and altered my ability to breathe properly.

The young man just grabbed the end of my parasol and held on, smirking. I tugged. He tugged back harder, and I lost my footing slightly. The edge of the tracks loomed close. The bone stays of my corset poked me in the ribs. His friends laughed.

"Now that's not nice, is it?" he said. I gave up the struggle and decided to follow with his last yank of the parasol. My sudden weight took him by surprise, nearly toppling him. One of them grabbed my elbow.

I opened my mouth to scream.

A gloved hand closed over my chin, fingers digging into my lips. "None of that now."

And then suddenly I was free, sailing backwards without warning.

"Get off her!"

I hit the trunks, bruising my shoulder. A hat box fell to the ground. I pushed my hair out of my eyes just in time to see Colin rearing back to punch the ringleader.

"No!" I leaped forward, grabbing his arm. The momentum of his swing had me sliding forward but at least it stopped his fist from connecting. They glared at each other as the passengers began to trickle around us, returning to their cars. Colin frowned down at me.

"Violet," he muttered, shaking me loose. "Are you daft?"

"Are you?" I shot back as the crowd pulled us away from them.

"I could've taken that tosser," he said, clearly insulted.

"I know that, but they were rich, or rich enough, anyway. Do you think they would have shrugged it off if one of them had had their nose broken by a manservant from third class?" And no doubt he would have done just that. He was taller than each of them and had broad shoulders, for someone of only eighteen years old. And he'd survived the alleys of London, whereas the others hadn't likely ever made it east of Covent Garden.

"Did they hurt you?" His voice was gentle, his blue eyes searching.

"No." I shook my head. "I'm fine. Thanks to you."

"What the devil are you doing wandering about alone?" he snapped. "And dressed like a bloomin' lady, the way you are. You have to be careful now, princess."

And there was the Colin I knew.

"'Tisn't proper," he insisted as he led me along the platform like a petulant child. His Irish accent always thickened when he was upset. I jerked my arm out of his grasp.

"Proper?" I echoed, nodding to my mother, who was flirting with no fewer than two earls from our compartment and three gentlemen from the car behind us. As if any impropriety I might muster could even hope to compete with my mother's expertise.

She still didn't know I'd discovered her real name: Mary Morgan. Mary Morgan was just another poor girl, scratching out a living, trying to keep her belly full while she yearned for pretty dresses and carriage rides. Celeste Willoughby was a gifted widow, crushed by the tragic death of her husband, leaving her young, beautiful, and with child.

Never mind that Mother had never married.

Or that she sometimes claimed my father was a great lord who had dallied with her when she had been a lady's maid in Wiltshire. I couldn't even be sure she'd ever set foot out of London. More often than not, she just muttered that I ought to be grateful she'd kept me at all. I'd only got that much out of her because she'd had one too many glasses of sherry.

Mother thought drinking sherry was dignified and sophisticated.

And if one glass was what the beau monde drank, then surely three glasses must be three times more sophisticated.

She was right, I supposed. Not about the sherry, of course, but that I ought to be grateful. She could have left me at some draughty orphanage or sent me to the workhouse—something she pointed out to me on a weekly basis. I was pretty enough to be useful now; pretty girls, after all, can marry rich no matter what their station. And even better, I was not so beautiful as to draw any attention away from her. My place was comfortably in her shadow.

If there was one thing she craved even more than expensive liqueur, it was to be the toast of polite society, to be invited to lavish dinner parties and weekends in the country. And Mary, with her Cockney accent and her questionable past, could never accomplish such a feat, whatever her physical attributes might be.

Mrs Celeste Willoughby, however, could.

Colin sighed. "You'd best go. And I should see how Marjorie's getting on."

Mother liked the idea of arriving with a manservant and our own lady's maid, even though Marjorie was actually just a maid-of-all-work. Mother had rescued Marjorie from a brothel just after we'd moved into our new house.

In my less charitable moments, I wondered if she'd rescued Marjorie and Colin so they would serve her out of loyalty and never ask for proper payment.

Colin acted as butler when necessary, servant boy when heavy things needed lifting, and guard for my mother when it would add to her mystique. She liked to tell people that her spirit guides had cautioned her to have her own protector, as her gifts were such a weighty responsibility.

I didn't believe in spirit guides. Or spirits.

Colin and I exchanged a commiserating roll of the eyes before I made my way to my mother's side. Her dark hair was coiled under a small black hat edged with a lace veil, carefully pinned back so it wouldn't obscure her face. To be fair, she was uncommonly beautiful; the trouble was, she knew it.

"Mo—" I cut myself off. She hated it when I called her Mother in front of handsome men. It made her peevish and sour for hours afterwards. I swallowed, trying not to notice the way she stood far too close to a man with prodigious whiskers and a neat moustache.

"Violet, come along," she said, scolding me. "Where on earth have you been?" The scolding was for everyone else's benefit. I knew full well she hadn't yet realised I had gone. "Inside now, and not another word." Which meant she was afraid I would give her away.

I hadn't given her away in the last seven years, since that first visit to Mrs Gordon, nor at any of the other sittings we provided. I didn't know why she thought I'd choose to do so on some train platform without a Spiritualist for miles. I found my seat as her giggle tinkled, like champagne flutes touching. Even one of the disapproving matrons in our car lifted her head, momentarily enchanted. Her scowl returned, dark as a thundercloud, when she spotted my mother stepping nimbly up the stair, wasp-waisted and beautiful.

Mother lowered herself gracefully into her seat. "I should have brought my own cushion," she said, a little too loudly. "I can't think who might have used this one before me."

The truth was, she loved the blue silk and would hide the cushion under her crinolines to keep, at the first chance she got. The warning whistle pierced through the steam and the train lurched into movement, jostling us. We left the station and the red roofs of the village, plunging once more into the green countryside. The sun glinted off a meandering creek as it set. There was something lulling about the motion of the train, once you got used to it.

I leaned my temple against the window, content to decipher shapes in the lilac-coloured clouds above us and then the
stars when it grew too dark to see anything else. We barely saw
the stars in London, because of the coal smoke. We barely
even saw the sky.

As we approached the village, the glass grew oddly misty,
then abruptly bloomed with frost.

It was nearly the end of summer and far too warm for frost
of any kind.

I glanced about but no one else seemed to notice anything
out of the ordinary. Mother was resting her eyes so she wouldn't
arrive with lines on her face. Most of the men were reading newspapers; one snored loudly. Two ladies bent over their
embroidery hoops. Everyone else appeared to be dozing.

The frost travelled slowly, thickly. The lamplight made it
look like lace, but it burned to the touch. I snatched my fingers away, sitting up straight, my heart thumping loud and
slow under my corset bones. Behind the thin ice, where the
glass was still glass, the hills and hamlets that ought to have
been dark glowed softly. It wasn't torchlight I was seeing, or
candles in cottage windows. We weren't that near to the village
yet; it was still all fields and oak groves. Otherwise I might
have taken the lights for hundreds of candles, even though they
flickered with a faintly blue glow, ghostly and cold.

The train cut through swarms of them, like giant fireflies,
but not a single passenger noticed. I was the only one gaping
at the scene outside. I'd read about corpse candles before, but
I'd thought them idle superstition. A quaint folk tradition.

I did not credit them to be the terrifying unearthly light that now fell on my face and made me feel wretched and ill and shiver as if I were up to my neck in a snowdrift. I understood the warning not to follow will-o'-the-wisps, to cast your eyes downwards when you walked at night.

I thought I saw flashes of pale faces, pale hands, pale teeth.

And then, a face was suddenly there on the other side of the window.

Long translucent hair drifted as if the girl were underwater. There was a cloying scent in the still air, like lilies wilting by green water. She dripped as if it were raining, floated as if she were made of dandelion fluff. She wore a white dress layered with flounces.

Her eyes met mine, cold as starlight. I jerked backwards, yelping.

My mother opened one eye crossly. "Violet, really."

The girl faded, tattering like mist under a spear of strong sunlight.

The ghostly candles guttered and went out.

CHAPTER 2

It was past dinner by the time we were handed up into Lord Jasper's carriage, which he'd been kind enough to send for us; otherwise we'd have been crammed into a public coach next to some sweaty man who smelled like ham. Lord Jasper's coach had plush velvet-covered cushioned seats and gleaming lacquered wood. The windows even had little drapes. We didn't speak much as the carriage rolled down the narrow streets and on to the open lanes. The hills spread out all around, the road edged with wild flowers and tangled blackberry hedges. I wondered if highwaymen still roamed these parts, and if one might stop us, face covered with a black mask. He would demand our jewellery, but one look at my mother and he would fall in love and carry her away on his horse.

Or not.

The carriage rattled over the badly pockmarked road.

After so much travelling my bottom was beginning to grow numb, and I was craving fresh air and sunlight. I envied Colin up on top with the driver, the warm summer wind on his face. I wished I could read one of my novels, but it always made my stomach uncertain to read in a moving vehicle.

I'd never been to a lord's country house before, of course, just as I'd never been on a train. I could imagine the wide gardens, the fat roses and the thick, dark woods. Finally the lane curved gently and we were afforded our first view of Rosefield, Lord Jasper's country house. It sat in a veritable moat of roses, all red and white and scattering petals on to the grass, lit with torches in the gardens and along the lane and the walkways. The house itself was mostly pale grey stone with towers and turrets and a small section off to one side that clearly dated back to Queen Elizabeth's time.

Mother looked distinctly satisfied as she surveyed our surroundings. She was already imagining herself as the lady of the manor. Lord Jasper might be a widower, but he showed no particular affection or matrimonial intent towards her, which was a source of bewildered frustration for her. He truly seemed to honour her gifts, such as they were. It made me sad to think about it.

I turned my attention back to the tall, handsome footman who was waiting patiently for me to take his hand and descend from the carriage. Colin looked at me blandly. I knew perfectly well that he was remembering last spring when I stumbled out of a hired hack and sprawled, rather spectacularly, into a muddy puddle. Rosefield's lane was dry and immaculately kept. No rain would dare fall on the first day of such a summer fete.

Rosefield's housekeeper, Mrs Harris, was a dour-looking woman, tall and thin as a lamp post. Her grey hair was scraped mercilessly off her face. Even my mother's loveliest smile only engendered a narrowing of the eyes.

"Mrs Willoughby," my mother introduced herself, steel lacing her tone. "And my daughter, Miss Violet Willoughby."

The housekeeper met the declaration with her own steel. "A pleasure, ma'am. I am the housekeeper, Mrs Harris. This way, if you please."

She led us past gleaming tables set with crystal vases full of roses, and up the carpeted staircase. Maids hurried up and down the hallway, which opened on to several chambers filled with chattering guests. Mrs Harris marched into one of the open doorways and paused, waiting for us to catch up.

"Lord Jasper picked this suite especially for you, Mrs Willoughby, and for your daughter."

The sitting room was all pale pink silk and velvet, with plush chairs and damask curtains. The door to the left opened on to a bed chamber, also done in roses and cream, with flowers on every available surface. The other bedroom was slightly smaller, with walls papered in green silk and my valises already set by the wardrobe. It was easily three times the size of my room back home, with paintings, lush carpets and my own mahogany writing desk.

"It's beautiful," I murmured, excited. I wasn't sure but I thought Mrs Harris might be trying to smile back.

"Lovely," my mother agreed from the sitting room. "Quite suitable."

I almost laughed. Our town house was decidedly sparse upstairs in the family rooms where no visitors went. We saved all of the best pieces for the parlour and the dining room, which, admittedly, looked well.

"Tea will be served shortly in the gardens," Mrs Harris announced. "Down the stairs and to your left, next to the conservatory." Her boot heels clacked all the way down the hall.

Mother hugged me briefly, smelling of lavender water and sherry. "If we play our cards right, my girl, this week could change our lives."

I knew what was behind that look she wore, smug as an alley cat with a bowl of cream. I smiled weakly and went to my room to change into a less rumpled dress.

<hr />

The gardens were immaculate, the flagstones swept clean and the potted flowers neatly clipped. Women wore silk dresses and pearl brooches; men stood smartly by in their sombre suits. Tea was served in china cups. Oil lamps burned on the tables and torches flamed at the edge of the lawns. It was like a fairy garden, and I was the changeling child. I tried not to look as nervous as I felt.

Mother pinched me. Hard.

Reverie broken, I curtsied to the guests who had just been introduced. I hadn't been paying attention and had no idea who they were. Mother sipped her tea demurely after declining an offer of wine or champagne. I ogled the cakes with the thick cream icing and the little sandwiches filled with ham or cucumbers next to bowls of watercress salad.

"I once fitted five of those little egg things in my mouth in one go," someone declared quite proudly from my right.

I laughed and turned to hug Elizabeth, despite our mothers' disapproving glances. We should have clasped hands or curtsied, we should have been quiet and polite, but I would have been bereft and adrift in a sea of dull old people without Elizabeth. We had met only a handful of times at various seances and Spiritualist events but had since written dozens of long letters back and forth. She was Lord Jasper's goddaughter and the most amusing person I'd ever met, not to mention my only true friend, since I wasn't afforded many opportunities to meet girls my own age. I had never been away to school where girls became fast friends and learned how to pour tea. I couldn't bear to think of how lonely I might have been without Elizabeth. Even if I did have to keep our secrets from her as well.

She was still grinning at me over the egg sandwiches. Her plump body had been stuffed into a steel-boned corset by her mother's maid. She was pretty, in a wholesome, cheerful kind of way. "Have some of the watercress," she said. "It's lovely."

I knew how watercress was grown in London, in the sewage run-off in Camden Place. "No, thank you."

"Just as well. I can't wait another moment." She took me abruptly by the hand, dragging me into the house. "I don't know what I would have done if you'd decided to have a rest. I'm turning blue as it is."

"Where are we going?" I asked as she pulled me through several sitting rooms and down a long corridor. She'd spent enough summers here to know exactly where she was going, but she stopped so suddenly that I crashed into her. She grunted as we stumbled into a tidy room with a massive desk in the centre and books lining the walls. This was the only room so far that didn't smell of roses. It was all ink and brandy.

"Oh, Lizzie," I said, drinking in all the books.

"Yes, yes—books," she said, hardly impressed. "You should see the library. Anyway, who cares about that? Help me!" She spun around, frantically pointing to the back of her corset. "I feel like a breakfast sausage," she complained. "Untie me, won't you?"

I knew the routine. This wasn't the first time we'd been in this situation—in fact, the very first time I had met Elizabeth we had been at a tea dance, where she cornered me under a shadowy decorative palm and begged me to release her from "the dark chains that bound her", her words exactly. It had taken me a moment to decipher what, precisely, she was asking me to do.

"Vi, stop daydreaming! I can't breathe. I'm joining the Rational Dress Society the very moment we are back in London, and I fully intend to leave their pamphlets under Mother's pillow and tucked into her corsets." She claimed this in every one of her letters, in spite of, or rather because of, her mother's vociferous protests. Lady Ashford was petite, barely reaching my shoulder, and still in possession of a decidedly girlish figure. She couldn't understand how her daughter was plump as a cinnamon bun.

"Vi!"

"Sorry." I hurried to loosen her stays, which required a rather ungenteel position with Elizabeth bending over a settee with the back of her skirts up over her head as I struggled to find my way through layers of lace and petticoats. I would have shed my own corset, if I'd dared.

"Stop squirming," I muttered, spitting a silk ribbon out of my mouth.

"Well, hurry up." Her voice was muffled. "Have you got it?"

"Almost." I pushed aside more fabric. "Your petticoats weigh a blasted tonne!"

"I know!" She wiggled again.

"Ahem!"

We both froze at the amused cough.

CHAPTER 3

Violet?" Elizabeth's bottom still tilted up like a sunflower seeking sunlight. "Vi, was that you?"

I swallowed, trying not to release the giggle welling up in my throat.

"Whatever are you two doing?" Frederic drawled.

Elizabeth jumped as if she'd suffered an electric jolt. There was a flurry of panicked movement and my hair became caught in one of the grommets of her corset. Suddenly, my face was pressed up against her backside. She squealed. Then she tugged. My hair pulled at my scalp. She tugged harder. I squeaked, and we both tumbled to the ground in a tangle of lace and ribbons.

"Bollocks!" Elizabeth shouted.

"Such language for a debutante," Frederic murmured.

Elizabeth's face was red when I finally freed myself and we pushed ourselves up from where we were sprawled across the rug. "I'm not a debutante yet," she muttered at him.

"I can see why."

She bit her lip. She had been nursing a *tendre* for Frederic for over two years, picturing him kissing her hand and declaring his love, while in reality he still thought of her as a child. His father had gone to school with Lord Jasper. Frederic was down from the same school for the week and thought himself quite above us. He was only back for his quarterly allowance. I hated that Elizabeth might suffer a single moment over him.

"If you must know, we were fixing a tear in her gown." I'd learned that a brisk tone and no trace whatsoever of a Cockney accent made most people pay attention. I'd practised elocution and diction for hours every day, along with how to pick a pocket and wash tea so it could be boiled a second time. "Furthermore, a gentleman doesn't laugh at a lady. And you might help her up, actually."

He bowed towards us. "I beg your pardon." He offered his hand to Elizabeth to help her up. Her eyelashes fluttered. Then he ruined it by speaking. "Up you go, Beth old girl," he said amiably as he pulled her up. "*Oof!*"

She blushed, looking down at her plump self. She nearly missed his wink before he turned and walked away, chuckling to himself. I scrambled to my feet, not waiting for assistance. I counted under my breath, waiting for the expected reaction: one . . . two . . . three—

"Oh, Violet." She sighed dreamily and right on cue.

"Oh, Lizzie," I mimicked, smiling to let her know I was only teasing.

"Isn't he utterly divine? Beautiful?"

"Somehow, I think he'd disagree with that last one." And not enough with the first.

"All right." She waved her hand dismissively. "Handsome then. Do you think he noticed me?"

"We were sprawled in a heap of twitching limbs and lace at his feet. He would have had to have been unconscious *not* to notice us."

She wrinkled her nose. "I meant, do you think he noticed I'm nearly ready for the marriage mart?"

I didn't know how to reply. I didn't want to hurt her feelings, but I wasn't sure Frederic noticed anything other than cards and port. He was twenty years old, after all, and quite wealthy. He was acting exactly as he was expected to.

Her cheeks were red. "We should return before Mother wonders where we've gone off to. Heaven forbid we might be somewhere enjoying ourselves!"

I pretended not to see her pick up the handkerchief that had fallen out of Frederic's coat and hide it in one of the pockets in her skirt.

⟫⟪

A knock woke me in the middle of the night.

I stumbled across the room, nearly tripping on the hem of my nightdress. When I opened my door, Colin stood on the other side. He cocked one eyebrow impatiently.

"Aren't you ready?"

I mumbled something unintelligible through a wide yawn and turned away to find my dressing gown. I knew he was smirking at me without looking. He always smirked at me, ever since we'd moved to a better address and I'd been given proper ladies' dresses to wear.

I found my slippers and he handed me a covered basket of supplies. We made our way down the hallway as quietly as possible. The standing clock ticked loudly, like a giant insect in the summer woods. It was so late that even the moonlight coming in through the windows was tired and pale. Everyone else was asleep, especially my mother, who claimed she needed to look her best for tomorrow's entertainments. It didn't matter as much if I was haggard with fatigue, and it mattered not at all for Colin.

"Stay on the edge," Colin advised as we descended the staircase. "The stairs won't creak that way."

I didn't ask him how he came to know that. I just wanted to get this over and done with and go back to my warm bed. If we were caught, there'd be no redeeming the situation. This part made me so nervous I felt a little ill. Not to mention that Rosefield was such a large manor house, we might wander about the rest of the night and never find the right parlour.

"Did you know your prince has finally arrived?"

"He's not my prince," I snapped. I didn't know why, but Colin always managed to get a rise out of me. At least he didn't slip toads in my bed the way he had when we were younger. He'd stopped the morning he woke up with a perfectly placed beetle on his face. If only it had been so easy to stop him from making sarcastic comments about Xavier Trethewey. Colin disliked him for no reason other than he liked to be contrary.

There was nothing offensive about Xavier, after all. He was kind and well-mannered and handsome. And his father was in trade, which mattered to the peerage but mattered not a whit to Mother because he was also wealthy. We were the last people on earth to look down on someone because of their situation. Xavier paid me several compliments and was seeking out my company with enough frequency that Mother had begun to look smug when his name was mentioned.

Which was never a good sign.

I was frowning so hard I nearly walked into a potted fern.

"Pay attention, princess."

I would have pinched Colin but he was noticeably out of reach. His blue eyes gleamed knowingly. He opened his mouth to make another quip and then shut it again with a snap. I frowned at him. He grabbed my elbow and hauled me unceremoniously into a miniature jungle of ficus trees and ferns near the stairs. His body wedged against mine. He'd been drinking mint tea; I could smell it on his breath.

"What are you—" His hand clamped over my mouth. I glared at him and contemplated biting his thumb.

"Shhh," he whispered, very quietly, so close I felt his lips brush my earlobe. I suppressed a ticklish sort of shiver.

Then I heard the footsteps. I froze. Colin nodded grimly. We couldn't be caught. It would ruin either Mother's reputation or mine. And we both knew she'd sacrifice mine without a second thought if it meant she could keep accepting invitations to country manor houses. I held my breath. Colin was a solid presence next to me, the warmth of his skin radiating through his thin shirt and my dressing gown. It was suddenly very warm in our little corner, as if we truly were in an exotic jungle full of orchids and tigers. I had to release my breath and for some reason it trembled.

A man I didn't recognise came down the corridor. He was very tall and thin, with shadows under his eyes. He looked wretched, muttering to himself. A snifter of brandy dangled from his left hand, spilling drops on the carpet, as he appeared to have forgotten he held it.

"Please," he begged out loud, even though he was utterly alone. He couldn't know we were hiding nearby. I crept an inch closer to Colin just in case. He shifted so his arm curled around me. His hand on my lower back was a distractingly pleasant feeling. "Please come back."

I looked away, uncomfortable. I'd never got used to seeing such naked grief. I thought it ought to remain private, despite what we did for a living. It was easy, after a while, to sort out the weepers who wanted dramatics and attention and the ones who were broken inside.

This young man, scarcely older than Colin, was definitely broken inside.

He passed us without a glance and stumbled up the stairs.

We waited a moment before hurrying to the drawing room and ducking inside.

"Do you know who he was?" I whispered, taking a paper packet from the basket. There weren't many preparations needed for tomorrow, but it was important for us to have a chance to investigate the room for the main event at the end of the week.

"No," Colin said. "Must be a guest. A servant wouldn't help himself to the brandy."

"I wonder what's happened to him."

Colin just shrugged. "We should hurry in case he wanders back down."

He was right. I emptied out the hairpins and then folded up the packet and slid it neatly under one of the legs of the large round table set in the back corner. With the lace table-cloth fluttering over the mahogany surface, the legs were mostly hidden from view. No one was likely to notice it, and we'd remove it straight away after we were done.

"There's a rug here," I said, crawling back out and standing up. "That'll make it easier as well."

"Good." He circled the parlour, looking behind plants and cupboards and paintings. He lifted the cushion off a chair. "This one," he said, "might do if we need to hide anything. But not for tomorrow."

I turned on one heel. "There isn't anywhere to hide the bellows."

He frowned, turning as well. "That'll be a problem."

I wrinkled my nose. "She'll think of something."

"She always does," he agreed.

We poked around some more, memorising the layout and the nooks and secret crannies created by the furniture. The fashion for long tablecloths and hangings on every chair and table helped our cause. I thought of Lord Jasper with his kind face, sitting next to my mother as she shivered and made dramatic pronouncements.

Colin glanced at me. "All right then?"

"I suppose so. There's not much else we can do tonight in any case."

"Chin up, Violet," he said with a smirk. "Maybe your prince will take you away from all of this."

<hr>

"Miss Willoughby." Marjorie opened the door. Her blonde hair was caught in a neat bun under a white cap and she was smiling conspiratorially. "Mr Trethewey is waiting for you in the parlour."

It was early for a visit, especially from someone like Xavier. Mostly, his kind slept past noon because they were awake until dawn, dancing in flower-decorated ballrooms. I slept past noon because I was up until all hours reading novels by candlelight. It was a habit no one could break me of, not even my mother.

I let Marjorie help me into my corset, leaving it looser than Mother liked. She tied hers so tight I wondered how she could eat, let alone breathe. "I suppose Mother's already told him I'll be down presently?" I tucked a wayward piece of lace back under my blouse. It needed mending.

"Yes, miss. And she's ordered tea and a pot of chocolate. She would like you to hurry." Marjorie helped me with my buttons. It wasn't my most fashionable dress, but anyone who called for me at nine o'clock in the bloody morning would have to take what he was given.

"Thank you, Marjie." I smiled at her. "I can manage the rest."

She bobbed a quick curtsy and hurried off to the rest of her chores.

Without time to brush my hair, I merely twisted it into a rope and secured it at my nape with a handful of pins. I was stifling another yawn and rushing down the stairs when I nearly bumped into a maidservant carrying a pile of clean linen.

"Sorry!" I mumbled around a pin I'd yet to put in my hair.

She ignored me. I stepped out of her way, watching her continue up the landing. Her gaze hadn't even flickered my way.

That's when I noticed I could see right through the hem of her dress, the glow of white from her blouse and pale skin.

I shivered under a sudden icy draught.

I really shouldn't be out of bed so early.

It clearly wasn't good for me.

I was still gaping when Colin frowned up at me through the railing from the chequered marble floor of the front hall. "What you doing, then?"

"What?" I blinked, forcing my mouth closed.

"Doesn't your prince know by now that you're not a morning person?"

"Oh, do be quiet."

"Are you wearing that?"

I just stared at him. "Don't you start," I muttered, feeling back to my normal self. Nothing like Colin's smirks to set things back to rights. "This dress isn't that old."

"Aren't you forgetting something?"

"What?"

"Shoes."

I looked down at my bare toes. I hadn't even remembered my stockings. If I'd been a duchess's daughter, it would have been shocking. As it was only me, and it was early in the morning, it was hardly surprising. Not that I thought for one moment that Xavier would have seen it that way. I made a sound of frustration and whirled round, dashing back up the stairs to my bedroom. Colin's laughter followed me the entire way.

By the time I'd reached the door to the parlour, with my shoes properly in place, I was awake enough to care that my hair was escaping its pins again. I stuffed it back in, scraping my scalp until every thick curl was ruthlessly secured.

Xavier stood up when I entered. "Miss Willoughby, pray forgive the early intrusion."

"Not at all," my mother said before I could reply. She stood up as well, a steely glint in her eye. I peered into her cup, wondering if it was filled with lukewarm tea or sherry. "Do excuse me," she added.

She swept out of the room, leaving the door open. We really ought to have had a chaperone, even for a morning visit over tea, but Mother was hoping Xavier would offer for me. She wasn't above unsubtly manoeuvring us all to fall in line with her wishes. Besides, I supposed it wasn't entirely risqué with the door open and servants rushing back and forth. I'd seen high-minded social mamas do far worse in the name of securing a husband for their daughters. An elderly, grey-haired grandmother once tripped up an eligible bachelor on his way to the gaming table so that he would fall at her grand-daughter's satin-slippered feet. Instead he'd landed on a footman and broken his arm.

"Miss Willoughby?"

I turned my attention back to Xavier with a start. His brown eyes were warm and focused entirely on my face. "I'm sorry . . . yes?"

"Are you quite well?"

"Certainly." I fought back a blush. Had I been staring blankly at the hideous cabbage-rose wallpaper?

"I shouldn't like to be forward, but I wanted a chance to see you."

"That's very kind of you." I didn't know what else to say. "More tea, Mr Trethewey?" I filled his cup and passed him the sugar bowl. He smiled, stirred, and tapped the edge of his spoon on the rim of his cup precisely three times.

"I hope you'll save me a dance at the ball this week?"

"Of course."

"And I should like you to meet my parents," he said. "They'll be arriving later today."

I swallowed nervously. "Thank you. I should be happy to meet them." In fact, I wanted nothing less. They'd know right away that I wasn't good enough for him.

He stood and came over to my chair, reaching for my hand. I'd forgotten my gloves again. The leather of his glove was soft and warm on my bare skin. He was always dressed impeccably and properly, no matter the hour. I stood up and we were very close.

"Mr Trethewey?"

"Violet," he exclaimed, even though we hadn't yet given each other leave to use our first names. He lifted my hand to his mouth. No man had ever been this close to me before, and certainly none had ever taken my ungloved hand in his. Except for Colin, but that had been to push my fingers into the jam pot.

Xavier kissed those same fingers. It sent tingles up my arm.

"Violet, you must know . . ." He shook his head. "Forgive me. Forgive me," he said again, seemingly startled by his own behaviour. It happened so fast, I didn't know what to think. I didn't even have time to reply before he bowed and rushed out of the parlour.

⌘

"Violet," my mother snapped. "Do stop squirming."

I wondered what else, exactly, I was expected to do with my petticoats up over my head and my mother and Marjorie crouched at my feet like goblins. Marjorie's mouth was full of pins. Mother tightened the rope around my thigh.

"Ouch," I complained.

"It needs to be secure," she insisted.

I grabbed on to the back of the settee so I wouldn't topple. "But I also need to be able to feel my legs so I can walk," I muttered. "It'll be rather obvious if I limp into the parlour."

She narrowed her eyes at me. "A little cooperation, if you please."

"Is this really necessary?" I shifted, trying to ease the chafing of the fireplace bellows now strapped to my leg. It was heavy and cumbersome. At home Marjorie stood outside in the hallway with the bellows, pumping air into a small hole in the wall, positioned just so. We didn't have that luxury at the moment.

"Yes," she said, checking the knots. She was beautiful in a black silk gown with white silk orchids along the frilled ruchings. Crystal beads glittered in her hair. I'd stolen those beads from a box outside a shop being fumigated for rats.

I knew from experience that there was a certain kind of beauty that made people shut their eyes to everything else. Mother had it in spades, and she assured me that I had it too; I only needed to learn to use it. I didn't think dragging my numb leg behind me would be a particularly good start.

"I should think you would be a little more enthusiastic, Violet. I am trying to secure you a good future. Or would you rather sew hats for fine ladies until your fingers bleed? Personally, I don't think you'd care for it."

She liked to lecture me that I was too soft, made that way by her hard work. It was virtually unheard of for a pregnant maid to return to London and make a better life for herself, but as it turned out, Mother had quite the talent for telling mourners exactly what they wanted to hear. And being in a state of perpetual half mourning lent her an air of gentility. Most Spiritualists preferred white for funerals; after all, they held it as one of their most important tenets that death, being just another journey, was nothing to be feared.

White, however, did nothing for Mother's complexion.

She was at her best with her pale skin delicately bordered with black silk. The contrived air of mourning was meant to curtail too many questions since my father wasn't actually dead. Though I suppose he might well be; I had no way of knowing since I wasn't exactly sure who he was in the first place. Nevertheless, she wore black silks and velvets and delicate cameos. And the only reason she hadn't forced me into a fictional half mourning too was because lavender made me look like week-old mutton.

And despite what one might say about her, she was clever and could read people's mannerisms the way I read novels. There was nothing so useful, as she was fond of saying, as knowing exactly what a gentleman or a rich old lady with more gold than family needed to hear.

Or nothing so useful, apparently, as being able to gracefully glide about the parlour with a pair of bellows tied to your leg. I didn't think they taught this particular skill at the finishing schools.

These kinds of tricks, along with Miss Hartington's dying kindness, were the only reason we were able to live nearer to Mayfair than the East End, where we belonged. If we walked from our new house we could see the peerage promenade through Hyde Park on chestnut bays. It was also how we became able to afford gilded mirrors and two new gowns in the most current fashion, with flounces and a matching bonnet trimmed with red roses. I loved those new dresses. I'd never had one before now that wasn't several years outdated and already worn at the seams.

But I still hated how we took advantage of people sunk so deep into their grief that any natural scepticism was lost. The curiosity seekers didn't bother me as much. It was the experience they wanted, along with the cachet of having sat hand to hand with a born sensitive. They seemed to care little for evidence of any kind once they saw my mother, all beautiful dark curls and eyes like warm chocolate.

I sincerely hoped these sitters fell into that safe category.

It wasn't long before Marjorie finished pinning the inside layer of my petticoats so that they wouldn't catch and bunch around the bellows. Then she shook out my skirts. Mother stepped back, eyeing me carefully.

"Very good," she said finally. "Now take a turn about the room."

The first step sent me sprawling across the carpet. I landed hard on my elbow and knocked the breath from my lungs for a moment.

Mother sighed irritably. "Violet, a little effort, if you please."

"Are you all right, miss?" Marjorie asked, helping me to my feet.

"She's fine." Mother waved her hand dismissively. "Try again."

By the third time across the sitting room I was walking more like a debutante and less like a wounded hippopotamus. I was feeling rather pleased with my efforts until Colin came in.

"What's wrong with your leg?"

I sighed. Mother scowled. "Try harder, Violet."

Colin met my eyes steadily before turning to my mother. "Lord Jasper is asking for you," he said. "Why doesn't Violet stay here a little longer and practise?" He was trying to give me some time to myself. He knew how flustered I got before a sitting, never mind one at Rosefield with my mother breathing fire down my neck.

"Very well." Mother smoothed her already perfect hair back. She paused before sailing out of the room like a glossy ship.

"No mistakes now," she warned us all.

CHAPTER 4

Even though Colin and I had searched every inch of it, the parlour was still intimidating with its velvet cushions and gold candlesticks. Lord Jasper was already sitting at the round table in the corner, his cane with its handle shaped like the head of a silver swan propped beside him. His hair was a shock of white, barely tamed into a queue with a matching white beard, closely trimmed. As he was our host, the etiquette books I'd studied said I should greet him first. Instead, I plopped down into the nearest chair. It was more awkward than I would have thought, because my left knee didn't bend properly alongside the bellows. I fixed one of those awful, excruciatingly polite smiles on my face. Elizabeth joined me, drinking from a glass of lemonade.

"What took you so long?" she whispered. "My mother's been trying to get me to flirt with Xavier even though I told her he was courting you."

"Oh." I didn't have any experience with this sort of thing. I liked him, of course. There was nothing to dislike. He was perfectly amiable. Elizabeth and I both looked in his direction. He was standing with Frederic, his blonde hair neatly swept back. He looked at ease, perfectly comfortable with his surroundings and his place in them. I rather envied him for that. He caught us staring at him and smiled, offering us a small bow from across the room. I blushed.

Elizabeth held back a laugh but only barely. "Have you met his parents yet?"

I shook my head. "No. Have they arrived?"

"That's his mother by the fern terrarium."

I glanced over and nearly groaned. She was dressed to the very pinnacle of fashion in blue silk with a lace-trimmed apron striped in a paler blue. Sapphires glittered on every possible expanse of skin and in her piled and scented hair. She was elegant and sophisticated.

"She's going to hate me," I muttered. "Even before I spill something on her."

"Oh, pish. They'll love you. Anyway, they're in trade. It's not like they can look down their nose at you because you aren't an earl's daughter," she said, even though her own mother looked down at me that way, knowing full well we didn't have the background to be associating with Lord Jasper and his ilk. The fact that he would invite families in trade was tolerated because of their combined wealth, but his inviting a medium and her daughter to a house party with the peerage was considered quite eccentric and worthy of prolonged gossip. He was very modern by all accounts. And since we were invited for scientific inquiry and entertainment, certain allowances were made.

Elizabeth's smile was wicked. "Mrs Trethewey cares about two things and two things only: fame and fortune. Right now, your mother is providing a fantastic amount of fame, so you have nothing to worry about."

If only that were true.

Still, Elizabeth was always so jolly, she nearly made me forget why we were sitting there in the first place, until Lord Jasper rose and cleared his throat. The conversations died and everyone turned towards him.

"Shall we begin?" he asked. "Mrs Willoughby?"

Mother was already seated at the cherrywood table. She smiled as if he were a king offering her a crown. She treated most wealthy men to that smile, but Lord Jasper especially. He was the reason behind most of the expensive cameos she wore and the silver candlesticks on our table at home. More important, he eagerly believed in her gifts and considered himself her most devoted patron and protector.

As the guests seated themselves, Colin busied himself with turning down all of the gaslights. It needed no explanations that a medium worked best in near darkness; where would any of us be without the suitable atmosphere? One of the candles was lit and placed on the mantle. A very small fire burned in the grate, reduced mostly to smoking embers. I took advantage of the shadows to hide my ungainly walk to the table.

Besides Lord Jasper there was Mrs Aberworthy and her daughter. Miss Elaine Aberworthy wore a dress in a most unfortunate shade of lime green, edged with pink ribbons. My eyes watered just to look at her. She giggled into her gloved hand. Elaine never stopped giggling. There was another gentleman, Mr Hughes, and his wife, who had the pale cheeks of the recently devastated. I had seen them all last week at one of the lectures Mother dragged us to. On her other side sat a girl, about my age, with reddish blonde curls. Her dress seemed very white in the gloom. The coals sparked behind her, like fireflies.

"Violet, there you are," Mother said pointedly. "Sit down. It doesn't do to keep the spirits waiting." She motioned to the chair in which the girl sat. There were no other empty spots at the table.

I halted, confused.

"Violet, do sit down." Mother's tone went sharp at my hesitation.

"I'll need a chair," I murmured, hoping Colin would bring one for me. I would never hear the end of it if I attempted to drag one across the faded carpet myself, even though I was perfectly capable. "I can't very well sit there. We won't both fit."

The girl's eyes widened when I nodded towards her. That was when I noticed the bruises around her throat and her wrists and the way she was dripping water on to the carpet. It ran from her long hair and her wet bodice, which clung to her, and there were dusky blue smudges under her eyes. She was as pale as jasmine petals. I could smell mud and fish and the thick, cloying perfume of lilies.

A heavy silence stretched between the sitters. Everyone

watched me eagerly. I took a step backwards before I could stop myself. Something wasn't right.

"That chair *is* empty," my mother said evenly.

I felt suddenly light-headed and foolish.

"But . . . the girl . . ." Surely a waterlogged girl with bracelets of bruises couldn't be ignored like a wallflower. She stood out. And not just because of the smell.

I must be coming down with a touch of the ague.

Or suffering the effects of bad beef.

Surely that was it. I wasn't sure which was preferable: hallucinations or illness or an actual psychical encounter.

I chose bad beef.

"A little girl?" Mrs Hughes squeaked, interrupting my inner turmoil. She clutched at her damp handkerchief. "Oh, it's my little Rose. Isn't it, Mr Hughes?" She turned pleadingly towards her husband.

In the time it took for me to glance at her and then back again, the chair was empty. Not even a water spot on the cushion remained. No one complained about the aroma of trout.

I didn't know what to do. I had to resist the urge to look under the table linen to see if she was hiding there. It seemed like a fine plan, actually; perhaps she could make room for me. My corset stays began to feel too tight. Lord Jasper looked at me sharply. Elaine giggled. It was high-pitched, like a goose at market. Mrs Trethewey stared at me.

"If Rose is here, we must begin straight away," Mother proclaimed. I sank into the chair, feeling a chill creep up the back of my neck.

Colin turned down the last light and we sat in shadows, the room quiet except for the ticking of the mantel clock and the wild runaway horse that was my heart. I clenched my fists and took a deep a breath. It wouldn't do anyone any good if I fell into hysterics. I did consider a false swoon and a long recuperation in the privacy of my bedroom, but Mother would never allow me to disrupt the evening for the other sitters. And she was likely to tell them I was suffering from the traditional malady that heralded psychical gifts.

Thank you, but no.

I already felt suffocated by the attention. I didn't know how Mother could love it the way she did. She sang the usual songs and I lowered my head to avoid the curious glances. Colin's stare dug into my shoulders.

We joined hands. Mother's palm was cool and firm. Mrs Hughes, on my other side, had damp and trembling fingers. Mother began to sway slightly. I knew the exact choreography of the evening. The candle flickered once and went out, taking with it the last of the reliable lighting. No one remembered it had been down to the last of the melting wax or had seen Colin replace the long taper with the worn nub. The fire fell in on itself in a shower of sparks, accented with Borax powder, which we'd discovered burned with a very dramatic yellow-green. Elaine gave a small shriek, followed by another giggle.

Mother continued to sway. There was a sharp *crack*, followed by several more that were nearly drowned out in a flurry of whispers. No one saw Colin stretch his neck in the way that always caused a popping sound. I nudged the paper packet with the toe of my boot. Gravity did the rest.

The table moved once, twice.

There were gasps, excited murmurs.

"The spirits are indeed here," Mother announced. "And they are eager to speak with us."

I squeezed my knees together slowly.

"A cold wind, Mr Hughes!" Mrs Hughes exclaimed. "A cold wind around my ankles. Do you feel it?"

There were murmurs of assent. Lord Jasper's sister looked suspicious but intrigued. I tried not to ruffle up Mrs Trethewey's skirts.

"A greeting from Rose, Mrs Hughes," Mother explained. "Did you not take her to the seaside?" We'd overheard her say as much to a companion last week while we stopped for a pot of chocolate. We frequented all the popular spots to eavesdrop.

She sucked in a breath. "We did. She loved it."

"And the wind off the water was cool, was it not?" As if the wind off the water was ever hot.

Mrs Hughes nodded, too overcome to say anything else. Another squeeze and everyone's ankles shivered. My leg muscles were beginning to ache. And I felt ridiculous.

"She would have me tell you that there is nothing to fear; she is quite happy where she is, and she has been eating sweets."

"Liquorice drops were her favourite."

"Of course."

"She had black curls, so sweet and always sticky with sugar when she ate liquorice."

I sniffed delicately. I could smell lilies again, sweet and thick, as if we were sitting by a sunlit pond. I was surprised when no one else mentioned it. It was quite strong; I could all but taste it. It was the sort of thing people generally reacted to immediately. I frowned.

Suddenly Elaine squealed, her hands twitching, as if by themselves. She stared at them, transfixed. "Mother!"

Mrs Aberworthy looked delighted. "It's the spirits!"

That happened frequently as well. Colin hypothesised that people sat so tensely, with their hands held so tightly together, that the muscles were bound to twitch.

Mother's head rolled back and she went still and rigid. She seemed to melt back into herself, standing up with the grace of smoke lifting and curving. When she opened her eyes again, they seemed different. Her hair slipped loose from its pins and she held the curls back, smiling seductively.

"Mrs Willoughby has left us," Lord Jasper said. "Who is it who joins us?"

She fluttered her lashes. "I am Tallulah, a temple dancer from the deserts of Egypt." The shawl slipped off her shoulders, leaving them bare.

Everyone watched her circle the table, as sinuous as Cleopatra might have been. I hated this part. It might unravel so easily and we would be exposed, reviled. I couldn't look at the others, especially Xavier. And his parents. Who would encourage the courtship of a girl whose mother pranced about as if she were from some ancient harem?

I hated Tallulah.

But as always, she captured their full attention. She offered them spirit apports, which were simply gifts—such as a scatter of roses, violets and larkspur. This was her favourite secret: how she kept the flowers in her shawl and no one noticed them falling into her hands when she began to dance, slow as a sunset. There wasn't a lily among them, for all that I still noticed their distinctive scent.

No one else noticed the girl standing in the shadows by the grate, water pooling under her bare feet.

She met my eyes and it was as if winter blew through the parlour. When she opened her mouth, the sound was muffled and high-pitched, like nothing I had ever heard before. She walked towards me, suddenly close enough that the hem of my skirt grew damp and cold. I cringed back in my chair, looking around wildly. Everyone was staring at my mother, except for Colin, whose eyes were narrowed and trained on my every flinch and wince. I wanted to get up and run from the room. Only Mrs Hughes's tight grip on my hand kept me there. Sweat pooled under my arms.

All the while, Mother was still dancing gracefully, brushing against the shoulders of the men. She stopped near the fire, where the glow was most flattering. She let her breath tremble. It was Colin's cue. He reached her side just as she swooned, crumpling softly. He caught her and laid her in her chair. It was the best way to end, we'd found, as it curtailed too many questions. Since it was understood that it was exhausting for a medium to give herself over to the spirits, we bundled Mother up and hurried her to her bedchamber.

I darted into my room and shut the door behind me before Colin could ask me any questions. I sank on to the chaise longue, not even bothering to loosen the bellows that were cutting off the circulation in my leg. My foot tingled but I barely noticed.

No one else had seen the screaming girl.

I wiped at my damp forehead. It must be a fever of some kind, I thought again. I did feel chilled and light-headed. There. That was a perfectly reasonable explanation.

Which didn't explain why the carpet squelched wetly under my boots. There was a puddle under my chair and I could hear the sound of dripping, as if the gutters were overflowing. I crossed the damp carpet and went to the window.

It wasn't raining.

Perhaps Lord Jasper had heated-water pipes installed and they were leaking. They were rare so far out of the city, but he was fantastically wealthy and could likely afford them. I turned back, intending to summon a footman or a housemaid to warn him before he lost all his best furniture to a flood.

That was when the water began to run in sheets down the walls, trickling over the floor towards me. I hurried to the door. The water followed me.

I frowned, taking a step to the side.

The water changed course.

It was still pouring down the silk paper, but when it hit the ground it followed me. It was cold, seeping into the soles of my boots. I didn't know what to do. I might not know very much about plumbing, but I was fairly certain it couldn't explain this particular phenomenon. The water rose to my ankles. I shivered.

"This is ridiculous," I muttered.

And if I stood here too long, I might just drown.

That galvanized me into moving. My steps churned up the water, splashing droplets into the air.

They froze there, hovering.

Which was utterly impossible.

My breath was loud and rasping in my ears. The beads stayed suspended around me, glittering in the light of the oil lamps. I wasn't suffering from some kind of influenza; I was going mad.

I was reflected in one of the drops—my frantic, pale face getting wider and more distorted as I got closer. I reached out a trembling fingertip. The very moment I touched the frozen drop, it fell like a marble. The splash sounded like ice cracking, and then all the water on the ground arced up in violent waves around me.

I leaped for the door.

The brass knob seared my hand, jagged ice bristling out of it as if it had turned into a porcupine. Tiny spots of frostbite salted my palm, tingling painfully.

And the water stopped.

Just stopped.

The next breath had it falling back to the floor and then sucking back towards the wall and up the paper.

I took a hesitant step forward. Nothing happened.

Nothing was wet. Not the rugs, the silk wallpaper or the ceiling. Not even my boots.

I slept on the settee in the adjoining parlour that night.

CHAPTER 5

I didn't believe in ghosts.

All the same, I avoided the downstairs drawing room the next morning and didn't linger in my room.

Just in case.

The rest of the guests had been arriving all morning, the carriages clogging the drive and the stable boys run off their feet. The footmen carrying heavy trunks made a constant parade, and the maids all looked out of breath. Mrs Harris was the only one who seemed to march her way through the controlled chaos without a hair out of place, the keys on her chatelaine rattling. It was all very normal and comforting. Clearly, I'd been overtired last night. And the stress of our first sitting here had frayed my nerves. That was all.

"Quickly!" Elizabeth pounced at me from behind the ferns outside the breakfast room. "My mother's looking for me."

"What for?"

"Does it matter?"

We rushed through a little-used door near the conservatory. Elizabeth's mother was rather imposing and stern. And she was determined to make a good match for Elizabeth after her debut, which involved a lot of lectures on proper posture and how to address a duke's son. I knew for a fact that she'd made Elizabeth memorise the names and holdings of every eligible bachelor of good breeding, not just the ones of our age but those two generations older as well.

We ended up outside, walking between two willow trees and then around the rose bushes along the side of the mansion. It was so large and grey, I felt like a fairy under the hulking shadow of an ogre.

"Elizabeth! There you are." A girl of about our age called from where she'd been sulking over by the pink globes of a hydrangea bush. The sun gleamed blindingly on the pond in the distance behind her. On one of the benches a woman with dark blonde hair in a plain bun watched us disapprovingly.

"Miss Donovan, her governess," Elizabeth whispered to me, making a pinched face.

The girl sniffed. "She is not my governess. I'm far too old for a governess," she insisted. She might have seemed delicate if it wasn't for the stony glint in her eyes. Her long hair was perfectly curled and the exact shade of pale daffodils. She seemed familiar in a vague way that irritated, like a toothache. She wore a pristine white dress, not a grass stain or mud spot in sight. "It's frightfully dull here. Everyone's too young or too old."

"I know," Elizabeth agreed. "Tabitha Wentworth, this is Violet Willoughby. Tabitha lives in the white house on the hill there, with her uncle Wentworth."

"*Sir* Wentworth," the governess corrected primly from her stone perch. Elizabeth rolled her eyes. Tabitha speared me with her gaze.

"Is your mother Celeste Willoughby? The medium?"

I nodded.

"I don't believe in ghosts and all that Spiritualist rot," she scoffed.

"Tabitha." Elizabeth frowned.

I just shrugged and didn't bother defending myself. I might have hated doing it, but I kept our secret as faithfully as my mother did. What else was I to do? How would ruining myself and my family help us in any way? No one would understand. Least of all Xavier. He would never forgive me. Perhaps if he truly did offer for me as Mother was convinced he would, I could leave all of this behind—all of the pretty, sneering girls like Tabitha, who looked down their noses at me. I would never have to take part in another seance again.

I just had to remind myself of that every time I felt the urge to confess everything to Lord Jasper.

The light flashed off the water behind Tabitha. I wouldn't have thought anything of it, except that suddenly my eyes felt painfully focused. My perspective stretched, then narrowed just as abruptly. It was the oddest thing. I shivered as goose pimples rose on my skin like a lawn of new grass poking out of the ground at springtime.

More distressing yet was the fact that Tabitha seemed to waver, as if she were standing in the oppressive heat of India instead of a perfectly pleasant English summer day. She wavered again and became two Tabithas, with the one on the left as pale as almond cream.

I suddenly knew why I had thought Tabitha looked familiar.

And I didn't like it one bit.

"Violet!" I could hear Elizabeth's worried voice, but it seemed to be coming from very far away.

"Why is she staring at me like that?" Tabitha snapped. "Is she having some sort of a fit?"

If only.

The other Tabitha opened her mouth and water streamed out, soaking into her already waterlogged dress and creating a puddle under her bare feet. There were lilies and long grasses caught in her hair. It was the same girl I had seen in the parlour last night.

And she was identical to Tabitha.

Except, of course, she was transparent.

So much for pretending none of this was actually happening to me.

I could see the outline of the decorative yew hedge behind Tabitha's double and, faintly, the distant pond. She reached out to touch Tabitha but her hand passed right through her shoulder. I flinched, waiting for the shrieking to begin.

There was nothing but the starlings singing from the rooftop. Tabitha didn't so much as twitch, though I did notice gooseflesh on her neck. I stared at Elizabeth. She came from a Spiritualist family; surely she realised what was going on.

Elizabeth just stared back at me quizzically.

"Miss Wentworth," I finally croaked. "Do you have a twin sister?"

I don't know who was paler, Tabitha or the suddenly excited spirit at her side.

"Excuse me?" Her tone was positively frigid, but I barely noticed. I was starting to feel faint. The governess made a strangled sound and rose to her feet.

"She drowned, didn't she?" I paused, thinking of the water that had inexplicably filled my room last night and then just as inexplicably disappeared. Around her wrists were bruises like jet beads. "No," I whispered, finally realising what I was seeing. "She didn't just drown. She was murdered."

I swayed slightly and had to grip Elizabeth's arm to keep from falling. Tabitha made an odd sound of fury and fear, like a wet cat. The girl beside her looked sad and then vanished.

Completely.

Only Tabitha remained, glaring at me with seething hatred.

"Stay away from me," she hissed before turning on her heel and marching away. I couldn't be sure but I thought there were tears on her cheeks. She pulled a small tin out of her pocket with trembling fingers, but I couldn't see what it was.

"Oh, Violet." Elizabeth sighed as I sank on to a stone bench. My head felt rather peculiar, my limbs weak.

"What just happened?" I asked.

She sat next to me warily. "How did you know about Rowena?"

"Who's Rowena?"

"Tabitha's twin sister." My stomach dropped into my shoes as she continued. "She died last year. Drowned."

I suppressed the violent shiver currently attacking my spine.

"But I overheard Uncle Jasper wondering aloud if it really was an accident, because who goes swimming in the middle of the night? He's forbidden me to visit Whitestone Manor at all, but he won't say anything else about it. And Tabitha is rarely allowed to leave the grounds. She hasn't been in London since it happened."

Ghosts were bad.

Mysterious ghosts were so much worse.

"What about her parents?" I asked.

"Her father was in India at the time and still hasn't returned. He's always been a bit of a rakehell, gambling and travelling all over the world. He's already spent all of the twins' dowry money, and most of the Wentworth fortune. That's why he travels so much, to avoid the creditors. Some families won't even receive them any more, can you believe it?" she added in hushed, scandalised tones. "Whitestone Manor is all that's left. Technically Rowena would have inherited it as she was three minutes older, but now it goes to Tabitha. She's frightfully rich because of it, despite everything else."

"What about their mother?"

"She died of consumption years ago, when we were barely

in pigtails. Whitestone was in her family, which is why it goes to the girls and their father couldn't lose it on a roll of dice. Their uncle has taken care of them for ages now, but he's become a little overprotective. He worries about fortune hunters. Tabitha's been begging for a Season in town but so far to no avail. She'll have to make do with a country coming-out ball, and it's made her even more cross than usual."

"Oh."

"You didn't know? Truly?"

I shook my head. "How could I?"

"And you really saw Rowena?" Elizabeth sounded excited, curious and a little afraid. "Perhaps you have the same gifts as your mother. How exciting, Violet!"

"I'm sure it's just a coincidence," I insisted. "A one-time aberration. A reaction to the sun, maybe. Or bad marmalade." I couldn't very well tell her the truth, which was that I *had* seen a ghostly Rowena, but that wasn't the real problem.

The real problem was that I didn't actually believe in ghosts.

But they clearly believed in me.

⁕

I waited until everyone had retired to their room for an afternoon rest or was otherwise occupied in the stables. I needed to think. Mother was lying down with a cold rose water compress over her eyes and was not to be disturbed.

I felt disturbed enough for us both.

I sneaked around the back of the house, through the herb garden and into the door leading to the kitchen. I shouldn't be back here, and I shouldn't be using the servants' door since I was pretending to be a lady. If Mother found out, she'd have a fit.

But I really needed the comforting chaos of the kitchen. I was the one who did the cooking and the baking at home and I missed the smell of warm bread, the crackle of the hearth, and the dangling iron and copper utensils. Hopefully, Marjorie was taking this rare moment for a rest and wouldn't be at the table. She was too timid and felt too indebted to my mother to keep secrets from her.

I felt the heat of the stoves in the doorway, blasting the scents of roasting meat and boiling plum puddings. Sugar and flour drifted in the air like snow. Lord Jasper's French cook was a fantastically fat man with a walrus moustache. I liked him immediately, even though he was bellowing. There was a long wooden table set in the back corner. It looked like a lovely place to sit.

I didn't even make it over the threshold.

"What are you doing?" Colin said from behind me. He pulled me back out of the warm kitchen. His eyes were the colour of the sea in the sunlight.

"I just wanted some tea." I scowled at him. "Don't be such a fidget."

He shook his head. "Violet, you can't sit in the kitchens. No polite lady would ever set foot down here. Servants' domain, innit?"

"I know," I said glumly. "I might hate it at home but right now it seems so cosy. I can't perch daintily on the edge of an uncomfortable chair and smile like a nitwit for the rest of the day, Colin. I'll bite someone."

"Savage." He sounded more appreciative than condemning.

I bared my teeth. "Yes."

He nudged me back. "Go on and hide in the herb gardens. There's a stone bench on the other side of the rosemary topiary. I'll bring you some tea."

I beamed at him. "You are not annoying at all today."

He just snorted.

In the garden, I picked my way around the thyme and sorrel and found the bench behind the rosemary. There was a small patch of grass under an apple tree, near the mint, that looked far more inviting. I was arranging myself so my corset bones didn't poke me in the ribs when Colin found me. He had a brown ceramic pot and two earthenware mugs. He passed me one of the mugs and I cradled it gratefully.

"Finally, a real mug," I approved, inhaling the lemon he'd added to my tea. We never got lemons at home; they were far too dear. And the delicate cups in the manor house were all fluted edges and gilt paint and I was constantly terrified I'd snap the handle right off.

"Your mother will fly into the boughs if you get grass stains on your skirt," he remarked, sitting next to me. I just shrugged. He handed me a spoon.

"What's this for?"

"Strawberry ice cream." He pushed the ceramic crockery pot between us. "The dairymaid's sweet on me, so she saved me the scrapings from the ice cream she made for your supper tonight."

"You're sweet on the dairymaid?"

"I didn't say that, did I?" He winked. "I said she's sweet on me."

Oh. The thought of Colin kissing the dairymaid made me feel queer inside.

He leaned on his elbow while I told myself it was ridiculous to feel cross. "Maybe I'll run away with the dairymaid and live in a cottage and eat ice cream all day long and you'll live in London with your prince and drink out of gold teacups."

"Gold cups wouldn't be at all practical," I felt the need to point out. He grinned. His black hair fell into his eye, as it always did. He could never be bothered to use pomade to sleek it back like the fashionable gentlemen did, and he was more handsome for it. His sleeves were rolled up, revealing strong wrists and muscular arms. He sprawled, utterly comfortable and utterly confident. I could see how the dairymaid might think he was a bit of all right.

I concentrated on scraping the pink ice cream at the bottom of the pot. It was cold and sweet on my tongue, melting away as it slid down my throat. I nearly purred.

Colin cleared his throat. "Like the ice cream then?"

I opened my eyes. I hadn't even realised I'd closed them. "Heavenly."

"Thought you might."

We ate in a companionable silence. A honeybee drifted between us. A warm breeze ruffled the mint. Birds sang in the hedgerows and someone was playing one of the pianofortes in the house. I refused to think about the ghost in the parlour, the water in my room, or Tabitha. I wasn't going to spoil this moment. I was sitting in grass with ants crawling over my boots and sticky ice cream on my lips and I was happier than in my best dress under the crystal chandeliers. It was the first time I'd felt myself since we'd left London.

I wondered if there really was something wrong with me.

CHAPTER 6

I barely slept that night.

Instead, I played the incidents over and over in my head: Rowena's ghost dripping on to the flagstones, the water running down the walls, Tabitha glaring at me. I'd made her angry and vulnerable and I didn't need to be told she wouldn't forgive me for it. I knew girls like Tabitha—I'd been brought up by one. She would need some kind of revenge. I didn't know how to tell her she needn't bother expending all that effort on my behalf; I was hardly competition. If I could convince her of what she already suspected—that I was beneath her notice—things would be easier for me.

And it was easier to worry about Tabitha than it was to wonder how I was going to keep all of this a secret from my mother. Because although I might not know very much about actual conversations with the dead, I did know my mother. She would have me talking to the deceased members of every influential family in the entire city of London, right down to the queen, if she had her way. I had no wish to pursue this newfound talent for seeing spirits. It was already getting me into trouble, and it had been only two days.

Referring to myself as a medium did nothing for my humour.

I had never really considered that other mediums might truly have psychical experiences. I assumed they used the same tricks we did, with varying degrees of success. But I couldn't deny, however much I wanted to, that something out of the ordinary was occurring.

I punched at my pillow a few more times before giving it up as a lost cause. Clearly, sleep would remain elusive. I sighed and sat up, reaching for my little book of Tennyson's verse, but even *The Lady of Shalott* couldn't keep my attention. It was too easy to imagine myself in a barge seeing visions and floating to my doom. I tucked the book under my pillow, feeling wild, as if I'd had too many honey cakes.

The moon shone through the windows. I'd left the curtains open as it seemed a shame not to take advantage of the view. My window at home was a quarter the size of this one and showed only a scraggly elm and the bricks of the house next door.

I pulled my shawl around my shoulders and opened the glass door leading out on to a wedge of balcony. The night was warm enough that I was comfortable in my faded night-dress and a mended lace dressing gown that had belonged to my mother. The stars flickered like candles and the wind was full of roses and larkspur.

I couldn't ignore the pale glimpse of moon-touched water where the hills gave way to the manicured lawns of Whitestone Manor.

The bushes rustled beneath my balcony. There was a muffled curse.

"Keep your voice down. Do you want to wake the entire house?"

I knew that tone, bitter and disapproving. Caroline Donovan, Tabitha's governess.

"Darling, you worry too much."

I didn't recognise the second voice, male and all smug condescension. I crouched down so I wouldn't be seen and peered through the gaps between the stone railings. The ground was cold under my feet.

"Everyone's asleep," the man reassured her, sounding vaguely bored. I could see only the cuff of his dark jacket and the gleam of his boots. Caroline was half wedged into the yew bush, staring all around her. What on earth was Tabitha's governess doing here at this time of the night?

"I don't know about this," Caroline murmured.

"It's too late now," he said cheerfully.

"Be serious, won't you?"

"Why bother? You're serious enough for both of us."

"We have to be careful."

"Did you pull me out here for that? I've cards to play and brandy to drink." The answering silence was strained, brittle. Not that he noticed, apparently. "At least give us a kiss."

I wasn't the only one with secrets. I shifted to ease the

pressure on my knees and tripped on the ribbon of my dressing gown. I tumbled with a muffled "oof".

"Did you hear that?" Caroline asked fearfully.

I froze, squeezing my eyes shut as if that would help me be invisible. I prised one eyelid open. From this angle I could see a third person watching them from the privacy of a rose arbour. I only chanced to see him because from this angle, the moonlight gleamed on his silver cravat pin. He scanned the gardens, his face hidden in the shadow cast by his hat.

"Probably nothing," Caroline's mysterious beau murmured. "All the same, you should get back."

They parted without another word, Caroline sneaking away across the lawn, the man easing back inside. After a few moments I straightened up, rubbing my elbow, which was now throbbing as much as my knee.

"Psst!"

I swatted away what I assumed was a fly. But the noise came again, from below me in the shadow-thick gardens. The white roses seemed to glow in the faint moonlight.

"Psst!"

I leaned over the railing. "What?"

It was hardly what Juliet might have said to Romeo, or indeed what any well-bred girl might say. I probably ought to have giggled enticingly or shrieked and dived under my blankets.

Instead, I leaned out further and nearly toppled over.

Colin emerged from behind a decorative hedge shaped like a mermaid. The gardens were as crowded as Covent Garden on market day. He looked as handsome as any young lord, even with the coarse wool of his coat and the calluses that I knew ridged his palms.

"Shouldn't you be in bed?" For some reason, saying it made me blush. He grinned.

"Shouldn't you?"

I almost told him why I couldn't sleep. I almost told him about the water in my room and about the drowned girl and the way she looked at me: hopefully, pleadingly, demandingly.

But I didn't.

"Someone will see us," I said instead. I hated how proper and prim I sounded.

I could have sworn he was disappointed. Since that hardly made sense, I ignored it. He bowed once, mockingly. I turned and sailed back inside, shutting the door pointedly behind me.

I couldn't say why he seemed to follow me, invading my empty bedroom and my thoughts.

Or why I found it comforting.

───✦───

I woke up scowling. I scowled through my cup of tea, I scowled when Marjorie brushed my hair, and I even scowled at the sunlight when it fell prettily through the windowpanes on to the carpet.

It was early. Too early.

I scowled all the way down the stairs, at each of Lord Jasper's ancestors in the portrait hall and even at a potted fern that fluttered across my hem as I passed. The fashion for ferns showed not the slightest inclination of fading if Rosefield was any house to judge by. Large green fronds grasped at me like hands as I marched down to breakfast.

I had just enough sense to pause before entering in order to collect myself. A headache pulsed viciously behind my eyes. I pasted on a polite smile before showing myself. Most of the guests were gathered at the long table. All of the men rose briefly. Frederic grinned. Since I didn't hear Elizabeth's customary stifled sigh, she must still be asleep, like any sensible person. One of the guests was a tall man, thin and with a predatory look about him. The effect was underscored by the way he stared, his black eyes peeling back the layers we all wore like shawls in polite society.

Something else about him made me uncomfortable: the silver cravat pin he wore. It was the same man who'd been hiding in the gardens last night, watching Caroline stealing kisses.

But why?

"There you are, darling." Mother's voice was decidedly crisp. She eyed me critically over her cup. Her smile was pointed. "Why don't you have a seat next to your Mr Trethewey?"

I instantly forgot about the man with the cravat pin and instead blushed violently. One of the ladies cleared her throat sharply.

"Mother!" I whispered. She was being too bold. I could see the censure in Lord Jasper's sister's expression and the gleam in Tabitha's eyes as she sat on Xavier's other side, smiling prettily at him. I stifled a groan. I had no wish to play the games Mother or Tabitha expected me to play. The headache jabbed at me mercilessly.

"It would be a pleasure," Xavier murmured. I could only be grateful his parents were still abed.

"Tell Jasper I miss him."

I blinked, looking at the guests. No one else seemed to have heard the breathy voice whispering.

"The locket is under the settee. Vera dropped it there last week."

I definitely heard that. I lifted a hand to my head, which throbbed mercilessly.

"Can you hear me?"

"And me?"

"Please, answer me!"

There were more voices, all layered on top of one another like a windstorm. I think I might have whimpered. I really didn't want this to be happening. Seeing spirits was bad enough; hearing them was no better. I clapped my hands over my ears. I had to get out of there.

"Violet!" Mother snapped.

Her voice, at least, was real, and it was sharp enough to cut through the haze of panic. Lord Jasper was staring at me quite intently. I smiled weakly and turned to the sideboard. I just needed to be alone, needed quiet. I was tired, that was all. The chattering and the clinking of silver cutlery frayed my nerves.

I reached for a plate, waving away the help of a footman. I'd never understood that. Surely I was capable of carrying my own plate, even though I felt tired and awful. I made my way back to the table with my eggs and toast, trying to breathe through the anxiety and the ache in my temples. I wasn't paying attention to Tabitha.

That was my first mistake.

The second was that when she surreptitiously reached back and yanked on my elbow, I let out an unbecoming yelp, like a monkey tumbling from a tree.

And third, I dropped my plate.

Or rather, I threw it.

It sailed out of my hand and I could only watch in horror as it proceeded to make its descent. Jam-covered toast turned over once, twice . . . and landed on Xavier's shoulder with a most undignified *splat*. The eggs rained on to the floor and the bacon slid across the pristine white tablecloth, leaving grease stains like skating grooves on an icy pond. There was a shocked silence before the ladies all gasped in unison, as if they'd just been thrown underwater. Mother sent me a glare, and Tabitha's laughter trilled out, delicate as a nightingale's song.

"I'm—" My voice was more of a croak. Why did Tabitha get to sound like a songbird while I imitated a toad? And was it entirely too late to crawl back into bed and refuse to come out?

"I'm terribly sorry," I finally managed to say as Xavier stood to wipe at his sticky shoulder with a napkin. Tabitha rose as well and all but purred.

"Oh, how dreadfully clumsy," she said. "I would be simply mortified. I would just *die*." She smiled at Xavier. "Let me help you with that."

"I'm sorry," I whispered again before fleeing the room. I stopped in the empty hallway, pressing my back to the silk-papered wall. Embarrassed, I closed my eyes. At least the pounding in my head had been reduced to a dull ache.

I wish Elizabeth had been there; it might have seemed a little funnier then. I'd probably laugh about it later. I'd laugh harder if I'd managed to smear jam in Tabitha's ringlets. That, at least, would have been amusing and worth the mortification. When the same event involved the handsome young man who was tentatively courting you, it rather lost some of its humour. I'd never seen Mother's eyes go so round. Lady Ashford's forkful of jellied fruit had landed on her plate with a *plop* and Frederic's tea had shot straight out of his nose.

It took me a moment to realise I was giggling. I pressed my fist to my mouth but the giggles wouldn't be stifled. Tears sprang to my eyes as I struggled to catch my breath. If there was a slight hysterical tint to my laughter, I decided not to notice. Laughing was still preferable to the panic, holding it at bay like an angry dog on a chain.

"Miss Willoughby."

I was still chortling like a deranged goose. My eyes flew open.

"Miss Willoughby, are you quite well?"

I just laughed harder when I realised it was Lord Jasper himself standing there in front of me, with his white hair and his polished boots. He was smiling quizzically.

"I'm so sorry," I squeaked. "I ruined your . . . tablecloth . . . and . . ." I kept having to pause, trying to breathe properly. "And . . . Mr Trethewey's . . . frock coat!"

For some reason it made me laugh even harder. Lord Jasper chuckled as I fought to regain my hopelessly lost demeanour. I wiped at my eyes.

"It can all be cleaned, I assure you," he said. "And I'm delighted, I must say, to see you haven't succumbed to a fit of the vapours and taken to your bed as many a young ninny has."

"Thank you." I'd always liked Lord Jasper. I liked him even more now. "I must have . . . tripped."

"Hmmm."

"I'm very clumsy," I assured him cheerfully. That, at least, was the truth.

"You needn't protect Miss Wentworth," he said drily. "I saw the remarkable angle her elbow took as she jostled you." He arched his brow, motioning for me to walk with him. The thump of his silver-tipped cane was soothing. "She's had rather a hard time of it."

I remembered Rowena, her bloated face and the lilies in her hair. It was my turn to make a noncommittal noise. "Mm-hmm."

"Do be patient with her." He turned a corner and stopped a few doors down the hall. "I thought you might enjoy the library."

I couldn't stop the appreciative gasp. The walls were lined with floor-to-ceiling mahogany shelves, crammed with books of all sizes. He smiled indulgently.

"I knew I sensed in you a fellow bibliophile."

"Mother doesn't like me to read as much as I do," I remarked with a sigh.

He winked. "Then we shan't tell her, shall we? It will be our secret. Feel free to borrow any of these volumes during your stay at Rosefield."

"Thank you," I whispered. A rope of diamonds would have

been less precious to me. And then, even though it was dreadfully improper, I stood on the tip of my toes and pressed a light kiss on his weathered cheek. He patted my shoulder gruffly.

I made a slow circle, drinking it all in. The hearth was deep, bracketed with two wide green leather chairs. I could have sworn I saw the shape of a woman, heard the rustle of cloth, the clink of a teacup. I could smell flowers, lemon.

"That was your wife's favourite chair," I said softly. "She drank lavender tea and read in it almost every night."

I didn't know what made me say it. I cringed when his gaze went heavy and intense. There was sorrow there, and speculation.

"She did," he confirmed.

I blushed. I felt like a fool, more so than at breakfast. "I shouldn't have—" I didn't want him to think I was like my mother.

"What else do you see, child?"

"Nothing. It was only . . . I smell lemons. I must be tired."

But he knew that wasn't it. In fact, Lord Jasper looked as if he'd have dearly liked to press for more details but restrained himself. Why on earth had I prattled on about his dead wife?

"The books on the shelf by the window might be of particular interest to you."

I nodded, knowing I would have stammered if I'd tried to speak. I felt as if I'd dipped a toe in a narrow river only to find myself swept out to sea. Something else was happening here, but I didn't know what it was. Only that the undercurrents were strong, dangerous. A person could drown in this particular sea.

When Lord Jasper left, I distracted myself by trailing my fingers over the leather bindings, skimming over the embossed titles. It would take a large dose of control for me not to lug a great big heavy pile of books upstairs to my room. Here was Jane Austen, Mary Wollstonecraft Shelley, Lord Byron. Here was *Alice in Wonderland*, *Frankenstein*, King Arthur—friends, every one of them.

I didn't realise I was no longer alone until there was the sound of a throat being cleared. Xavier stood not three steps away in a new coat, with the chain of his pocket watch hanging just so.

"I apologise for the intrusion, but Lord Jasper said I might find you here."

"You know very well it is for me to apologise," I said, returning his smile. "I'm terribly sorry. I had a ghastly headache and, well, I don't quite know what happened."

I knew exactly what had happened: wretched Tabitha.

"Think nothing of it," he said graciously. "I trust you are quite recovered?"

"Yes, thank you." There was a small silence. I wasn't certain how to fill it. Elizabeth would have made a jest of some sort and Colin would have made teasing remarks. Xavier, however, probably thought I had delicate and cultivated sensibilities.

"The gardens are lovely this morning," he said finally, glancing out of the window. The roses were fat and still damp with dew. A butterfly floated past. "Would you like to take a stroll?"

His smile was sincere, his blonde hair brushed back from a

handsome brow. A walk would be lovely, uncomplicated. And it was kind of him to ask me, even after he'd had to wash jam out of his ear. My stomach tingled nervously, pleasantly, when he held out his arm to me. I laid my gloved hand over his cuff, just above his wrist. He smelled of soap and strawberry jam. I could get used to the way he looked at me, with admiration.

"Thank you, Mr Trethewey. A turn about the garden would be lovely." And he wasn't likely to slip earthworms down the back of my dress, as Colin had. True, that had been six years ago, but still.

It wasn't until we passed the window that I noticed the books Lord Jasper had recommended: *The Yearbook of Spiritualism for 1871*, *Spirit Drawings* by William M. Wilkinson, *History of the Supernatural* by William Howitt, as well as pamphlets from numerous psychical and Spiritualist societies.

It made perfect sense. He would assume, given my mother's interests and his own, that I might be interested as well.

And yet I couldn't account for the barest of shivers that skittered like a nervous cat over my spine.

Xavier didn't notice. He led me outside where the swallows were dipping and diving over the hedges. It smelled like roses and rain and we meandered slowly along the path, as if I hadn't thrown toast at him less than an hour before. I felt a little shy and couldn't think of anything to say, but his company was pleasant. He guided me carefully around a puddle. We stopped at a stone bench under a hedge of lilac bushes. There was a large fountain with rabbits and herons dipping their stone feet in the cold water. Lily pads drifted in the basin.

Xavier didn't sit too near or try to kiss me—that would have been terribly ungentlemanly, and he was nothing if not polite. But his hand on the bench was near mine, his gloved finger nearly pressing against mine. The ruffles of my hem waved in the breeze, touching his leg.

"Miss Willoughby, say you'll join my parents and me for tea," he finally blurted out. "I've told them all about you."

I licked my lips, my mouth feeling suddenly dry. I wasn't sure I was ready for this. "Of course."

His hand closed over mine gently. I turned my palm up under his. He smiled down at me. I tried to smile back.

"Xavier . . . that is, Mr Trethewey . . ." It was horribly awkward to have to discuss this, but I had no father to do it for me and Mother would lie. And asking Colin was just too mortifying even to contemplate.

"Yes, Violet?"

"I feel I ought to . . . that is . . ." I sighed, irritated with myself. There was no sense in having a fit of the vapours over simple facts. "I don't have a dowry."

He looked briefly taken aback, but I couldn't be sure if it was due to what I'd just told him or merely the blunt delivery of it.

"Perhaps you no longer wish for me to take tea with your mother?" I said, my spine very straight, my expression as bland and amiable as I could make it, despite the uncomfortable burning beneath my breastbone.

"Oh, Violet!" He clasped my hand to his chest, startling

me. "You are quite ten times more beautiful than any other girl in England. Let that be your dowry!"

I felt sure there was a compliment in there somewhere. I couldn't say why it made me want to do something shocking, like slide down the banisters or take off my shoes and itchy stockings and frolic in the fountain under the stone rabbits. I might be the one wearing the stifling corset, but Xavier would be the one to swoon if I did any such thing. He misunderstood my silence and picked a handful of roses for me with an eager smile.

"Violet, Mother expects only a title or else some kind of fashionable coup she can lord over her friends," he explained. Elizabeth was right about that then. "Your mother is the most famous medium in London right now," he pointed out proudly. "And no one can deny your beauty."

That was the second time he mentioned my beauty. I should be flattered. A thorn pricked my thumb through my thin summer gloves.

"Let's go to them now," he urged, "so you'll know you needn't worry. They'll love you as I do."

He was earnest and dashing and I was a horrible girl. I should love him. Or I should at least feel the inclination for it. I felt only a vague sense of indulgence, as if he were a sweet boy. But maybe that was love—a soft slow feeling and not the passionate fiery melodrama of novels. Determined to make this work, I took his arm and we went back towards the house and his mother's private sitting room.

"Oh, my flowers!" I stopped so abruptly I nearly jerked him off his feet. His fine polished shoes must not have had a very good tread. He flushed under his collar. "I'll be right back," I promised him and turned back.

I didn't break into an undignified trot until after I'd gone past the hedges and was hidden from his view. The roses lay like a painted silk fan on the bench. I cradled them gently; they really were beautiful and the first I'd received from a boy. I couldn't help a secret delighted smile as I buried my nose in them, careful to avoid the prickly thorns. They smelled like summer and perfume and sunlight. I'd have to remember to press them in a book when we got home—perhaps in my treasured copy of *Jane Eyre*, which I'd bought the day after we'd drugged Mrs Gordon's hot chocolate. I hadn't been able to drink hot chocolate since.

I took another deep breath of the roses, determined not to ruin the moment for myself.

I had Colin for that, after all.

"You'll get a beetle up your nose," he said. I jumped, dropping one of the roses.

"Colin, for heaven's sake! Were you hiding in the bushes?" Had he heard my conversation with Xavier? Did it matter?

He dropped down from a low branch of an oak tree where he'd been lounging and looking up at the leaves. "I miss the green," he said with a shrug. Sometimes I forgot that he hadn't always lived in London. "And Jasper won't thank you for stripping his gardens bare," he pointed out, combing an oak leaf out of his dark hair. He wore his usual trousers and shirt. I'd seen him in them a hundred times before, but after so many starched collar points and cravats, the small V of his bare throat and chest was distracting.

"They were a gift," I said.

"Why would an old man—" He cut himself off, standing suddenly as straight as any duke. "Trethewey."

"Yes," I replied, refusing to blush. "Aren't they romantic?"

His jaw clenched. "He's in love with your pretty face and has no idea who you are, pompous bastard that he is."

"I'm sure that's not true," I said stiffly. "Excuse me."

"Fine, then. Run after your prince."

I turned on my heel, grinding rose petals under my boots.

"Violet, wait."

I frowned at him. "I don't have time to bicker just now."

"Just be careful."

"Of what?" Surely he couldn't mean Xavier.

"I'm not sure," he admitted, frustrated. "But I hear stories from the servants."

"Stories? About Xavier?".

"Aye, about this house and Jasper, even. I don't think everything is as it seems."

"Lord Jasper is a kindly old gentleman, not to mention an earl. You can't be serious."

"He's a nice enough bloke, I reckon. But that doesn't change the facts," he insisted stubbornly. The dappled light made his blue eyes like water, mysterious and hard to read.

I tilted my head. "You've never been the sort to jump at shadows."

"I'm not jumpy," he grumbled. "Just cautious. And you should be too."

"Fine," I said. "I'll be careful. I have to go."

He caught my hand as I turned to leave. He wasn't wearing gloves, of course, and I'd taken mine off so I wouldn't stain them with the tiny thorn-induced wound on my thumb. "He's not good enough for you."

"What?" I stared at him incredulously. "I'd say you have that backwards. He's from a good family. I'm not." His fingers slid away from mine. A swallow darted past us. "So if you'll excuse me, I have to go and convince his mother that I'm not a desperate fortune hunter with a liar for a mother and a disgusting talent for drugging old ladies."

"No."

I frowned. "What do you mean, no? What's the matter with you?"

He just stepped closer to me, right on my shadow, which had been the only thing between us. His eyes were angry and conflicted but his hands were gentle on my face, wrapping around the back of my neck. He pulled slightly and I stumbled forward. His mouth closed over mine, the kiss sending warmth shooting all the way from my belly down into my knees. His tongue was bold, sliding over mine as if I were strawberry ice cream. I felt devoured, delicious, decadent.

He stopped abruptly, pulling back, his breath ragged.

"I'm not good enough for you either."

CHAPTER 7

Xavier waited on the patio to lead me to a table in the corner of a deserted parlour. I repeated etiquette rules to myself as we crossed the wide expanse of the room, so that I wouldn't replay Colin's kiss in my head. I felt warm, too warm. Had Colin really just kissed me?

A lady does not cross her feet when seated.

And had I kissed him back, just as eagerly?

A lady does not shake hands at a ball.

"Mother, Father, allow me to introduce to you Miss Violet Willoughby," Xavier said, stepping aside to present me as if I were a particularly shiny new toy. I had to force myself to pay attention.

"Miss Willoughby," his father said pleasantly, lowering his newspaper. He wore gold rings and a gold pin through his elaborate cravat. "How do you do?"

I made a small curtsy, then immediately wondered if a

short bow would have been more appropriate. "It's a pleasure to meet you, sir."

Xavier beamed proudly. "Isn't she just as beautiful as I said?"

I didn't know what to say to that. Or where to look. My smile didn't fit quite properly.

"Xavier, you're embarrassing the young lady," his mother admonished. "Do sit down, Miss Willoughby."

"Thank you." I tried not to flop on to the settee. Women always lowered themselves so gracefully. I had no idea how they managed it while wearing a corset. I nearly toppled over but caught myself by bracing my foot against the leg of the brocade chair. Xavier sat beside me, smiling.

"I think Miss Willoughby loves hot chocolate best of all, don't you, darling?" he asked, nodding to the silver tray in front of us.

I wondered if he had me confused with another girl or if he just assumed all girls preferred chocolate. And if I had to drink chocolate now, I might be sick all over his mother's very fine silk shoes with the embroidered buttons. My fingers ached at the sight of those buttons. I felt sorry for the poor seamstress who'd had to manage those stitches by gaslight.

I swallowed thickly. "Tea would be lovely."

Blast.

Did a lady remove her gloves to take tea or only at the dinner table? I couldn't remember.

"Milk or lemon?" Mrs Trethewey's dress was yellow and matched the gold curtains. Citrine stones dangled from her ears and hung heavy around her neck. Her gloves were folded primly next to her.

I hurried to pull mine off, nearly elbowing Xavier in the kidney. "Lemon, please."

This was already the longest tea in history. The cup in my hand was painted with roses and doves.

"Xavier tells us you are from London, Miss Willoughby."

"Yes, ma'am. Near Wimpole Street."

"Is that near the park?"

"It's not far," I hedged, taking a hasty swallow of tea and burning my tongue. At home I'd have eaten a spoonful of sugar to soothe the burn. I could just imagine what Xavier and his parents' reaction would be were I to dig into the sugar bowl. I nearly snorted a laugh right there at the painted table and shocked their elegant sensibilities.

"Your mother is very popular there, I understand," Mr Trethewey said. "In the Spiritualist circles?"

I nodded. "She is accounted a good medium, sir."

"Better than good," Xavier bragged lightly. "I heard tell if this sitting of Lord Jasper's goes well, there's a duke who's interested!"

I'd hadn't heard that rumour yet, and I sincerely hoped my mother never did.

"And you're from a good family, aren't you?" Mrs Trethewey asked, stirring her tea carefully so that the spoon never made a whisper of sound against the cup. I couldn't recall if my spoon had clattered. Probably. "Who are your people?"

The illustrious Willoughbys were confined to a series of

portraits in the stairway at home, all lined up in a row to watch over us. Mother told people they were her husband's ancestors, but the truth was, she'd found them behind a stall in Covent Garden one morning. My favourite was the old woman with her cocker spaniel, which was dressed ignominiously in a lacy white christening gown with a ridiculous pink bow on each floppy ear. I wasn't sure Mrs Trethewey would take to her.

"Yes, my father died when I was very young," I replied, not quite answering either question. Telling someone your father had died usually ended that particular train of conversation.

"Oh dear, I'm very sorry," Mrs Trethewey said. "Have some more tea."

"And what do you do for pleasure?" Xavier's father asked. "Horseback riding? Collect seashells? You're not one of those rarefied girls afraid of a little exertion, are you?"

I was the best pickpocket this side of London Bridge, I made an excellent plum pudding and I knew how to string flowers on thread so they looked as if they were floating. And, apparently, I now saw ghosts and heard voices.

I didn't think those would count as pleasurable pursuits.

"I am very fond of reading," I said.

Mrs Trethewey set her cup down. "Reading."

Xavier winced.

"And seashells," I hastened to add. "I love making seashell lamps." I'd never made a seashell lamp in my life, but I'd read all about them in a ladies' periodical. They'd been touted as a dignified pastime. "And I assist my mother," I said, hating myself a little for playing the game. "She did a reading for Lady Charleston just recently." Lady Charleston was considered a very fine lady and arbiter of all things fashionable.

Mrs Trethewey's eyes lit up, my suspicious reading habits instantly forgotten. "You don't say!"

Xavier nodded, and the two of them proceeded to discuss the new fashion for silk flowers, calling cards with silk borders and a new shop on Bond Street I'd never heard of. I drank tea and smiled and nodded and drank more tea. Finally, Xavier stood.

"I ought to return Miss Willoughby to her mother, I suppose, so they may change for the picnic."

"I suppose so," I agreed, rising reluctantly. I had every intention of slipping into some dark corner with a book and no intention whatsoever of spending the afternoon with my mother. Plus, I didn't have an extra dress to change into. "Thank you for the tea."

"I am very much looking forward to your mother's demonstrations," Mrs Trethewey said. "She is quite famous. Quite famous indeed if she has sat for Lady Charleston."

"You really are uncommonly pretty," Mr Trethewey said, smiling jovially. "I understand what my son sees in you."

I smiled weakly.

❧❧❧

The picnic was chaperoned by Lord Jasper's more amiable sister, Lady Octavia. Some of the neighbouring families attended and so Tabitha was there as well. I refused to let her glower ruin the afternoon. My mother elected to stay behind, not being fond of the outdoors, and I felt very nearly free despite my precarious position and imminent ghost-madness. The sky was as blue and delicate as a porcelain teacup, and the hills rolled gently in all directions, intersected occasionally with the silver ribbon of a river. Robins sang in the beech trees.

Tables waited for us on a hilltop, set with white cloths and ceramic pitchers filled with lemonade. There was cold ham and pigeon pie and bowls of blackberries and custard. I wondered if Colin had been pressed into helping the footmen move all of the food and if he'd noticed the very fine cutlery. It would have been so easy to slip one of those silver spoons into the slit in the hem of my skirt. I might have sold it back in London and got enough money to buy food for the week. We might even have been able to afford beef. I clasped my hands behind my back to avoid the temptation.

"Violet, you simply must try one of these tartlets!" Elizabeth brushed crumbs off her hands. There were pearl beads on her gloves. "On second thoughts, perhaps you should stick to the sweets. It wouldn't do to eat leek tarts now when Xavier might kiss you!"

I glanced about. "Elizabeth!"

She just laughed. "No one's near enough to hear us. So how did it go with his mother? She loves you already, of course." Sometimes Elizabeth's optimism took me by surprise. She had no doubt that Xavier loved me and that we'd be married and everything would turn out swimmingly. But she didn't really know my mother, or how close I had come to stealing the silverware.

Still, it had gone better than I'd thought. Xavier's mother seemed disposed to think well of me. And apparently his father wouldn't stop telling Xavier how pretty I was.

I couldn't help but wonder if Colin was thinking about our kiss at all.

I ate a slice of pineapple before answering her and then lost my train of thought completely. I'd never eaten pineapple before. It was even better than strawberry ice cream.

"This is the best food I have ever eaten," I said reverently, taking another bite. "I would marry this pineapple, if I could."

"Well, have at it then, before Lord Furlinghew creaks his way up here. He's notorious for eating it all and leaving none for anyone else."

I ate two more slices so fast I nearly choked.

Elizabeth grinned and slipped a handful of sugared almonds into her reticule for later. "They've set up a croquet field on the other side of the hill. Let's see if a match has started yet."

"I don't know how to play," I said apologetically.

"Oh, I don't actually want to play." She waved her hand dismissively. "I just want to see if it gets warm enough that Lord Fitzwilliam has to remove his coat. He has the *nicest* shoulders."

The *thwack* of mallets led us around a copse of ash saplings to a meadow bordered with cowslips and daisies. Dress flounces and hair ribbons fluttered and polished boots gleamed as guests laughed and attempted to knock the striped wooden balls clear out of the allotted playing field. The long grass fluttered around our calves. The pond between Rosefield and Whitestone Manor gleamed like a silver coin dropped into the palm of summer.

If Xavier and I really did marry, we might have many afternoons like this one. Lazy and content, full of pineapple and elegant friends. Never mind that Elizabeth was the only person here I was really comfortable with—it was still a nice daydream. I tilted my head up to the sky, letting the dapple of sunlight make the insides of my closed eyelids dance with colours.

"I knew he'd have to take off his coat eventually!" Elizabeth giggled. The sound pierced the quiet moment, jolting me back. "And his cravat. I may swoon. Violet! You have to look."

I opened my eyes lazily. "Mmm?"

"Fitzwilliam over there. The handsome one." She sounded fluttery.

I obediently followed her gaze and also went fluttery.

Only I wasn't looking at Lord Fitzwilliam but Rowena Wentworth.

She came towards me, stepping out of the ash saplings, trailing a soaked hem that left water in the grass like dew. No one else saw her. Elizabeth continued her excited, hushed chatter, a mallet cracked against a ball, a blackbird cried as it dived towards the pond. Rowena stared at me hard.

I blinked but the blasted girl remained.

I shook my head once at her and tried to ignore her. She

should have the decency to stay dead. Not to mention she'd nearly drowned me in my own bedroom. I counted to ten under my breath before looking back.

She was still there, water dripping from her tangled hair, wearing a crown of lilies and grass, bruises on her arms, her fine dress ragged.

Elizabeth paused, sniffed. "Do you smell lilies?"

I looked at her sharply. "Do you?"

She took another breath and shrugged. "Not any more. Must have been the wind off the pond." She went back to her enamoured fluttering over Lord Fitzwilliam's shoulders.

Rowena's pale face turned towards me pleadingly.

"Please, not here," I muttered under my breath. "Go away. Just go away."

She opened her mouth but only water came out, falling over blue lips. I shuddered, feeling water soak into my boots. I clenched my hands into fists, digging my nails into my palms, willing the queasy feeling in the pit of my stomach to go away. I felt odd all over, as if I were standing on a ship in the middle of a storm. My vision wavered. I blinked frantically, but there was no stopping it. I felt as if I were falling. I wondered if I was swooning, but Elizabeth didn't cry out and I didn't feel the impact of the ground.

In fact, I couldn't see the grassy field at all.

Instead, I was standing on broken flagstones overgrown with white lilies that glowed blue in the strange twilight. There was grass all around and apple trees raining pale pink petals everywhere. There was a huge stone staircase, the kind that belonged to a crumbling castle, only this one just stopped, leading to nowhere in particular.

Rowena stood on the third step near a candelabrum. A light at the top of the stairs grew bright as the moon, bright as a thousand candles. I could feel the warmth even as far away as I was. Rowena was shivering in her wet dress, her lips faintly blue. I couldn't imagine why she didn't want to get closer.

"Please, sweetheart," a woman begged from the top step. She was standing silhouetted against the light, but I caught glimpses of long blonde hair and diamonds. "I've been waiting for you."

I knew without any logical sense that this was Rowena's mother, who'd died years before. I felt it.

Rowena wouldn't go to her. She covered her eyes as if the light was too bright, as if it hurt her to look at it. She was crying and shaking her head violently.

"Tabitha." I saw Rowena mouth her sister's name but couldn't hear her over the sudden rain that beat down around us, flattening the grass and tearing petals from the apple branches. The light dimmed. Rowena was still weeping, and I was too, though I couldn't have said why.

"Tabitha."

The rain blurred my vision and between one blink and the next, I was back in the field. The *crack* of the croquet balls seemed too loud. There were tears on my cheeks. Rowena was gone.

But Tabitha stood in front of me, her smiled barbed. Several young gentlemen in white cravats and windswept hair trailed behind her.

"What's the matter with her?" she asked Elizabeth disdainfully. I had no idea how long I'd been standing there, unresponsive. I shifted, embarrassed.

"Are you ill?" Elizabeth asked me.

I shook my head. "I felt faint—that's all. Too much sun."

"Allow me." One of Tabitha's beaux offered me his arm gallantly. Tabitha's eyes narrowed as I placed my hand on his wrist.

"Violet, weren't you wearing that same dress this morning?" She smiled at Xavier, who was talking to one of her gallants about cricket. "Mr Trethewey, I do hope Miss Willoughby didn't ruin your coat with her clumsiness."

"Not at all, I assure you." He bowed in my direction. I smiled and tried not to flush red. He'd think I was embarrassed when really it was my temper boiling under my skin. I was in no position to vent it here. I swallowed hard; it was like I had one of Elizabeth's candied almonds stuck in my throat.

Tabitha smirked. She was an earl's daughter and knew exactly what she could get away with.

"Oh, Tabitha." Elizabeth sighed. She was also an earl's daughter and therefore unimpressed. "Stop being such a flibbertigibbet."

Tabitha sniffed. "Well, if you're going to be like that," she said, "I'll take my new friends elsewhere." They circled her, offering to fetch lemonade or clear a spot free of leaves under the branches so she might have some shade. The sun flashed off a cravat pin. I recognised the young man from the gardens who'd been spying on Caroline. And he'd been pacing the hallways when Colin and I had hidden in the ferns. He wasn't smiling and flirting with Tabitha like the others. In fact, he looked quite desperate. And I couldn't help but notice that his suit, though neatly pressed, was not nearly of the same quality as the others'. He stood out against the lounging aristocrats, especially near Frederic, who was drinking from a silver flask he pulled out of his pocket, an emerald ring gleaming on his finger.

Elizabeth stood up straighter. "Hello, Frederic."

He toasted her absently. Tabitha fluttered her eyelashes at Xavier, who blinked, ears red. "Mr Trethewey, I should love to sketch those pink lady's slippers we saw growing near that little cave. Perhaps you might fetch some for me? I'd be ever so grateful."

He glanced at me helplessly. He was no match for her. "Of course, Miss Wentworth."

She flashed me a look of pure smug triumph and then flounced away, the gentlemen eagerly placing bets as to who would pick the most flowers for her. Elizabeth and I were left alone, watching miserably as Xavier and Frederic disappeared to do her bidding.

"She'll be unbearable for the rest of the week now," Elizabeth said apologetically. "She never gets to flirt any more, and all of those gentlemen are single and wealthy. Well, except for the one on the end. I'm not sure who he is." She shook her head. "Her uncle won't like it one bit when he sees that lot. And she'll be staying overnight in one of Jasper's guest rooms as often as she can now." She swung her arm through mine. "Come on, let's see if there's any pineapple left."

❦

There was a scratching at my door that night, followed by what sounded like a hedgehog choking.

When I swung the door open, Elizabeth stopped mid-cough. "Quickly, before someone sees me." She darted inside, a shawl draped over her nightdress and something tucked under her arm. "My mother took for ever to fall asleep. I couldn't risk creeping past her room when she was still awake. No matter how quiet I think I am, it's like she has some occult sense when it comes to the possibility of me having any fun." She sailed past me and took up residence on the carpet in front of the open window where the crickets sang in the rose gardens. The flame of my candle flickered in the draught.

I joined her on the carpet, eyeing the lump under her arm suspiciously. "What have you got there?"

"I found it in Uncle Jasper's library. In the cabinet on the balcony."

"The *locked* cabinet?"

"Naturally. There's nothing to picking a lock—anyone with a hairpin can manage. It's a spirit board," she explained before I could come up with a plausible reason why a Spiritu-alist medium's daughter wanted nothing to do with spirits. The moon afforded us just enough milky blue light that the white of our nightclothes glowed faintly and I could make out the figures on the board in front of us if I squinted. "Uncle

❦ 99 ❦

Jasper has access to the best things. He says this will be all the rage as soon as they perfect it, but he doesn't approve of its parlour use just yet."

"Perfect it how?"

She wrinkled her nose. "It's apparently not as safe as it could be."

I looked dubiously at the painted wooden board on the carpet between us. "Looks safe enough to me. It's only a piece of oak."

"Exactly! I knew you wouldn't come over all missish."

It seemed a simple enough object, painted with the alphabet in black and roman numerals from one to nine. YES and NO were in each corner and GOODBYE on the bottom. A curious triangle piece with little legs stood off to the side. "How does this piece work?"

"I'm not sure exactly. It's called a planchette."

"You don't know? How are we meant to make any use of it?"

"I am sure we can work it out. I do know we're meant to use the planchette." She lifted the triangle piece and set it on the board. "And from what I can gather, the spirits push it to letters in succession and spell out messages from the afterworld." She shivered dramatically. "Perhaps we can persuade Boadicea or Anne Boleyn to speak to us. Or Aphrodite might tell me if Frederic will fall in love with me." I didn't think even the goddess of love herself would dare say no to Elizabeth. "Ooh, perhaps she'll tell you exactly when Xavier will propose. I do hope he goes down on one knee and recites a sonnet to your beauty."

I wondered if it said something unsavoury about my character that the image of Xavier reciting love poems made me want to laugh. That was hardly romantic of me. I didn't mention it out loud; instead I pulled my shawl tighter around my shoulders and made myself more comfortable. "Let's get started, shall we? I'm all shivers."

"I know. Isn't it deliciously frightening? We might speak to Napoleon—or Catherine Bathory, who bathed in the blood of virgin girls."

"I meant that I'm getting cold, you goose."

"Oh." She pushed her hair back off her shoulders and met my eyes. "Ready?"

I swallowed. It was silly to be nervous about a parlour game. But what I was really nervous about was being forced to admit, sooner rather than later, that there really were spirits and that, yes, they liked to talk to me.

One could deny the obvious for only so long.

A little longer might be nice though.

"Spirits," Elizabeth whispered. "Speak to us through this talking board. We are listening."

We waited expectantly. I stared so hard at the planchette, waiting for it to move, that my eyes burned.

Elizabeth's shoulders sagged. "Nothing's happening."

I wiped my palms on my knees. "Perhaps we're doing it wrong. Are we meant to sing, like at a seance?"

"I don't know. I couldn't very well ask Uncle Jasper, now, could I? Perhaps it's broken." She crouched down, her nose practically touching the planchette. "Hello?"

She looked so ridiculous, I couldn't suppress a giggle. It came out more like a snort and the sound startled Elizabeth so that she squeaked and leaped away, as if the planchette had turned into a spider. I laughed harder.

She glowered, thumping her chest as if her heart had stammered to a stop. "Don't *do* that!"

"Sorry!" I couldn't stop giggling. She tried to hold on to her glare, but after a moment she was chortling as well. She wiped her eyes.

"Perhaps we can ask your mother," she suggested, once she'd got her composure back. "Surely she has experience with such things?"

"No!" I answered, perhaps too quickly. Elizabeth blinked at my severity. I tried to smile, to soften my tone. "I happen to know she's never had any experience with spirit boards." I cast about for something else to say, to break the moment before she began to wonder at my discomfort.

I might have told her the truth then.

I didn't. Instead, I turned my attention back to the planchette.

"I saw a drawing once, in one of the Spiritualist papers," I said, remembering the sketch of sitters around a table, hands resting on the wooden triangle. "Everyone was touching the planchette, the way sitters hold hands. Perhaps to join us together with the energies."

"Brilliant!" Elizabeth said. "Perhaps you really are a medium, just like your mother."

I couldn't explain to her why the notion depressed me so.

We leaned forward to try again. The crickets stopped singing the moment our fingertips rested on the planchette. I tried not to take it as an omen. Elizabeth smiled nervously.

"Ready?" she whispered. When I nodded, she raised her voice a touch higher. "Spirits, we are listening."

The same silence stretched between us.

"We await your presence." She sounded sharp, like a governess.

A tingle skittered across my brow, like a beetle. But there were no spirit voices or faces peering back at me.

"How rude." Annoyed, Elizabeth huffed out a breath. "As I'm not the medium's daughter, they clearly won't speak to me. You try."

I worked to relax my fingers so they wouldn't cramp. "Spirits."

"You could ask to speak to your father," Elizabeth whispered.

I shook my head. I knew there would be no answer; we would call out until our tongues turned blue.

"Spirits," I repeated more forcefully, suddenly just wanting this to be over so I could crawl back under my blankets. If I hadn't had to keep my fingers so still, I would have scratched at my forehead. It felt tight, tingling as if my skin was burned with too much sun. At first I wasn't convinced anything was actually happening. The planchette moved infinitesimally, but it might have been the way we were hunched over the board.

"Is anything happening?" Elizabeth asked in hushed undertones.

"I'm not sure. Maybe." I leaned slightly so that the moonlight fell past my shoulder on to the spirit board. "Please, speak to us!"

"It moved!" She grabbed my arm, startling me. The planchette stuttered, as if it had slid from a waxed floor to a carpet.

"Put your hand back!"

She scratched me in her haste to grip the planchette again. I kept very still. It moved again, just a little.

"Did you see that?" Elizabeth breathed.

I nodded, not trusting my voice. The triangle moved so slowly, sweat beaded under my arms as I strained not to shift my hands or influence it in any way. Opposite me, Elizabeth was similarly flushed. It seemed to take an age for it to travel just a few inches, towards the first letter, *R*.

"*R*," Elizabeth breathed. "For what? Rheumatism? Retinue? Richard the Third?"

The planchette continued to move, towards the *O*.

"Romantic? It's going to tell us our husband's name! Or else . . . rotund?" She paused. "Is it calling us fat?"

W.

"Someone's going to have a row?" She blinked, inhaling sharply. "Oh." She met my eyes. I nodded, not looking up from the movement of the planchette.

The rest of the name was painstakingly spelled out.

Rowena.

I felt odd, light-headed and short of breath, and the spot between my eyes burned.

Elizabeth was trembling, her eyes glistening. "Truly? Rowena?"

I'd forgotten that, to Elizabeth, this was an old friend who had died tragically last summer, not some ghost tormenting her. The planchette was moving much more quickly, like a beetle on the surface of a pond.

"N-o-t s-a-f-e."

Elizabeth and I stared at the board.

"What's not safe?" she whispered, looking at me with wide eyes.

The planchette continued its eerie journey.

"N-o-t a-l-o-n-e."

Both of us looked over our shoulders. My breath felt thick in my throat. I could very easily imagine someone sneaking up behind us even though there was nothing but a painted clothes cabinet behind me. Rowena must have meant herself. There was someone else with her, trying to control the board. Or else there was someone else searching out her murderer, and we weren't alone in the investigation. Or there was someone in the hallway listening to our conversation. There were so many interpretations, I felt as if we now knew less than when we'd started.

The pointer stalled. I could feel the connection wavering; the burning on my brow became a distracting pain.

"Rowena, don't go!" Elizabeth cried. "You have to tell us what's going on!"

The planchette spelled out *M-r* and then *T-r-a*.

And then it went suddenly fast as a top. It spun and spun in place and then stopped abruptly and would not move again no matter how much we concentrated or pleaded. Elizabeth looked nearly as flabbergasted as I felt.

"Poppycock," she whispered.

I nodded mutely. But at least we knew something we hadn't known previously. There was a person of interest whose name started with "T-r-a", perhaps the spirit clinging to the board with Rowena, perhaps someone else altogether.

It wasn't much. But at least it was something.

———— ✺ ————

The next morning I tried to ask if Mother knew anyone with a name starting with "T-r-a", but she told me not to bother her while she was preparing for the ball. Without any new sightings, I managed to forget about the voices and the spirit board for a little while. A ball is a most wonderful distraction when one concentrates hard enough. Elizabeth spent hours preparing, which mostly consisted of arguing with her mother about corset stays versus the physical need to breathe. Neither she nor I were debutantes just yet (and I never would be), but we were allowed to wear our best gowns and put our hair up with pearl-tipped pins. Should anyone ask, we were even allowed to dance. It was considered perfect practice for when we officially came out. If I felt a little like a show pony, I was proud enough of my off-the-shoulder periwinkle blue gown not to mind it terribly.

The ballroom was spectacular, as expected, lit with bees-wax candles and oil lamps. Giant ferns and orange trees had been brought from the conservatory and placed in all the corners, creating shadowy and secret jungles. And, of course, there were roses everywhere—white ones hanging from the ceiling, red petals scattered over every surface: floor, table and punchbowl. Even the orchestra was hidden behind rose-draped screens so that the music seemed to float from nowhere at all. In the adjacent room, the buffet table was piled high with cucumber sandwiches, little sponge cakes and éclairs. Footmen circulated with trays of lemonade and champagne. There were easily a hundred guests, as Lord Jasper had invited most of his neighbours as well as his friends and family. Couples waltzed in a large circle in the centre of the room. It was beautiful.

But something wasn't right.

The ballroom was far more crowded than the guests alone could account for. Next to or behind each of them was an extra person: misty, cold, thin as glass and just as transparent.

I rubbed my eyes but the spirits remained, waltzing, walking and singing. A few were dressed as the rest of us, some were in chitons and one woman was in a full Renaissance gown.

A man waltzed by in the striped waistcoat of a dandy, another in a doublet and hose, followed by a lady in a dress such as Marie-Antoinette might have worn, with her hair piled high around a small gilded cage complete with singing bird, a girl in a gypsy skirt and a man who looked decidedly like a pirate. His ear hoop gleamed and he moved like smoke.

Some wept, some laughed. One appeared to be screaming into an old man's ear but he didn't so much as blink. Indeed, none of the other guests could see them, judging from the lack of fainting and shrieks.

I could see them perfectly.

And they could see me.

I'd never felt the way I did in that moment, when they all turned in unison to clap their phosphorescent eyes on me. I felt light and yet heavy as stone. My stomach turned upside down, as if I was riding far too fast in a broken carriage. I felt somehow far away from my body and yet utterly trapped in it through fear and awe.

Rowena, on the other hand, barely acknowledged me, which seemed odd. She was usually far too eager to insinuate herself into my company. Instead, tonight she hovered protectively by Tabitha's side, water pooling under her feet. She wore a crown of white lilies. She looked at me, at last, as she tried to place herself between her sister and a man whose back was turned to me. I couldn't recognise him; he wore the same dark suit as every other man here, with indistinguishable brown hair cut in the current style. He could have been anyone.

And I didn't have time to wait for him to turn round.

Because the other ghosts abandoned their posts, no longer dancing with unknowing partners, watching over wallflowers, or pressing close to widowed dowagers.

They rushed at me, all at once, as if some beacon only they could see had been lit above me. Their expressions registered countless emotions: relief, excitement, anger, fear, longing.

The force of it crashed over me like icy water.

Their mouths moved but I heard no words: only something like thunder and a high-pitched screech, like metal on metal, which had me clapping my hands over my ears. The ribbons on my dress fluttered.

The rest of the party carried on, sipping lemonade, gossiping, smoking cigars outside in the still garden. I barely heard the sweeping music or the scuff of silk shoes on the floor. There was nothing but those ghostly faces, those misty bodies.

Hands reached towards me, dozens of spirit hands touching me with all the weight of winter. I'd never felt such cold in my entire life, not even the day I'd fallen into the river in February.

"Stop it!" I stumbled back a step, trying to bat them away. A prim-mouthed guest looked at me disapprovingly. I didn't know how long I'd been standing there, frozen at first and then pushing at imaginary hands.

I moaned once before a warm hand, palm comfortingly callused, closed around my upper arm and yanked me back out into the hallway. He dragged me or I stumbled after him, until he stopped in a shadowy alcove. I pressed my back against the solid wall and slid down to the floor, heedless of my new gown and the pale silk flowers sewn along the hem and trims.

CHAPTER 8

"Violet."

I admit I was too afraid to open my eyes. At least that awful grating sound had died away.

"Vi! You're pale as a ghost!"

He had no idea.

"Violet, for God's sake, open your eyes."

Colin sounded worried, sharp. He was a little watery around the edges when I looked at him, wavering faintly before returning to reassuring solidity.

"What the bloody hell happened?"

"I . . ." I had to struggle to find my breath. He crouched down in front of me, blissfully alone. No pale face loomed behind his shoulder or whispered in his ear. I was so grateful for it that I clasped his hand. He looked briefly startled before returning the light squeeze. "I wasn't feeling quite right."

"Evidently."

"Did anyone else notice?"

He shrugged. "I don't think so. You just looked frightened, like you were going to swoon."

"I never swoon," I quipped back at him.

"It's what I like best about you."

"How very flattering."

He went serious for a moment. "Do you need a doctor?"

"No! No, I feel better already. Must have been the excitement."

He didn't look particularly convinced. "There's something you're not telling me."

I tried for a breezy smile, getting to my feet and putting my dress back to rights.

"Maybe you should lie down," he added.

I made a face. "And miss the ball? Mother would be as furious as a bag of wet monkeys." Actually, I had no idea if wet monkeys were known for their anger.

Colin's eyes seemed to close, like shutters over a window. "You'd better get back then," he said sarcastically, "and trap your prince."

I narrowed my gaze at him. "Stop calling him that. He's a perfectly nice gentleman."

"So his mama liked you well enough then? Isn't that fortunate. And how long do you think he would have paid you compliments if his mother disapproved?"

I scowled. "I can't keep up with your moods, Colin Lennox. You're either kissing me or snapping at me. I wish you'd make up your bloody mind."

I stomped off, back to the ballroom. The music was softer now, slower. It took every ounce of courage in my possession to step through the doorway. I let out a sigh when it appeared that no one spared me much of a glance. And they seemed quite alone, dancing as one did at a ball, quite unshadowed by spirits—which meant I could go back to being a girl at her first fancy ball. And though it was tempting, I managed not to shove anyone out of my way in my haste to find Elizabeth. I could just imagine the reaction if I'd knocked some old widow with pearls in her hair into the punchbowl.

I finally found Elizabeth on the edge of the dance floor, near her mother, who was whispering feverishly behind her hand to a woman dripping diamonds. My lower back was still damp with perspiration. I hoped it wouldn't mark the silk. Elizabeth was very pretty in a plum gown with lilac satin trim. She wore a lovely necklace of amethyst and pearl loops. My own neck was bare. I hadn't anything appropriate for a fancy-dress ball, only a simple cameo brooch an admirer had once given my mother. She'd grown tired of it and now it was mine.

I tried to ignore the glances thrown my way as I moved through the crowd. I ought not to be unaccompanied, but I'd slipped out before Mother could notice. She'd been drinking her "medicinal" tea all afternoon and I had no wish to catch her attention.

"Violet!" Elizabeth clasped my hands. "Oh, thank God. I was beginning to feel like a veritable ninny standing here alone all this time, and Mother wouldn't let me wander, not even for lemonade. Where have you been?" She blinked. "You're rather pale."

"I'm sure it's the excitement, nothing more." I smiled weakly, determined to enjoy the night and pretend I was like any other sixteen-year-old girl, one who didn't see spirits or dead girls dripping on to the carpet.

"Well, you look lovely anyway," she added. "Xavier won't be able to keep his eyes off you."

We waited until the music had faded and started up again before Elizabeth took my arm. "Mother, we're going for a turn about the room."

Lady Ashford nodded, engrossed in some titbit of gossip we weren't allowed to hear. We circled the dancing couples, admiring handsome sideburns and pretty tucked flounces. We stopped several times so that Elizabeth could murmur politely to her mother's friends, and once for Tabitha's uncle, Sir Wentworth, with his bushy sideburns and rotund belly, to tweak her cheek and slip her a piece of chocolate wrapped in gold foil. Apparently he had been doing that since she was a child.

Elizabeth sighed in that way I knew all too well. "Do you suppose Frederic will ask me to dance?"

I followed her gaze to where he was laughing with several friends over glasses of port. It wouldn't be long before they escaped to the gaming halls. Most young men of his age considered these balls to be tiresome affairs, forever being forced into asking wealthy single girls to dance, regardless of whether or not they had horse teeth or fainted at the sight of a moth. It was worse for the debutantes: they had to dance with wealthy old men who smelled like stewed onions and stepped on their toes. I didn't think Frederic noticed us, even when we wandered with excruciating slowness past him, lingering practically under his nose.

"Elizabeth," I whispered. "A lame donkey could walk faster than this."

She tried not to laugh and ended up snorting instead. "Shh," she added. We giggled and continued to make the circuit of the room. I'd never seen so many beautiful gowns in my life, or so many jewels. Everything sparkled. We accepted crystal cups of lemonade from a passing footman.

"Can you imagine? Wearing that colour at her age?" We heard a woman sniff disapprovingly. She was regal in a silvery grey gown with several ruffles and flounces. Her companion wore green silk and an equally disgusted expression. The crowd parted, allowing us a view of the woman in question.

My mother.

She wore pink, from her bustle to her square rose-trimmed neckline, with darker pink for an underskirt. It was silk and she all but shimmered in it. Her dark hair was coiled on top, with long ringlets down her back. She wore garnets at her throat and was surrounded by younger men, all no doubt lavishing her with praise.

It wasn't that she didn't look very becoming in the pink dress. I'd rarely seen another colour do more for her complexion, but that shade of candy pink was generally reserved for younger girls. Mother always wanted to appear much younger than she was. She was never happier than when some handsome lord mistook her for my older sister. And it was quite a dramatic departure from her widow's weeds.

"Shameful," said the lady in green silk. "And she's a widow, is she not?"

"She's worn the black for years, as I hear it. Except for formal balls."

"A lady of good breeding would know better. Honestly, what can Lord Jasper be thinking, parading his mistress about like that? As if we'd believe she's just some Spiritualist he's taken a scientific interest in."

She tittered. I'd never actually heard someone titter before. Beside me, Elizabeth winced.

"He's lonely, poor old thing."

"And rich enough not to care what the rest of us think," came the dry reply.

They laughed together while I stood, rooted to the floor. Mother laughed as well, and it was like silver bells, but too loud. Her cheeks were flushed. I knew, even from this distance, that the sherry she'd been drinking all day had been followed by several glasses of fine champagne.

"Never mind them," Elizabeth said. "You know how people get. They're just jealous that they already look like wrinkled old prunes."

I nodded, feeling even more awful because I agreed with what they'd said about my mother. She always behaved this way when there were wealthy men around, whatever their age.

The man smiling at her just now was barely older than I was, which didn't seem to bother her one whit. She glanced at him through her lashes. For all that she craved respectability, Mother was a consummate flirt. Even though I knew it would do no good, I went over to her.

"Mother."

She pouted. She didn't want me to remind her admirers of her age.

"Impossible!" one of them cried out. "You couldn't have a grown daughter."

She smiled demurely and tapped his chest with the tip of her folded fan. "You flatter me, sir."

"And such a beautiful daughter," Lord Marshall murmured. I shifted uncomfortably.

"Mother, perhaps one of these gentlemen could fetch you some lemonade. You must be thirsty."

She just giggled. "I don't want lemonade," she said. "But a kiss to the first one to bring me champagne."

Half a dozen men rushed off like wild buffalo. There were squeaks of protest from women who didn't flirt nearly as well as my mother and therefore had to all but leap out of the way. Lord Marshall remained at her side, kissing the palm of her hand in a most indiscreet manner.

"Mother," I groaned, mortified. She shot me a look that made me fall back a step.

"Don't be tiresome, Violet. I knew you were too young to attend a ball. I should send you to your room."

I bit back tears even though I wasn't sure why they stung my eyes. She'd certainly said worse to me. It was just something about the way she'd looked at me. If I hadn't known better, if she hadn't been my own mother, I would have thought I'd seen resentment, even a touch of hatred. I didn't know what to do.

"Come on, Vi," Elizabeth whispered. "Let's take another turn."

"Yes, do run along, children," Lord Marshall murmured.

Mother giggled again, and Elizabeth and I left to stroll the circuit, arm in arm. Suddenly the ball was less exciting, less magical.

"Excuse me," I said, when we passed the double doors to the hall.

Elizabeth looked concerned. "Shall I come with you?"

"I'm fine, only a little overheated." I forced a smile for her benefit. She didn't believe me, of course, but she didn't follow me.

The hall was deserted and it was a relief to leave behind the hot, scented air of the ballroom. I wandered down towards the conservatory, pausing to admire a massive bronze urn on a marble table. It was large enough to house what looked like an entire rosebush, with space left for peacock feathers, fern fronds and stalks of white lilies. I circled it, using its bulk to conceal myself—but only for a moment. I wouldn't give either my mother or the other ladies the satisfaction of running away to hide in my room. I'd be perfectly fine in a moment. My throat felt less constricted already. And if my mother wasn't going to be embarrassed about her own behaviour, why should I? If nothing else, I had to keep her away from Mrs Trethewey.

I lifted my chin and prepared to pretend I was a sheltered girl without a clue as to what was going on. I was determined to salvage what was left of the evening. Even muffled by the closed doors, the music was beautiful, haunting.

And then all I knew was the sound of bronze against marble, an odd screeching scrape, and the shadow of the urn toppling towards me. I stared at it uncomprehending, even as a small part of me realised I was about to be crushed. I didn't have time to decide whether I should steel myself for impact or try to leap to safety.

The decision was made for me. A hand closed over my arm, digging painfully as it yanked me out of the way. The urn tipped to the floor with a resounding *crash*, spilling water and lily petals. My breath was still caught in my throat, like a lump of dry bread, when I recognised the man towering over me.

"Have a care, Miss Willoughby," he murmured, his silver cravat pin gleaming. I stumbled back out of his hold, trembling. I recognised the cravat pin from the gardens.

Several footmen raced towards us. "What happened? Are you hurt, miss?"

I shook my head, trying to find my voice. "The urn fell."

"You ought to be more careful," the man with the pin repeated to me in a way that made me think he was actually saying something else. In the shadows of the hallway, he looked gaunt. His suit may as well have hung on a scarecrow. He finally looked at one of the footmen. "This urn ought to be better secured. Lord Jasper will need to be informed. One would assume he doesn't plan to have his guests flattened." His gaze swung back to me. "Do you wish for us to summon your mother?"

"No!" I could just imagine her response should she be taken away from her admirers. "I'm perfectly well, thank you. My friend is waiting for me." I swallowed, my heart still racing inside my chest. My corset felt tighter than usual. Even though the stranger made me uncomfortable with his staring, he had saved me from injury. I curtsied. He bowed and left.

I stopped the footman. "Who was that man?" I asked him.

"Mr Travis, miss. Right kind fellow he is too, but tormented. Paces the halls all night and doesn't sleep."

Mr Travis.

I must have gone pale because the footman peered at me nervously. "Are you ill, miss?"

"No, just the shock, I expect." I gave him a wobbly smile before fleeing into the safety of the ballroom. Inside the doors, Xavier stopped me before I could find Elizabeth and tell her I had found our Mr Tra—, though I was no nearer to knowing what that actually meant. He was clearly up to something; men didn't lurk about gardens in the middle of the night or pace endlessly for the good of their health. And he stared a lot.

But he *had* saved me just now.

"Good evening, Miss Willoughby." Xavier smelled of soap and cologne. He was safe, polite and unlikely to push an urn on me. I felt my pulse return to normal.

"Miss Willoughby, would you do me the honour of this dance?" he asked as the strains of a waltz fell like soft rain around us. I took his arm and he led me out on to the dance floor. The evening might yet regain some of its lustre. Xavier held me close enough that I could feel his breath on my hair. His hand was warm on my waist. I could forget about everything else and let him spin me in circles, the other dancers a blur of colours around us. It was like being caught in a kaleidoscope.

"I've never seen you more beautiful," he said. He held me as though I was delicate, made of porcelain and lace. I was neither of those things but I smiled nonetheless.

"Thank you."

We danced until I felt flushed and nearly dizzy. When the music faded, Xavier bowed again and I curtsied. "Miss Willoughby, if I might be so bold as to ask you to accompany me into the gardens? The moon is quite lovely on the roses, or so I hear."

I smiled, placing my hand on his forearm. Everyone knew couples stole away into the gardens at a ball to kiss. I widened my eyes at Elizabeth as we passed her. She muffled a giggle behind her glove. I hoped I wasn't blushing.

The evening was warm with a bright moon pouring light like milk on to the trees and the flowers. The white roses glowed. Fireflies darted between the oak trees in the grove, barely visible. Couples meandered over the lawn and a handful of gentlemen smoked cheroots and laughed in the corner of the veranda. Xavier and I walked along the flagstone path and I trailed my fingers over the flowers, releasing the scent of petals and perfume.

"I think you must know, Miss Willoughby, that I admire you greatly." I looked away, blushing for certain this time. "I hope you feel the same way I do." He stopped and turned so that he was standing in front of me. His hair gleamed in the pale light. "When we return to the city, I should like to speak to your mother."

My breath caught. He could only mean one thing by talking to my mother—he meant to offer marriage. Marriage to me, barely sixteen and not even out yet. My heart was beating erratically. Part of me was thrilled and flattered and eager to be out of my mother's house. Another part of me was nervous and scared. What would happen if he ever found out about mother's "gifts", and my part in the deception? Would he ever forgive me? Would his parents and his friends snub me? And what would Colin say when he heard? Would he ever stop sneering when he said Xavier's name? Or was he even now giggling with the dairymaid?

I wanted to wipe my damp palms on my skirt but I knew it would leave streaks on the silk. I should be ecstatic. And it wasn't as if I had other options. We couldn't carry on deceiving widows for ever.

And a declaration of love in a moonlit garden was what all girls dreamed of, wasn't it? I was just giddy with nerves and tired. Between screeching ghosts and falling urns, it was no wonder I was having difficulty catching up. And besides, Mother would no doubt push for a long engagement. She would want to enjoy all of the benefits of a society nuptial while she could. I would have plenty of time to accustom myself to the idea.

Xavier must have misread my silence. He pressed my hand to his mouth. "Violet, if I may call you that?"

I nodded. If we were going to be married, I suppose I ought to allow him permission to use my first name.

"Violet, you are so lovely. I know we will suit. I just know it."

He leaned down and kissed me then, pressing his mouth against mine. His hands cupped my shoulders, holding me upright as if he thought I might swoon. His lips were soft, warm. He pulled me closer as music from the ballroom coiled around us like mist, all harps and weeping violins.

And I wished I was the kind of girl to be swept away into the moment.

CHAPTER 9

I woke early the next morning again. It was becoming a very bad habit.

Luckily Elizabeth was the only one in the breakfast room. She ducked teasingly when I took a piece of toasted bread and reached for the jam pot. I stuck out my tongue at her. It was so much more pleasant without the adults about or girls who sat up straight and smiled demurely even when they were alone. Elizabeth yawned hugely. I was exhausted too. I should have been still abed, cosy under the counterpane. We chewed between more yawns.

The sun was glistening on the last of the dewdrops when we decided to go for a walk over the hills. It was warm already and the birds sang cheerfully from the hedgerows. We left behind the roses and the hydrangea and the oak trees, cutting through the green fields.

"I can't believe he kissed you!" Elizabeth exclaimed once

we were carefully out of earshot. We were the only ones for miles, it seemed, the house sitting sleepily on the hill behind us. It made me want to tear off my petticoats and run until my legs burned or spin in circles until I fell down.

"I know." I could still feel his hands on my neck, smell the smoke and leaf of him.

"It's so romantic. And he's *handsome*. Not as handsome as Frederic," Elizabeth said as we walked arm in arm. "But still a very good-looking young man, don't you think? And his family's quite rich."

Xavier. She'd been talking about Xavier, not Colin.

"Quite handsome," I agreed. Xavier really was handsome in his navy frock coat and gold pocket watch.

"Do you really think he's going to propose?"

My stomach tingled, not unpleasantly. "Maybe. Why else would he want to speak to my mother?"

Elizabeth squealed and hugged me. Then she jumped up and down. Laughing, I jumped up and down with her, seeing as she was still holding on to me.

"Oh, what will you wear? Will you carry flowers?" I wasn't going to tell her we couldn't afford a new dress. I'd just have to wear my best gown and hope not too many people noticed I'd worn it before. "You'd look lovely with orange blossom in your hair."

"I think lilacs would be nice," I said, letting myself get distracted with the details. We would have a wedding break-fast with lemon cake sprinkled with sugared violets. Mother would wear white, like a proper Spiritualist, instead of her customary black. Elizabeth would be my bridesmaid.

"A spring wedding then. Perfect." She sighed again, her whole body heaving with emotion. "I wish I were engaged."

"I'm not engaged!"

"Not yet, *Mrs Trethewey*." She giggled. I would be Mrs Xavier Trethewey. I'd always found it a little curious that I should go by a man's first name. Violet Trethewey. I giggled too. I felt as if there were champagne bubbles in my throat.

"Perhaps he'll take you to the opera," she added as the damp grass soaked the bottom of our day dresses. "And oh! Perhaps you'll go to Italy for your wedding trip! I've always longed to see Rome. You could get heaps of new gowns made. You'll be so fashionable. Though it would have been nice if we'd been able to have our come-out together."

"Elizabeth," I said gently, "I'm not from the peerage. I wouldn't have been making my curtsy to the queen and coming out, regardless." That much we'd never tried to hide.

"Oh." She pouted. "Well, you still have to help me practise. How can we be expected to back out of the room with such a long train on our gowns? What if I fall over? What if I take the rest of the debutantes with me?"

We looked at each other and giggled. I could picture it perfectly.

We crested the last hill between us and the pond that glittered between Rosefield and Whitestone Manor. Fields full of fat sheep stretched out on either side. Valleys were dark crevices filled with oak trees and mushrooms. Closer to the pond, long grass waved, dotted with wild mint, buttercup and lady's smock.

And a man standing in the lilies.

He was tall and thin, his shoulders bowed as if he were in pain. He shuddered violently, even from a distance.

Mr Travis.

"What's he doing there?" I asked Elizabeth.

She shook her head, shielding her eyes with her hand. "I don't know. Perhaps he's out for a walk."

"To the pond where a girl drowned?" I frowned, suspicious. "I don't like it."

"He does look rather . . . odd."

We approached quietly, descending the hill and climbing back up the slow incline to the pond. By the time we reached it, Mr Travis was gone. I saw him cross into the woods that led back to Rosefield.

"Do we know why he's here?" I asked as we stopped by the pond. "How did Lord Jasper come to know him?"

"His family lives in the village, I hear. His father's a tailor or haberdasher or some such thing. I think he's the only Spiritualist in the lot though. I can't think how Rowena would have known him, though I admit I thought at first that he might be familiar."

"How?"

"I can't quite put my finger on it. Perhaps it's only my imagination. Mother has always claimed reading so many penny dreadful stories is bad for the disposition. And he's not peerage, so she won't allow an introduction, even here."

Pale lilies nodded their heavy heads when the breeze rose around us briefly. The water was deep and dark. We stepped on to one of the large rocks on the bank, balancing carefully. All around us were hills crossed with low stone walls and Whitestone Manor glowing like the moon. I felt peaceful for the first time in days, despite Mr Travis. I could spend all day here, watching the birds dive for water bugs, listening to the crickets, waiting for the odd brave bunny to hop out of hiding for a bite to eat.

And then, of course, Rowena had to go and ruin it.

If I could have found a finishing school for ghosts I would have forced her to attend. She might have been an earl's daughter while she lived, but as a dead girl, she had ghastly manners. And I was going to tell her so, just as soon as I worked out how not to choke on my own terrified heart.

The water trembled only faintly at first, and then, under the surface, the pebbles at the bottom of the pond became eyes, brown eyes watching me. Her pale face bobbed to the surface followed by her wrists, ringed with bruises.

She reached up out of the water and tugged on my ankle. Hard. Since Elizabeth was looking down without any reaction, I knew she didn't see anything but weeds. I, however, had felt the insistent touch of cold fingers, even through my boot. I hadn't thought ghosts could be corporeal.

It was not a comforting realisation.

I jerked back but she yanked hard enough that I stumbled, slipping off the rock. I waved my arms uselessly, like a hysterical windmill, screaming. My ankle felt as if it was wrapped in ice. Elizabeth shouted and grabbed for me. Instead of stopping my fall, she joined me, adding momentum. We tumbled headfirst into the cold water with an unladylike splash. I flailed about, trying to remember which way was up.

The sun faded, as if swallowed by storm clouds. There was no light to pierce the water and guide me to the surface. I felt sluggish, as if I was moving through honey. It was the same odd feeling I'd had at the picnic, only worse, much worse.

The pond wasn't this deep.

I should have hit the bottom by now, or bobbed back up, but I was caught floating in between. I tried to kick but I could barely move. Water filled my mouth and my nose and I wanted to cough but even that seemed like too much effort. There was a shadow on the edge of the pond, standing in the grass, the moon a sudden bright glow behind it. I couldn't tell if it was a man or a woman, but I felt as if I knew them. Or as if Rowena did. I was confused.

And drowning.

I struggled harder, my hair floating like seaweed as it escaped its pins. My dress was heavy, weighing me down. My corset felt like iron hands clasped too tightly around my waist. My wrists were bruised and my throat burned. I had an odd taste in my mouth, medicinal and cloying. Letters rained down to bob on the pond's surface, catching fire when they landed.

And then Elizabeth grabbed my shoulder and yanked me up, sputtering with laughter. Her hair was plastered to her neck and face.

"You look like a drowned rat!" She splashed at me, grinning.

I coughed up water, desperately hauling air into my starved lungs. I hadn't been drowning. I'd only been under for a few seconds. *Rowena* had drowned.

We already knew that. She needn't have been so violent in her reminders. My teeth chattered as I pushed the panic down.

Rowena drowned, I reminded myself. Not me.

I wished I could laugh at our clumsy tumble into a summer pond, as Elizabeth was doing. Instead, I was frantically wondering if we were floating above a dead body, if something else was going to grab me. I couldn't get out fast enough. I slipped and went under again, landing hard on my backside. I dug for a handhold in the thick mud, palms scraping pebbles and stones. Water filled my mouth. I resurfaced, sputtering, panicking despite myself.

"Clumsy!" Elizabeth teased me, leaning back to use her feet to churn up the pond water.

"What," a voice asked with icy disdain, "are you two doing?"

Elizabeth just laughed louder. Tabitha looked down her nose at us. A nervous giggle burst in my throat. I had to fight the urge to pull her into the pond with us. Somehow, I didn't think it would improve her disposition. She looked elegant in her pale dress. We looked like startled cats and smelled like green water.

"Tabitha, you managed to escape both your uncle and Caroline!" Elizabeth crowed as we climbed out, using the long grass for a handhold. It was an ungraceful affair all round. Something tumbled from the mud caked on my hands. It glittered dully until I dipped it to rinse off the worst of the grime. My boots squelched when I moved.

"I've found something," I muttered, swallowing. It was a gold ring set with pearls in the shape of a daisy.

Tabitha paled. "Give me that." She grabbed at it so viciously her nails left thin red welts. Her eyes were suspiciously bright.

Elizabeth tilted her head. "Is it yours, Tabitha?"

But I knew with sudden, certain clarity that it wasn't hers at all. That ring had belonged to her sister. The white lilies shivered at her feet, etched in impossible light.

"It was Rowena's," she whispered, mostly to herself. When she looked up, her gaze was hot, like a burning ember tossed right at me. "Get off my uncle's property," she said between her teeth, "before I set his hunting dogs on you."

Elizabeth's eyebrows rose practically up to her hairline as Tabitha stormed away. "Well," she huffed. "Really." She sat back in the grass, letting the sun warm her face. "What was that all about?" she asked curiously. She looked at me pointedly.

"What?" I asked, looking away.

She rolled her eyes. "Violet, I'm not a featherbrain. I know there's something else going on here that you're not telling me. I saw the spirit-board message too, remember, and it isn't very sporting of you to leave me out."

I bit my lip for a moment before deciding. And then I told her everything: seeing Rowena before I'd even met Tabitha, the voices in the breakfast room, the spirits at the ball—everything. Being a good friend and, more important, a girl from a Spiritualist family, Elizabeth believed me straight away, and probably would have even before we'd used the spirit board. I doubted my every word, but she just nodded.

"Oh, Vi, how thrilling. What does your mother say? Surely she went through something similar when she received her gifts?"

"She must never know." I stared at her. "Promise me."

She blinked and then nodded slowly. "All right. But then what are we going to do?"

"I don't know." I groaned, flopping down on to my back and scattering buttercup petals. "I really don't. But I have to do something. She's getting more persistent." I hesitated. "When I see her she has bruises round her neck and wrists."

"No!" Elizabeth sucked in a startled breath. "She really was murdered."

I'd been avoiding that particular part of the conundrum as carefully as I would have avoided a hornet. "You said she drowned," I reminded her, even though I didn't believe that for a moment.

"Girls who drown don't bruise like that, surely." Her mouth trembled. "She must want us to find her murderer."

I lifted my head. "Us?"

"Of course, us. Did you really think I'd just sit here and let you go on with this alone? Especially since she was a childhood friend of mine? Honestly, Violet." She sounded thoroughly disgusted.

I didn't know what to say. I'd had few friends. We moved frequently and had too many secrets. "Thank you," I whispered.

"Where do we start?"

"I wish I knew." I ran my hand through my tangled hair. "I can't very well tell Tabitha. She hates me as it is."

"She really does."

I made a face. "Thanks for that."

She patted my arm. "It's only because you make her feel vulnerable and she hates that above all else. Oh, and she's accustomed to being the prettiest girl in the room—and you're much prettier than she is."

"She's a lady, an earl's daughter."

"That might be, but she's terribly vexing."

"True." I twisted my hair into a rope and squeezed it until it wasn't dripping down the back of my collar any more. "I forgot to tell you. I think I found our Mr T-r-a last night. Mr Travis is the man with the silver cravat pin who was at the pond just now."

"And you waited all this time to mention it?" She gaped at me, then shoved my shoulder.

"I did just get pulled into a pond by a dead girl," I muttered. "And possibly proposed to. And nearly crushed under an urn. I've been rather busy."

"Oh, very well," she grumbled. She paused. "Wait. An urn?" she asked quizzically.

I told her about the urn and Mr Travis.

We got to our feet, shivering in our damp dresses. The sun might be warm on our shoulders but it was definitely time to put on something dry. We made our way back over the hills and across the tidy lawns with their perfectly groomed weeping willows.

"You know what we have to do, don't you?" Elizabeth asked finally, with an eager grin.

I instantly felt uneasy.

"What's that?"

"We are going to have to snoop." She rubbed her hands together. "Finally, my mother's training will be put to good use. Never mind finding an eligible bachelor, I mean to find a murderer."

CHAPTER 10

I had the library to myself. Elizabeth went off to gather gossip in a more conventional manner. Mother was still abed and likely wouldn't rise until the afternoon. Champagne always did that to her—mostly because she was rarely presented with the opportunity to drink it and so she overdid it every time.

I wandered through the huge room with its towering walls of books. There were so many to choose from. It was better than chocolate cream biscuits, better than Xavier's kiss—and nearly as good as Colin's. I pressed a hand to my nervous stomach at the thought. I could hardly believe it had happened, even now. I would have liked to dwell on it a little more, but it was somewhat dwarfed by the sharper reality of ghosts and spirit boards and murderers.

I made a small pile of books on a scrolled table and kicked off my shoes, tucking my feet under me. The sun slanted through the windows, pooling on the leather chairs. I skimmed thick vellum pages, drinking in the smell of parchment and sunlight. The windows were thrown wide open and the breeze brought in a waft of roses. How lucky Elizabeth was to have spent so much time here. I envied her that, almost as much as I envied the simplicity of her life and her family. Her mother might be dreadfully overbearing at times, but I didn't even know who my own father was: lord, butcher, candlestick maker. Elizabeth's father bought her gowns and satin ribbons and Arabian horses.

I turned back to the balm of poetry and prose. It wouldn't do any good to sulk about it. My mother was my mother; I couldn't very well stroll down to the shops and purchase myself a new one. And I was lucky to have Colin to stand between us.

I picked up a copy of *Alice in Wonderland*, the spine barely creased. It was my very favourite novel but I hadn't yet been able to buy my own copy. I had just about enough saved up, tucked away in one of my boots at the back of my closet. Some of the older ladies who came to Mother's seances would press a coin into my hand when I helped them with their canes or brought them tea. Lord Jasper sneaked me shillings on a regular basis, always when Mother was otherwise occupied. She might have expected me to buy lace fichus with the money or potatoes for supper. I suppose I ought to have shared it. Instead I saved every shilling for books. There was a copy of *Jane Eyre* next to *Alice in Wonderland*, which I couldn't help picking up, returning to it like an old friend.

I lost myself for the better part of an hour in the red room at

Thornfield Hall with the taciturn and handsome Mr Rochester. Xavier wasn't a bit like him. I just knew he didn't have any
secrets. He wouldn't snap at me and tease me, but he'd never
dress up like an old Gypsy woman for entertainment either. I
didn't know why I was comparing the two. Or why I was perfectly able to picture Colin with a treasure chest of secrets.

Jane was just fleeing the church in her best dress with the
news of Mr Rochester's dead wife when Elizabeth cleared her
throat, her shadow falling over me.

I jerked, yelping loudly. Startled, Elizabeth yelped right back,
louder.

"Why are we screaming?" she shouted, clutching her heart.

We paused, stared at each other, and then burst out laughing. As always, tucking my nose into a book made me completely oblivious to my surroundings. I would have made a
terrible spy in the army—the first person to hand me a novel
would have been able to shoot my head clean off without me
noticing. Elizabeth dropped down into a chair and blew a
stray curl out of her eye.

"I've talked to every old biddy here and drunk enough tea
to widen the Thames," she muttered. "I know every gouty
foot, bunion and putrid throat intimately. And that half the
people here are dreadfully tired," she mimicked, slumping in a
way we'd never have dared if either of our mothers had been in
the vicinity. "But I know precious little about Rowena's tragic
demise."

I put my novel down reluctantly. "Nothing?"

"Nothing but the story everyone already knows, that she

drowned last autumn. There were lots of sighs and 'oh dear's'
but nothing useful. What's become of good, proper gossip?
I'm heartily ashamed of the whole dull lot of them. Even the
bits about her father were the same complaints about gambling and creditors."

"And Mr Travis?"

"Nothing we didn't already know. Neither my mother nor
any of her friends will deign to talk to him, and they're quite
put out that Lord Jasper would invite him at all. So I still
can't think where I might have seen him before now."

"Blast."

"They feel the same about Xavier, I'm sorry to say, but he's
rich enough that they'll pretend otherwise. And you're so beautiful, they think him quite lucky." I could just imagine what
they would think of me if they knew the truth.

I rose and went to the shelves by the window. I couldn't
avoid it any longer. "Maybe these will help," I said, bringing
a tower of books and pamphlets over to the big round table.

"It's too fine a day for reading," Elizabeth groaned.

"There's no such thing," I said decisively.

"You're the bluestocking, always with your nose in a book,"
she said, sighing dramatically. "Besides, reading gives me a
headache."

I arched an eyebrow and pushed a pile of pamphlets
towards her. "Read."

"Mother says I shouldn't act too intelligent or no man
will have me."

I snorted.

She leaned her chin in her hands and grinned. "Perhaps I won't marry then. Instead, you and I shall live as spinsters in a cottage by the sea. We'll burn our corsets, eat chocolate morning, noon and night and grow fat as hedgehogs."

"Sounds lovely. But I'd rather have books than chocolate."

"Criminal," she declared. "Would you rather books over pineapple, even?"

"Even that."

We read for a couple of hours, discovering more about spirits than we'd previously thought possible: that sometimes they took over the body and wrote on slates—and the medium had no control over what was being written, that flowers appeared out of the air, that they blew cold winds (without the help of bellows), that women were more susceptible to their powers and better suited to lead seances, that spirit messages were to be followed exactly, and that illness often predated the development of Spiritualist gifts. We read until even I was cross-eyed but felt no less confused. Finally Elizabeth slammed her book shut in a puff of agitated dust motes.

"No more!" she exclaimed. "My head is full and if I develop wrinkles around my eyes, Mother will kill me. And you, I suspect. She is convinced that is why my cousin Mary has never married. Even though it's far more likely that it's because Mary is always cross and eats too many onions." She leaped to her feet. "Let's go for a walk."

"But we need to do more research."

"We'll go back to the pond, see what we can find. That's research."

"And probably a bad idea." I stood up and smiled. "Let's."

She grabbed my hand before I could change my mind.

"We have to put the books away." I laughed, tugging back.

"One of the maids will do that. Come *on*."

I slipped a small book into my pocket. I hadn't yet had a chance to finish the section on contacting spirits and it seemed promising. It might be helpful. We stumbled out into the bright garden, blinking like baby owls.

"Not that way," Elizabeth hissed when I went to turn. "They'll be taking tea outside and if I hear one more word about how bad the damp is for the bones, I swear I shall scream."

She ducked behind a yew bush carefully clipped within an inch of its life. It was shaped like a rabbit, if rabbits were rigid and perfect. Behind it was a narrow path that wound around the patio, hidden from view by several trellises dripping with more roses and morning glories. We passed the conservatory, with its small orange and lemon trees pressing glossy leaves against the glass. A shadow moved between them. I recognised the mane of white hair.

"Uncle Jasper!" Elizabeth said triumphantly. "And he's alone. Perfect."

"We shouldn't disturb him." I wasn't sure why I felt so uncertain. And I was annoyed with Colin that his vague warnings were making me hesitate.

"Don't be a goose. How else are we to get information? This way we can ask him as many impertinent questions as we like. He never minds."

The glasshouse was warm and humid, all moist earth and fragrant blossoms. There was a bank of lilies and several shelves of roses in painted pots. Even in winter Rosefield would live up to its name. Clay pots big enough to hide a grown man inside cradled ficus trees, hibiscus and pineapple plants. Lord Jasper walked up and down the narrow aisles, cane thumping rhythmically and large leaves brushing his shoulders.

"Ah, girls!" he said, glancing at us though I had no idea how he might have known we were there. We hadn't made any noise. "Good morning, then."

"Good morning, Uncle Jasper," Elizabeth said, poking her finger into a pot. She grimaced at the soil when it clung to her nail. I folded my hands at my waist and dropped a polite curtsy. I had a hard time meeting Lord Jasper's gaze.

"Are you enjoying your stay, Miss Violet?" he asked. "I can call you Violet, can't I?"

I nodded. "Of course, your lordship."

"Your mother's sitting ought to be even more spectacular than our little country ball was last night." He was looking at me carefully, shrewdly.

I made a noncommittal sound as Elizabeth stroked the thick leaves of a peace lily.

"Perhaps you and Violet might like to take the horses out." Lord Jasper snipped off a few wilted fronds from a nearby fern.

I'd never learned to ride, which was a necessary accomplishment for all young ladies of the peerage, but we couldn't afford to keep a horse. I was getting tired of navigating the cramped alleys left to us by the lies, by the state of our finances, by everything, really. The guilt sat like spoiled milk in my mouth.

"It's very kind of you to offer, Lord Jasper," I rushed in before Elizabeth, easily sidetracked, could accept. "But we've decided on a walk and I shouldn't like to trouble your groom." To be more precise, I had no wish to trouble him by landing in a heap at his feet.

"Excellent. Perhaps you might ask Tabitha to join you."

Elizabeth slid me a knowing, triumphant glance. "But Tabitha is so vexing." She pouted at her godfather.

"She's still grieving," he reminded her. "You know how her family has suffered."

She nodded, twirling a rose in her hand until the petals drifted to the floor. They looked like blood on the white stones. "She may as well be a nun now." She sighed, and there was real sadness in the sound. "I liked Rowena," she added softly.

Lord Jasper merely patted her hand.

After a long silent moment she wrinkled her nose in frustration. "I was away with *Maman* then," she tried again. "We went to Paris for the summer," she explained for my benefit. "I never did hear any details." Her brown eyes were utterly guileless and as innocent as a kitten's. She could have trodden the boards at Drury Lane with that kind of playacting. We abandoned eye contact when I had to swallow a nervous giggle and her lips twitched. I stared hard at an elegant pink orchid growing out of a round pot, fighting another untoward giggle.

Elizabeth surreptitiously pinched me before turning to her god-father expectantly.

"Uncle?"

"Yes, dear?"

She tilted her head. I could tell she was curious as to why Lord Jasper was suddenly being so evasive and absent-minded. It wasn't like him at all—even I knew that. "How did Rowena die?" she pressed.

"She drowned."

"But she knew how to swim," she said. "We used to sneak out sometimes when it was too hot to do anything else."

He looked at her steadily. "Promise me you won't go to the pond by yourself. Both of you. And stay away from White-stone altogether. They've troubles enough."

We exchanged a brief glance. I tucked the little book further into my pocket.

"Unc—"

"Promise me!" His cane smacked the ground for emphasis.

We both nodded, even though I knew full well we were lying.

"Good. Go on, now, girls. Enjoy the sunshine."

We turned to go and Elizabeth paused, turning back. "But what about the bruises round her throat?" she asked quietly.

A heavy silence filled the room, making the air feel like molasses. I held my breath. Lord Jasper took two big steps towards us, his face stern. I had to fight not to scramble back-wards. He could be remarkably intimidating for an ageing lord who spent his days at Spiritualist lectures and drinking port at his clubs.

"Where did you hear about that?" he demanded.

Elizabeth shrank a little. "N-nowhere. Really."

His pale gaze speared me. "Violet?"

I just shook my head mutely. I wanted to tell him, but I couldn't. His eyes narrowed. He all but barked at us.

"Leave it alone, girls. Or I'll send you both straight back to London."

CHAPTER 11

We stared at each other as Lord Jasper stalked out of the conservatory and back to the house. We followed at a slower pace, crossing the lawn towards the gardening shed. Birds sang from the hedgerows. A grasshopper bumped off my knee, disoriented.

Elizabeth linked her arm through mine, shivering. "I've never seen him like that," she murmured. "He's hiding something."

"Something definitely isn't right." I chewed on my lower lip. "Perhaps this is more dangerous than we thought. Perhaps you oughtn't to help me."

"*Pfft*," she exclaimed. Well, it was more of a rush of breath than an exclamation, but it conveyed her meaning clearly enough.

"We'll have to be careful," I said, taking out the little book from my pocket. It might not look like much, but the leather was worn, the spine loose. Someone had clearly read it more than once.

"Careful about what?" a voice called out suspiciously. I froze, stifling a groan. I knew that voice all too well, and the tone. I knew before looking that Colin had his eyes narrowed.

"Nothing," I said sharply.

Colin was behind the shed, leaning back against a tree. Frederic sat on a stone nearby, resting his arms on his knees, a flask in his hand. Another young man of a similar age stood nearby, smirking.

"Rowena's old beau," Elizabeth hissed at me. "Peter Burlington, eldest son of the Earl of Berkeley. Beastly temper when he doesn't get his way."

Peter was handsome, smouldering. But I didn't like the way he looked at me, as if I were an iced scone fresh from the oven.

"And Rowena loved him?"

"Hardly. Oh, she liked him well enough, but it was their fathers who were well and truly enamoured of each other and the connections they'd make marrying their children off to each other. Even her uncle approved, but only because there was still Tabitha at home, wanting several Seasons to meet eligible young men and show off her gowns. He only has access to the Wentworth fortune while he's their guardian."

Frederic straightened, took a large swallow, and handed the flask to Colin, whom he wouldn't even have noticed anywhere else but was certainly happy enough to while away the hours with at a country party. He stood and executed a sloppy bow. "Ladies." He grinned unrepentantly. "What are you whispering about?"

Elizabeth straightened immediately, combing the curls off her face. "Frederic." She sniffed once. "Are you drinking Madeira?" she asked, aghast, neatly changing the subject. "At this hour?" It was barely noon and they were clearly already tipsy.

He shrugged as Colin took a gulp and passed the flask back.

"Bloody little else to do around here," Peter drawled.

I knew that drawl.

I'd heard it in the garden coaxing Caroline for a kiss.

One mystery solved, several more presented. Why was Mr Travis spying on them? And what did an earl's son and a governess have to whisper about in the dead of night? Did Caroline know something about Rowena's demise that she wasn't telling anyone? Or did Peter, who apparently had a beastly temper? I'd have to ask Elizabeth, but for the moment I'd lost her to Frederic's questionable charms.

"You hate Madeira," she said to him.

He blinked at her. "How do you know that?"

She shrugged, blushing. "Are you enjoying your stay?"

Peter laughed. "He'd be enjoying it more if Tabitha's uncle hadn't just booted him off the estate."

Elizabeth's smile slipped. "You went to see Tabitha? Why?"

Frederic shrugged. "She's pretty, rich, and bored."

"Like you," I muttered under my breath.

"Wentworth wouldn't hear of it though," Peter added.

"He booted us both off, if you'll recall," Frederic felt compelled to say. "He didn't exactly ask you into the library for a glass of port, old boy."

Colin moved away from the oak as the two boys bickered. "Pretty Violet," he said. "What are you up to?"

I tried not to blush as well. It wouldn't do for both Elizabeth and me to giggle and tumble like lovesick puppies. Besides, it certainly didn't matter a whit to me if Colin thought I was pretty. Really.

I scowled.

"Solemn little flower," he said, too softly for the others to hear. He reached out and traced the lines on my brow. I had to swallow, my throat inexplicably dry. I thought for one wild moment that he was going to lean over and kiss me, right there in front of everyone.

Xavier was about to propose. He was the one I ought to be kissing.

Still, Colin was close enough that I could smell the sweet wine on his breath. And then, just as I wondered how much closer we were going to get, he reached out and snagged the book from my hand, quick as a spring storm. I made a grab for it, but too late. "Damn it, Colin."

He clucked his tongue. "Such language for a young lady."

"I am about to kick you in the shin."

He ignored me, reading the book's title. I lifted my chin. I had no reason to feel embarrassed or vulnerable. So there.

"What are you up to?" he asked me quietly.

I flashed him a brief and patently insincere smile, which

basically amounted to me baring my teeth like a wild dog. I snatched the book back. "Nothing," I declared with false dignity. I stuck my nose up in the air for good measure as I grabbed Elizabeth's hand. "We are taking a turn about the gardens."

He took a step toward me. "Violet."

I hurried away. I did *not* like how my breath was suddenly hot in my chest.

"He's very handsome," Elizabeth whispered. "I never noticed. Even with the accent."

I didn't reply.

"You two bicker like brother and sister."

"He's not my brother," I snapped.

She didn't say anything else as we rushed across the cropped grass. By the time we reached the pond, we were out of breath. And now that we were here, with the instruction book in my hand, I felt a little silly. "Perhaps this isn't such a good idea."

"It's our *only* idea, Vi."

"True." I skimmed the pages one more time before tucking the book away again. I pushed my hair off my face. I shifted from foot to foot.

I felt like an idiot.

Elizabeth grinned. "Have you got fleas?"

I wrinkled my nose at her and stopped fidgeting. "Fine. Here we go."

I rolled my neck back and forth to loosen the muscles.

"*Vi.*"

"All right," I muttered. I tried to calm the blood rushing

in my ears, tried not to remember the feel of ghostly eyes turned my way at the ball. Part of me hoped this wouldn't work at all. I'd spent so long fighting to be nothing like my mother that the irony of having actual medium talents hardly sat well.

"Sp—" I had to stop and clear my throat. "Spirits, I invite you." Elizabeth motioned for me to keep going when I hesitated again. "Rowena Wentworth, we call you to speak to us. Rowena!"

A breeze ruffled the surface of the pond. The grasses billowed, tangling. The mud at the bottom loosened, thickening the water. The sun shone brightly over us, indifferent.

"Rowena!"

The pond went dark, as if it were full of storm clouds. The water was the colour of hyacinth and lilac blossoms, the reflection of my face blurring and changing. The eyes I looked into were no longer my own, my violet-blue's turned brown as chestnuts, my dark hair unravelled from its knot, like daffodils around the pale throat.

Rowena floated peacefully in the pond.

"Rowena, why do you keep coming to me?"

She pointed to her throat. Her lips moved but no sound emerged. I'd heard all of those other ghostly voices, but I'd yet to hear hers, though I assumed it was the same as Tabitha's, if less caustic.

"Can't you speak?" I asked.

She shook her head. There were lilies in her hair again.

"Because you drowned? Or were strangled?"

A nod.

"And you won't rest until your murderer is found?"

She nodded again. This was work for a constable or a private detective, not the two of us.

"Do you know who did this to you?"

Her face changed, turning angry and fierce. Clouds gathered, rushing towards us like spilled ink. It was growing colder and colder. Elizabeth and I took a step closer to each other. My palms were damp.

Rowena rose so that she was drifting on her toes, leaving trails in the water. She turned once, her arms out as if she was dancing a waltz. She mimed a laugh, drinking from a teacup, fluttering her eyelashes, flirting. Then she pointed behind us to Rosefield Manor. I gaped at her, not liking where this was going. "Your murderer is at the party?"

She nodded. I was beginning to hate that nod.

We'd been waltzing and eating teacakes with a murderer.

I shivered as the clouds released a spatter of cold rain and a burst of icy wind. "Was it Peter?" I asked. "Or Mr Travis perhaps?"

She looked angrier still.

"Was it Mr Travis?" I repeated. Ice pellets stung us through the unnatural wind. My heart stuttered. The rain fell harder, like little arrows. The water churned. We stumbled back, away from the edge.

"We should go back!" Elizabeth yelled over the sound of the storm. Rowena looked terrified. Her mouth opened on a silent shriek, her eyes like stars burning. There was a sound such as I'd never heard before. She appeared to be struggling, fighting, cursing.

And then she was gone.

We stood for a long moment, startled and quiet. Fear opened inside me like a dark, sticky mouth full of teeth as a new face formed under the pond. It was someone I didn't recognise.

He reared up out of the water, coming straight at me. His expression was wild, hungry and savage. He wore the torn remnants of a frock coat, smeared with blood. His hair was pale and dishevelled, his cheeks gaunt and sharp as knives. There was a gash on the side of his head and more blood in his hair.

The storm raged on around us, unappeased. The rain added weight to my gown as if lead had been sewn into the hem. The steel ribs of my corset iced. I could see right through him, could make out the grass and the pond and lightning on the hill behind him, and, even more distressing, I could feel him too. He was cold, colder than anything I'd ever felt, clutching and clawing at me.

I heard Elizabeth screaming, and still his voice was worse— icy and dark. "Revenge," he murmured, almost as if he was singing a lullaby to himself. It lifted every hair on the back of my neck and along my arms; it was every bit as terrifying as his attempt to take me over. "Revenge, at long last."

I batted him away but made no contact. I was starting to feel as if my veins were frozen rivers. My breath was a white cloud, drifting away. I was weak, dizzy, as if he was pulling me straight out of my body, as if he were either going to toss me out altogether or, worse, trap me inside while he took control. Already, my hand lifted of its own accord. And if he succeeded, I would be worse than dead. I knew this for a fact, even if I didn't know how to stop it.

"No!" I thought I screamed it, but it came out more like a gurgle. My eyes rolled back in my head. I swung my fists as if he had a corporeal body with eyes I could blacken, but I slipped on the wet grass and crashed into Elizabeth. We toppled to the ground. It was enough to dislodge the angry ghost.

"Oi!" Colin launched himself at us. The collar of his coat was near my nose, already stiffening with frost, as my dress had. I gasped for air. "What the bleedin' hell was that?" he demanded. The rain continued to fall, but it was softer, warmer.

I just shook my head, letting the heat of his body chase the last of the shivers away. He smelled of smoke and wine and blackberries. I wanted to curl up into him like a kitten.

"Oh, Violet," Elizabeth whispered.

Colin jerked slightly, as if he'd forgotten she was there. He sat up and then put his arm behind me when I struggled to do the same. When I stood up, my knees were soggy, weak. I felt as if I'd swum in the sea for days without rest. Everything hurt. I limped away from the pond, wanting only a warm fire and buckets of hot tea. Colin cursed, stalked over to me and then swept me up into his arms. I could tell that Elizabeth, despite her recent fright, thought it all very romantic. I just scowled up at him.

"I can walk," I said. My voice was decidedly rusty.

He didn't even glance at me. "Shut up."

I opened my mouth to argue but something in his face stopped me, and anyway, I hardly had the energy. He shook his head.

"I knew you were up to no good," he muttered.

<hr/>

None of us spoke until we were back on the estate grounds. In the privacy of the grove, he set me down on my feet. The oak trees dripped around us and the sun was already coming out, falling between the gnarled branches like honey.

"This way," Elizabeth said, leading us down yet another secret walkway, this one winding past the kitchens to a little-used door. Everything smelled like wet roses. We took the servant stairs and hurried down the hallway towards a small family sitting room. "No one ever comes here," she assured us, shutting the door behind her. It was hardly proper for us to be behind closed doors unchaperoned, but none of us cared much. Damp wool, soggy petticoats and angry ghosts tend to put things in perspective.

Colin crouched and lit the wood prepared in the grate. Soon we were huddled in front of the flames, sprawled like puppies on the ground, fighting for every ounce of warmth. It was so much nicer than the coal fires in the grates of London houses. The smell of the woodsmoke was like a warm scarf on a winter day. We left our damp boots on the carpet. I was still racked with the odd violent shiver even though I was beginning to feel warmer. I let my hair down and wrung it out like a rope, holding it out to the fire to dry.

"Are you going to tell me what that was about?" Colin asked grimly.

I hadn't told him before now because I'd been afraid he would only mock me. We'd set up too many tricks of our own. But given what had just happened, there seemed little chance of him teasing me about it now.

"I..." I bit my lip and stared into the flames. I could feel him looking at me. I tried to picture Xavier's polite and proper smile and couldn't. "I...I've been seeing spirits," I finished in a rush, as if daring him to make a comment. There was a long beat of silence and then another. I didn't know what he was thinking. Finally, I had to give in and look at him. I arched an eyebrow defensively. "Well?"

Which, I admit, was hardly a gracious way to thank him for rescuing me.

But I really hated having to be rescued.

He nodded. "All right."

I gaped at him. "All right? That's all?" I glanced at Elizabeth, whose eyes had drifted shut. Her breathing was even and slow. I knew she wasn't pretending because she never would have let her mouth hang open like that had she been awake. "After everything?" I whispered.

"I believe you, Vi." For some reason it made tears burn behind my lids, but I blinked them away. Bad enough I'd nearly fainted; I wasn't about to become a watering pot as well. I picked at the lace of my petticoat, tumbling like frothed cream out from under my hem. His ears went red, which was odd. He was hardly the prim and proper sort. I knew full well he'd been to Covent Garden to mingle with the unsavouries. He was eighteen years old, after all. "But you have to be careful." I looked down when he touched my hand. "What were you doing at the pond?" he asked.

"We went to contact Rowena," I explained, telling him about the ball and the fact that a murderer had waltzed among us and ending with the apparition that had flung itself out of the agitated water.

"You little eejit," he cursed, shaking his head. "Didn't I tell you there was something off? Did you not even think to protect yourself? Not a speck of salt on you, I reckon."

I only blinked at him. "What does salt have to do with any of this?"

"It protects you from evil."

"Salt?" Disbelief all but dripped from my voice. I couldn't help it. "Table salt? How is seasoning myself going to help? This isn't a dinner party."

"It may as well have been, the way you invited that spirit like you did. You leave yourself open that way, as you found out. You have to be careful, Violet."

"How do you know all this?"

He shrugged, looking uncomfortable.

I tilted my head. "How, Colin?" I asked again.

He jerked a hand through his hair. His blue eyes gleamed. "Because me mam had the gift." He said it so fast I almost didn't understand him.

"Your mother?" I repeated uselessly. In all the years I'd known him, he'd never talked about his family. "Truly?"

"Aye," he said quietly.

"But . . . you don't believe in spirit gifts."

"I don't believe in your *mother's* spirit gifts."

I made a face. "Fair enough."

"Me own mam saw things," he said, looking at the fire as if she might be there behind it. "And they always came true. She didn't say anything about spirits. She just called it the Second Sight. Said it was hereditary and dangerous sometimes, if you didn't take care."

"Do you have it? Do you see things?"

He shook his head.

"Colin." If he thought I was going to be fobbed off with a vague reply, the day's events had clearly addled his wits. He had to know I had no intention of letting this lie.

"She told me about a girl with violet eyes," he said quietly, rising to his feet.

I looked up at him, startled. "She did?"

"Aye." He nodded. "I should go." He stalked towards the door, opening it slightly to make sure the hallway was deserted. His hair was still damp, tousled. I couldn't help but remember the weight of his body pressing me into the grass.

"Colin?" I said quietly.

"I have to go." He didn't turn round.

The door closed behind him.

CHAPTER 12

The next day, Elizabeth leaped out at me from behind a wall of ferns on my way to the library.

I only shrieked a little.

She grinned at me. "Are you ready?"

"For what?" I asked suspiciously.

She tugged on my arm. "Come on."

We sped through the drawing room, pausing for a quick curtsy to Lord Jasper's sister Lady Lucinda and another woman I didn't recognise. We were out of the back doors and into the garden before they even finished a return greeting. We ran across the lawns and through the fields, clambering over the fences. The sun was out again, shining on the last of the raindrops clinging to leaf and grass. A startled rabbit dived under a hedgerow.

"Where are we off to? Back to the pond?" I asked, lifting my hem clear of a mud puddle. "Is that wise?" I could still feel the cold push of the spirit trying to enter my chest.

"We're going to Whitestone Manor."

"Aren't you forbidden to go there?"

"I can't worry about that. There's something going on and I mean to find out what it is. You could have drowned yesterday."

"What are we going to do once we get there? I can't imagine Tabitha will be overjoyed to see me," I pointed out.

We climbed over another fence, this one with a few wooden steps on either side, which made it much easier. Corsets were not conducive to wriggling.

"No, she'd probably have you thrown out."

"Thank you," I said drily. "That's very helpful."

Elizabeth just laughed. The field was dotted with fat cows, all placidly munching away. There was easily a thousand acres of orchards and farmland. No wonder Tabitha's uncle was so concerned about fortune hunters marrying her for her wealth.

"We're going in through the back where no one will see us. Old Mrs Moon is still the housekeeper, and she's always been kind to me. Maybe we can get some information from her."

The house was as big as Rosefield, made of pale stones that gleamed like pearls. The windows shone brightly, like dozens of eyes watching our progress. All the flowers in the gardens were white as well: roses, foxgloves, dahlias. It was lovely, like a fairytale. We followed a wide dirt path around to the servants' entrance. Elizabeth didn't seem to mind overly, even though ladies never used the back doors. She just smiled as if we were being naughty. The servants curtsied as we passed or tugged their caps. I felt awkward, as if I were intruding. I was more like them than I was like Elizabeth. Three years ago I would have been curtsying to her in the same manner. Oblivious, Elizabeth just sailed right through the kitchen.

"Wentworth has a French cook," she whispered. "He always made the most delicious sauces. Better even than Uncle Jasper's chef."

The cook was standing behind a huge wooden table, slicing a leg of meat. A kitchen girl handed him brightly polished utensils off a white napkin. Something delicious-smelling bubbled in a pot on the stove. In the scullery on the far side, two maids washed a pile of dishes in a deep sink. Their hair was damp, arms red and chapped. I looked away. One false move and I might end up here, as Mother was so fond of telling me.

We passed through to the still room. Elizabeth stood in the doorway smiling widely until Mrs Moon looked up from the flowers she was crystallising. There were violet and rose and marigold petals, all coated with sugar. She wiped her hands before bustling over. She looked just like her name, round and cheerful with white hair carefully curled and pinned under a white ruffled bonnet. She smelled like violets and tea.

"Bless me, child, we haven't seen you here since . . . well, it has been a long time, hasn't it?"

"Oh, I've missed you!" Elizabeth hugged her briefly.

"And look at you, all grown up. Don't you look smart in that pretty dress." She clicked her tongue. "I'm all covered in sugar—mind yourself."

"Oh, I don't care a fig about that," Elizabeth said. "Besides, we're covered in mud as it is."

Mrs Moon smiled, her blue eyes crinkling at the corners. "So you are. And who's this, then?"

"Violet Willoughby, this is Mrs Moon. She makes the best berry tarts in all of England."

"Flatterer. Come on, then, I expect you're thirsty."

We followed her into the housekeeper's parlour, where there was a hearth with a single easy chair in front of it and several baskets of knitting. The cupboards on the opposite wall were packed floor to ceiling with the manor preserves, jams, spices and sugar. She lowered herself carefully into a chair at the small table, motioning for us to do the same. A maid hurried in with a tray of tea and berry tarts.

Elizabeth all but fell on the tarts. She ate with a little moan of delight before she recollected why we were here in the first place.

"Tell me, then, have you been keeping out of mischief?" Mrs Moon asked.

Elizabeth smiled breezily, licking a bit of raspberry off her lip. "Of course."

"Mmm-hmm."

We drank our tea with fresh milk and ate tarts. It wasn't until she'd reached the bottom of her cup that Elizabeth remarked on anything other than the weather and fond memories of Mrs Moon chasing her and Rowena out of the kitchen with a broom when they accidentally turned over a pot of bubbling jam. At the mention of Rowena's name, Mrs Moon sighed. "Poor lamb."

"I still miss her," Elizabeth said quietly.

Mrs Moon patted her hand. "Of course you do, dear."

"I still don't understand how she drowned. She swam quite well."

Mrs Moon looked away. "A dreadful accident," was all she said.

Elizabeth leaned forward, rattling her empty cup. "But it doesn't make sense, Moony." I gathered this was their childhood nickname for the housekeeper.

"Tragedies never make sense. Have some more tea."

She poured the rest of the pot out and pushed more tarts towards us. Chewing wasn't going to stop Elizabeth from asking questions though. She just took smaller bites and swallowed more quickly. "Do you remember that day? When Rowena drowned?"

"'Course I do. She'd had another row with her beau and couldn't sleep. Tabitha was sulking because her father sent word that he'd stay in India for the foreseeable future. Miss Donovan was here too, though the girls were too distracted for lessons, it was that hot out."

"Was there no one . . . strange about?"

Mrs Moon frowned. "What do ye mean, strange? Sir Wentworth had guests and even your own Lord Jasper's house was full to the brim with summer visitors. It's always like that in the summer."

"But no one . . . sinister?"

"*Hmph.* Don't go getting wild ideas in your head, Lizzie. You always were one for storytelling. Rowena had an accident. I expect she was tired or else suffered a cramp of some kind. The doctor said it would have been peaceful-like." Mrs Moon touched a napkin to her lips. She stood up with a warm but firm smile. "Shall I go and see if Miss Tabitha is at home?"

"But we came to see you," Elizabeth said.

"Oh?" She raised her eyebrows. "And not even a hello for your old childhood friend?"

"I've seen Tabitha all week at Uncle Jasper's," Elizabeth muttered. "And she's cross as two cats."

"Well, I expect she's just tired."

Elizabeth gave a long-suffering sigh as she dragged herself into a standing position. "Very well, if we *must*."

"It's what ladies do." The housekeeper said it very decisively. "Now, come along."

We followed obediently behind her, making faces. The last thing I wanted to do was call on Tabitha. The rooms were huge, every surface polished and dusted. The curtains were heavy velvet, but here in the country, they were pulled back to let in the sunlight. There was no danger of the city's coal fog smearing every nook and cranny with soot. We were left in a sunny parlour, vases of orchids and gladioli sharing their heavy scents.

"So both Caroline and Peter were here," I whispered. "And they have a secret between them—I heard them in the garden one night."

Elizabeth's eyes widened. "Really? But he's a gentleman. And she's too dull to have secrets."

A few moments later the sound of footsteps echoed down the hallway. Tabitha stopped in the doorway, wearing a beautiful yellow dress with a white underskirt. She looked exceedingly tired.

"What are you two doing here?" she asked suspiciously.

"I came to eat Moony's tarts," Elizabeth said, lounging back with a hand on her stomach. She groaned. "And I ate too many."

"You never did know when to stop," Tabitha said, but not unkindly. She sat down on the edge of a scrolled chair, as if she wasn't sure if she was going to bolt. She eyed me with distrust. I just smiled as inoffensively as I could. I'd been dealing with Mother's temper all these years; I wasn't going to be cowed by a debutante, no matter what her family connections might be. There were crystal vases everywhere, overflowing with roses and irises and larkspur. Elizabeth stifled a sneeze.

"Why all the flowers?" she asked.

Tabitha lifted her chin haughtily. "They're from my admirers." There were enough of them to stock a flower shop twice over. She looked over them proudly. "Almost every eligible bachelor at Rosefield has sent some, even Fitzwilliam." I wondered briefly if Xavier sent any but wouldn't give her the satisfaction of peeking. "There are even some from London, though I haven't been there in over a year and I'm not even officially out yet." She preened like a cat.

"Your uncle must have had a fit of nerves," Elizabeth snorted.

"A little," she admitted.

"Shall we call on him?" Elizabeth asked, still rubbing her too-full belly.

"No, he's in a dreadful temper. He lost at cards and then saw all the flowers. And father sent word that—" She glanced at me. "Well, never mind. He's in a temper."

"Just as well. I don't think I can move."

"Are you enjoying your stay in the country?" Tabitha asked me stiffly.

"Yes, thank you." I nodded.

"Would you like some tea?"

"No, thank you."

Polite parlour conversation always made me feel itchy. Colin and Frederic, though of different classes, were allowed to sneak off and drink Madeira behind the shed. No one expected them to smile and sit politely. I suddenly envied them and their choices. I wanted to stroll through Vauxhall Gardens and visit the gaming hells and the opium dens. I wanted to walk in Hyde Park without a maid, or ride too fast in a carriage down St James Street. I suddenly wanted it all.

And I was going to start by throwing off the pretty shackles of drawing room chatter. It was probably a bad idea. I wasn't sure why I did it, but I couldn't seem to help myself. I leaned forward.

"Tabitha, your sister wants us to find her murderer."

Not precisely how I'd meant to begin.

"Not this again," Tabitha snapped, turning to Elizabeth, who had sat up from her lounging as if a stray spark from the grate had set her skirts on fire. "Why did you bring your lunatic friend with you if you can't control her?"

"Tabitha, please just listen to her," she pleaded.

"I've already told you, I'm not a Spiritualist. I don't believe in ghosts." She whirled towards me. "Is she here right now?"

I shook my head. "No."

"How convenient."

"It doesn't work that way. Actually, I'm not entirely certain how it works," I admitted.

"It doesn't work at all," she said. "And my sister wasn't murdered. She *drowned*."

"You know as well as I do that your sister was far too good a swimmer to drown in a little pond." Elizabeth scoffed.

Tabitha narrowed her eyes. "You didn't think so before you met *her*." By which I gathered she meant me.

"Perhaps that's true. But it's only because she made me think, not just blindly accept what I was being told. And you can't deny people have been acting strangely about it."

"I don't know what you mean." Tabitha was trying to sound uninterested but it was too late. I'd caught the flicker in her eye. I just wasn't entirely certain as to how to decipher it.

"Perhaps I'm wrong then," I said. "I *hope* so. I only know that she's trying to tell me something, and that she's trying to protect you."

"From what?" I don't think she knew she was chewing anxiously on her lower lip.

"I'm not sure. But she won't rest. Not until we find out what happened to her."

"She drowned. She was tired."

"Do you really believe that?" I asked softly.

She leaped to her feet and paced to the window. "I have

to." It was the most honest thing I'd heard her say. Although I didn't like her much, I could at least admire her for that alone.

"Can you remember who was here that week?" I asked. "We have to start somewhere."

"Start what?"

"Our investigation," Elizabeth replied, eyes shining.

"I think you're both daft," Tabitha said.

Elizabeth shrugged a shoulder. "Perhaps. But try to remember which guests were here anyway."

Tabitha sighed, as if she were greatly put upon.

"We didn't spend much time with the guests. We were still in the schoolroom, you'll recall. Caroline was here, of course, and Peter was courting Rowena, though she was sweet on someone else. She only paid him any attention because they've been betrothed since we were seven years old."

"She was sweet on someone?" Elizabeth caught the scent of gossip as a hound caught the scent of deer in the woods. She would have put her nose to the ground if she'd thought it would help. "Who was she flirting with? She never told me a thing!"

"I still don't know," Tabitha admitted. "She wouldn't tell me either. Anyway, no one ever spoke up afterwards, or seemed more upset than the others at the funeral."

Elizabeth nodded, clearly trying to remember. "I was at Highgate Cemetery for the London service," she said quietly. "I don't remember any young man in particular either." She tapped her fingers on her knee. "That's going to bother me now."

I nudged her. "Focus."

"Right, sorry. Who else was here, Tabitha?"

"I'm not sure. I think your cousin Frederic was at Rosefield with his sisters and both your aunts. Uncle's town friends came down, but I don't remember their names. Lords Winterbourne, Underhall and Fitzwilliam as well, of course. They always come to a good party." I recognised them from Rosefield. They spent most of their time gambling and hunting.

"Fitzwilliam," Elizabeth sighed. "He's utterly divine, isn't he?"

He was rather handsome, with dark hair and a proud profile. He winked at all the debutantes to make them giggle. And he'd taken his coat off during the croquet game.

"Rowena thought so too," Tabitha said. "I think he's far too old."

"And Mr Travis?" I asked casually.

She frowned. "Who?"

"He's one of the Spiritualists visiting Rosefield," Elizabeth explained. "Very tall and rather thin? From the village?"

Tabitha shrugged. "I don't know him. Hardly sounds worth an introduction."

Elizabeth rolled her eyes at me. "Is that all?" she pressed Tabitha.

"Yes. We were busy reading Greek myths and Caroline was an absolute bear about letting us out to mingle with the adults."

Tabitha wavered in front of me, but only for a moment. Then Rowena was there, streaming water and lily petals. Her hand was pale and fluttered up to her neck. On her left hand, the gold ring with the tiny pearls that I'd found in the mud. The one Tabitha had grabbed from me. The one she was wearing right now.

"Rowena's ring," I murmured questioningly. Tabitha curled her finger into the palm of her opposite hand, as if to hide it.

"I said as much," she answered defensively. "So?"

"Tabitha," I said gently. "What are you hiding?"

"Nothing. She wouldn't tell me who gave it to her, and she wouldn't take it off." She looked as if she might say something else, but at that moment Caroline rushed in, flustered.

"There you are," she said. "I wondered where you'd gone off to."

Tabitha clamped her lips together. "I've hardly run away," she said, annoyed. "You needn't hover like a mother hen. I'm perfectly capable of being alone for an hour."

Caroline murmured placatingly and sat on a settee in the corner. Tabitha looked away, her entire posture changing. Whatever she might have been getting ready to tell us wasn't going to be revealed now. Not with her governess watching her every movement. Tabitha stiffened, as if her corset had just been tightened.

"Thank you for visiting," she said, "but I'm feeling a little off colour."

"Perhaps you ought to lie down," Caroline suggested softly.

"No, I'll go for a walk in the garden." She was pale. She pulled a tin of lozenges out of her pocket and slipped one under her tongue.

Elizabeth frowned. "Are those laudanum sweets? Why are you taking those?"

"I have black headaches," she answered tersely. She walked away without another word. I tried to ignore the hazy presence of several ghost-maids, winking in and out of sight by the window, all staring at me beseechingly.

I didn't like the way Caroline watched us go, her expression determined and even more pinched than usual.

CHAPTER 13

None of our subtle espionage had done us much good. Even our more deliberate questioning hadn't revealed anything particularly helpful. At this rate, I'd be an old lady in my rocking chair with Rowena still flitting about me like an annoying gnat. The image alone was enough to keep me awake for hours.

I finally gave up and decided to go downstairs to the library. I went as quietly as I could, bringing a candle with me so I wouldn't stumble into any furniture and wake the household. I was being so careful, I knew instantly that the creak of floorboards wasn't the result of my own footsteps. I froze. Another creak. I had no idea if it was a ghostly footstep or a more mundane human step. Either way, I had no wish to be discovered.

I blew out my candle and slipped into the shadows cast by a tall mahogany armoire and a cluster of ferns at the top of the stairs. I held my breath and waited. The creaking became louder and finally a figure came round the corner.

Mr Travis.

He looked positively dreadful. His eyes were red as if he'd been drinking, but he seemed perfectly sober. Weeping might have caused such redness, but I didn't know what he could have to weep about. His slouch was more pronounced, as if it was a struggle to hold his posture. I frowned as he passed by me and went down the stairs. I debated fetching Elizabeth but there was no time. I eased out of the corner to follow him. He was clearly up to no good.

Mr Travis passed the parlour without pausing. I raced from the shadowy safety of fern to fern to clock. I avoided the urns altogether. I hadn't thought he was moving very quickly but I lost sight of him around the corner past the library. The ballroom was an empty cavern. Frustrated, I turned on my heel, wondering how I was going to find him now.

I'd lost him entirely until I heard a murmur of voices from the men's private smoking room. The door was closed. I knelt silently in front of it, pressing my eye to the keyhole. I could see the flicker of a small fire in the grate and oil lamps on the tables. Lord Jasper puffed on an ebony pipe, reclining in his chair.

"Can't sleep again, old chap?" he asked Mr Travis.

Mr Travis ran a hand through his dishevelled hair. "I'm afraid not."

"You look awful," Peter slurred cheerfully. "Come and

play at cards. I could use some more pocket money, if you've got any to lose. Ran clear through all my monthly allowance already."

Mr Travis joined them at the polished table, passing around a decanter of port and playing cards. I wouldn't get a better opportunity to suss out their secrets. I made a special point to seek out Lords Fitzwilliam, Winterbourne and Underhall. Winterbourne was the only one of them not playing. Sir Wentworth's face was flushed, whether from sitting so near the fire or too much port, I couldn't tell. Frederic and Peter were definitely suffering the effects of too much port. If they swayed into each other any closer, Frederic would be sitting in Peter's lap. I entertained the notion of going to fetch Elizabeth but decided against it. At the sight of Frederic's undone cravat and open collar she'd squeal and we'd be found out for sure.

"Is that wise, Sir Wentworth?" Lord Underhall said mildly. "You've already lost your favourite horse."

Tabitha's uncle drained his glass and set it down forcefully enough that the glass stem snapped. He wiped his hand on his trousers. "Bah, I'll win yet. Mark my words."

If it wasn't for the edge of tension hanging between each of the players I would have thought it a dreadfully dull thing to watch. Sir Wentworth lost that hand and pieces of parchment, which I assumed were notes signifying a debt owed, were exchanged.

"Your niece is rather lovely," Lord Fitzwilliam drawled to Sir Wentworth. "And about to be launched on to the marriage mart, isn't she?"

I couldn't help but think that Rowena had, after all, been as beautiful as Tabitha, whom he was now complimenting. It was worth further investigation. Sir Wentworth stopped scowling at his cards and scowled at Lord Fitzwilliam instead.

"Not for the likes of you," he said darkly. "You haven't the coin to afford her. Not with my bloody brother at the reins of the family fortune. So keep your distance, Fitzwilliam."

Fitzwilliam only laughed. The night stretched on. Peter looked as if he barely knew his own name, but he still managed to win the next hand. Mr Travis didn't appear to be drinking, only swirled his port in his glass in a manner that made Sir Wentworth grit his teeth. Lord Jasper offered his guests coffee. Peter switched to brandy. Sir Wentworth won a gold watch and lost a pouch of coins. He rubbed his face. Mr Travis ate a piece of cheese. I yawned, bored. The floor was hard under my knees, and I shifted slightly to ease the pressure.

"Deuced cold in here," Peter muttered, slurring slightly.

Cold didn't quite explain it.

Rowena appeared at the table, drifting in between the players, trailing her hand over the table. The cards ruffled. Peter shivered.

"Shut the window," he told Frederic.

Lord Jasper frowned, eyes bouncing around the room, as if he knew the chilled air had nothing to do with an open window. Rowena circled, her expression softening, then sharpening, seemingly at random.

I knew the exact moment she realised I was on the other side of the door.

She turned and abandoned her pacing around the table, moving so quickly I thought she'd vanished. She reappeared, very suddenly, her eyes staring right into mine. The iron plate of the handle frosted as I yelped and fell backwards. I cracked my elbow on the edge of a table. A candlestick wobbled and fell over, silver thudding into the parquet floor.

"What was that?" Mr Travis enquired. There was the sound of chairs being pushed back and men getting to their feet.

I ran all the way to my room, cradling my injured arm and praying no one would follow. The fear of being caught didn't fully dissipate until a full half hour had passed without a knock sounding on my door.

◦◦◦◦◦

"It's not a good idea."

"I *know* that," I told Colin again. We were huddled in a dark corner behind a terrarium of ferns outside the parlour. Elizabeth peered around the edge of the glass to be certain we weren't about to be discovered. "But we have to do *something*."

"Not this," Colin insisted.

Elizabeth hissed at us. "Keep your voices down." Laughter spilled down the hall from the parlour. "Besides, it will all be perfectly safe."

"You should listen to Jasper if you won't listen to me," Colin muttered. "He said to leave it alone. It's too dangerous."

"Well, we can't sit around much longer waiting for a mute ghost to tell us everything we need to know. She's being irritatingly cryptic, if you'll notice." Colin was very close to me; he smelled like rain. "We've made a list of suspects but it's hardly of any use if we don't do anything with it."

"You made a list of suspects?" He groaned.

"Yes," Elizabeth told him pertly. "We're very clever, actually."

He closed his eyes briefly. "Who's on this famous list then?"

I explained what we'd discovered, listing only the most prominent names: Caroline, Peter, Mr Travis, and Lords Fitzwilliam, Winterbourne and Underhall.

"Frederic is, of course, not a suspect," Elizabeth felt the need to warn us sternly.

"'Course not," Colin said dryly.

"Oh, and Rowena had a secret beau," I added. "We need to find out who he was."

"Ha!" Elizabeth nodded triumphantly. "Told you we were clever."

"And reckless."

"It's only a few questions here and there," she scoffed. "And I know everyone here, have since I was a baby."

Colin shook his head—"Everyone has secrets."

"Not the peerage."

"*Especially* the peerage."

Elizabeth looked shocked. "Surely not." She shook her head. "I'll go in first."

We watched her go. Colin rubbed his face. "Doesn't it seem

strange to you that every single person accounted for at the party last year is here now? In Lord Jasper's country house? With a purported medium?"

I froze. He had a point. And Lord Jasper had been vehement in his warnings when we'd tried to question him.

Our list of suspects had just got longer.

"Violet, I don't like it."

"I know, but I don't see that we have a choice." And we couldn't mention it to Elizabeth. She'd never believe it of her godfather.

"Consider this then: what if you end up asking the actual murderer a question that makes him nervous? He'll think you know more than you do. Then what?"

Again, he had a point. *Blast.*

"We'll be very careful," I promised, smoothing out my skirt. The day had been rather hard on my clothes. My last clean dress was a plain dark brown gown a few years out of style, but it would have to do. Mother had not been pleased. At least her head had stopped pounding so she wasn't yelling at all the maids any more.

"Do you have salt?" Colin asked me finally.

"Yes." Feeling foolish, I pulled at a pocket until a small trickle of salt poured out. I wasn't entirely convinced it would help, but I was willing to try anything to prevent a repeat of the events at the pond.

"There's that at least," he said grudgingly.

We eased into the hall and then into the parlour where everyone had gathered for post-supper tea and games. Colin waited inside by the door, as he always did. I joined Elizabeth on a settee, trying to pretend we'd been sitting there all along. We'd have to mingle a little before we did anything. A maid handed me a plate of iced biscuits and a cup of tea. I smiled and sipped at my tea, watching everyone and trying not to be obvious about it.

I let the murmurs about archery the next day and shopping in the nearby village and how certain dresses had a dreadful lack of silk flowers flow over me. There were well over a dozen couples; I had no idea how we were supposed to find out anything useful. One hardly spoke to sixteen-year-old girls, and we weren't meant to speak at all unless asked a question directly. Elizabeth lifted her cup and used the rim to hide her mouth.

"Uncle Jasper you know, and Lady Octavia and Lucinda. Lord Francis in the creased breeches is the family embarrassment. He drinks and swears and smells like fish. Most alarming. Lord and Lady Kearlsey are neighbours; they'd have been here as well. He drinks and she gambles, but only secretly. She lost a pair of bays and her favourite carriage last year on a hand of whist. Frederic," she couldn't help a little sigh, "and the other boys are all at Oxford. Both Ellen and Diana are betrothed and will talk of nothing else. Lord Furlinghew has a mistress in town. Or is it two? Tabitha's uncle you know—he always sneaks me an extra pudding at Christmastime. Lord Fitzwilliam is making Lady Marguerite blush. I wonder what he could be saying." She squinted, as if she could read their lips but soon gave up with a sigh. "Lord Winterbourne there is a little paunchy, but he's terribly rich. Lord Underhall doesn't say much but by all accounts is very kind." I hadn't heard him say a word at the card game, even when he won a hefty sum that had made the other men groan.

Colin was right. It was strange that they were all here, the same people at nearly the same party.

I caught Mr Travis sipping coffee and watching us with a half frown. "Mr Travis is staring at me again," I murmured.

"Perhaps he thinks you're pretty."

"Or perhaps he knows we suspect him."

"Well, don't make eye contact then. And don't glower! You'll give yourself away completely." She went on with her appraisal of the guests. "The Tretheweys you already know, in trade but not bad altogether." She nudged me knowingly. I ignored her.

"And Tabitha's father hasn't been back since the . . . accident." It seemed more prudent to say "accident" instead of "murder", no matter how hushed our voices were. I couldn't help but feel sorry for Tabitha, even though she was flirting with Xavier and shooting me mocking glances. Her gown was utterly perfect, pale pink with cream-coloured lace and pink stones edged with diamonds around her neck and wrists. The stones rested exactly where Rowena's bruises had been. She was very pale. Caroline stood nearby, stiff as an iron poker. I half-expected someone to take her by the feet and use her to stoke the fire.

When Tabitha moved slightly, Rowena appeared behind her like a pale, damp shadow. I swallowed. Goose pimples scattered across my arms.

Elizabeth followed my gaze. "Don't worry, she doesn't care a fig about Xavier. She only wants to vex you."

"It's not that," I whispered. "Rowena."

"Oh," Elizabeth whispered back. "That's good, isn't it? We need her." She pulled her shawl over her shoulders. "It's rather chilly all of a sudden."

"Try and make it seem as if we're deep in conversation," I told her. "And tell me if I go cross-eyed."

"Where's the fun in that?"

"Rowena," I intoned, hoping Tabitha didn't think I was staring at her and decide to create some sort of fuss over it. And wouldn't that just complete my day. Rowena glanced at me and nodded her head but remained exactly where she was.

How was I supposed to have a conversation with her all the way over there?

Mr Travis leaned forward, staring at me even more forcefully than usual. I hoped I hadn't spoken too loudly. He'd think I was mad. And it was no way to stay undetected in my efforts.

"Mr Travis is still staring," I said out of the corner of my mouth.

"Do you think he heard you?" Elizabeth asked.

"I don't know. Laugh loudly."

She laughed.

"Rowena," I repeated sternly, under the cover of Elizabeth's chortles.

Xavier moved away after a short bow to Tabitha. Rowena ignored me.

The dead girl sopping into the carpet *ignored* me.

"Oh, I don't think so," I muttered peevishly. "You're the reason we're in this mess in the first place."

I cleared my throat warningly. "Rowena Wentworth, you blasted girl, is your murderer in this room?"

She nodded but remained where she was, her eyes keeping track of all of the guests and their movements.

"Show us."

She didn't so much as float an inch away from her position. I'm sure it was very touching that she missed her sister, even if that sister was horrid, but she could be a little more inclined to help us.

"You're going to have to *move*," I muttered.

Xavier looked bemused. I hadn't noticed that he'd come over and was now standing right in front of us.

"I beg your pardon," he said.

Elizabeth's giggle was perfectly genuine this time.

"Oh. Uh..." I couldn't think of a single word that rhymed with "move", which might explain how he'd clearly misheard what I'd just hissed at him.

"I was sitting on her sash, Mr Trethewey," Elizabeth lied cheerfully. "She was just asking me to move. And how do you do this evening?"

"Very well, thank you." He bowed to each of us. "I wonder if you might care for a glass of lemonade, Miss Willoughby."

"Yes, thank you" I stood and took his offered arm even though what I really wanted to do was march over to the recalcitrant ghost and shove salt up her nose. Instead I followed Xavier to the table at the back of the room, where the silver punchbowl and glass cups waited. My mother watched us triumphantly. I tried not to glance at Colin to see what he was doing. I probably didn't want to know anyway.

Xavier and I made polite chit-chat about the weather. He was very handsome and attentive, his blonde hair glinting in the light of several oil lamps. It wasn't his fault he was rather bland. I nearly clapped a hand to my mouth. Clearly, this ghost business was pickling my brain. I should be grateful and flattered that he paid me compliments and might possibly wish to marry me.

And I *was* grateful. *And* flattered.

Truly.

I smiled more brightly at him, determined not to be a goose. He smiled back. His gloved hand brushed mine as he handed me a cup.

"You are beautiful as always, Violet," he murmured. His parents smiled at us from where they sat sipping wine. There. Every single one of us was smiling.

It was all very pleasant, even if my cheeks were starting to hurt.

And then Rowena left her post without warning.

She really was becoming quite a bother. She'd had all that time to acknowledge my presence and instead waited until I was comfortably secluded with Xavier, who was telling me a charming story about his aunt's poodle. It was a story he'd already told me, but still, that was hardly the point.

Rowena hovered over me until I shivered. Xavier led me to a chair, thinking he'd been keeping me standing in a draught. I tried to ignore her.

"In a moment," I mumbled out of the side of my mouth.

She pressed against me in a most uncomfortable manner. A transparent white lily bobbed into my face, narrowly missing my eye. I felt cold, damp; even my bones wondered why winter had come so suddenly. I clenched my teeth to keep them from chattering. The room tilted suddenly and I was caught in another vision. I wished Rowena had another way of sharing information with me. One that was clearer.

And made me less inclined to cast my accounts on someone's shoes.

The small comforts of the parlour faded.

I was being dragged through the grass outside Whitestone Manor in my nightdress. The white cotton material caught the moonlight and made me glow. I felt faint and disoriented, with that medicinal taste in my mouth again. Rowena's mouth. It was hard to remember that this wasn't happening to me. I wasn't being pulled towards the pond, didn't have shards of pain in my throat from being choked. I couldn't tell who had my wrists, who was even now shoving me under the water and holding me down. I couldn't see properly. Panic and whatever drink I'd been forced to swallow made me hazy. The cold water was soft. I tried to struggle, kicked futilely. My lungs ached.

I snapped back into my own body with a strangled gasp.

"Violet, are you quite well?" Xavier asked me, clearly concerned.

I sipped at my lemonade to calm my throat before speaking. My hands were trembling. "A stitch in my side," I explained. "My corset must be too tight."

He flushed and I remembered belatedly that ladies weren't supposed to mention their corsets. I followed his embarrassed gaze to the hem of my skirt, which was becoming damp, water unfolding like a blue rose. Rowena.

I smiled weakly. "Oh dear," I mumbled. "I must have spilled some of my drink."

I tried to keep my expression pleasant, even as Rowena flew through the room like a violent wind, scattering lily petals and water droplets as she went. Her mouth was stretched open, hideously wide as she keened. I could think of no other word for it. It was thunder and rain and ice shattering into a thousand sharp, angry pieces.

The soiree went on, as if everything were perfectly normal.

Tabitha accepted her shawl from a maid; Caroline stood just as straight-backed as she always did. Lord Jasper laughed at some jest, Wentworth ate another handful of macaroons. Mother flirted with a young man half her age and then turned to repeat the procedure with a man twice her age. Young girls giggled; young men continued to play cards at the tables under the window. A woman in white satin played Mozart at the piano without missing a note.

Water hammered at the windows. The fine hairs on my arms stood up, like soldiers at attention. I suppressed a shiver. I stuck my hand in my pocket and scattered salt as unobtrusively as possible on the ground by my chair.

"Strange," Xavier murmured, and for a moment I thought he'd seen me. "I hadn't thought we'd get a storm tonight," he continued to my great relief.

I kept my eyes on Rowena while trying to smile at Xavier. She circled the room over and over again, trying to catch my attention, clearly distraught. But she wouldn't stop or pause long enough to single anyone out. I was starting to feel dizzy and overstimulated.

"Are you sure you're well, Miss Willoughby?" Xavier asked solicitously.

Then in one sudden moment Rowena came apart like rain. There was a massive clap of thunder that rattled the windows. Several people jumped, spilling drinks. Rain hissed at the glass and shook the roses.

"I believe this storm is giving me a bit of a headache," I said, scrambling to my feet. "Perhaps I should say goodnight."

"Goodnight, Miss Willoughby." Xavier bowed over my hand. His hand was warm, soft under mine. Rowena followed me out into the foyer. I'd had enough of her theatrics for one night so I ignored her, gritting my teeth. I ought to have known that wouldn't work. She made a whirling of cold and blurred lights around me.

Lord Jasper was at the front door, shaking Lord Kearsley's hand. Xavier straightened and went to help his mother to the stairs. Mr Travis stood in the doorway to the smoking room. Elizabeth and Colin waited impatiently for me by the potted ferns.

All too far away to be of any help at all.

Even the shout from Mr Travis and the sight of Colin fighting his way out of the fern fronds didn't quite make sense. Only Rowena's face coming at me so suddenly, shrieking soundlessly, had me staggering back a step.

That one step was just enough to get me out of the direct path of the heavy chandelier, dropping from its hook in the ceiling and scattering lit candles as it fell.

Sir Wentworth appeared out of nowhere, yanking me out of the way. The crystal drops of the chandelier shattered and skittered in pieces across the floor, like icicles falling from a tree in winter. A candle landed near my foot, extinguishing itself with a plume of dark smoke. The smell of burning wax filled the foyer. The other guests stood where they were, frozen and shocked. Lord Jasper was the first to break the moment.

"Violet!" His cane scattered glass shards. "Are you hurt?" He took me from Sir Wentworth's grasp, eyeing me carefully, as a grandfather might. Colin came next, face pale.

"Oh, Violet!" Elizabeth gasped.

Goose pimples pebbled my bare arms above my gloves and over the back of my neck. Rowena dissipated like smoke. I met Mr Travis's dark, serious gaze and knew he was remembering the urn nearly falling on me. I was starting to be suspicious about his presence at both events. I might have wondered some more but I was distracted by the pounding of my pulse in my ears and the fact that my heart seemed to have lodged itself firmly in my throat.

"Thank you, Sir Wentworth," I said, my voice scratchy.

"Violet! My darling!" My mother clutched Xavier's arm,

dragging him towards me. Her eyes were too bright and I knew there'd been more than tea in her cup. She only realised something was happening when attention veered away from her. "We were so worried." She patted Xavier's shoulder. "You look faint. Perhaps Mr Trethewey might lend you his arm."

"I'm not faint." She glared at me, then shot Xavier a side-long glance. I knew what I was meant to do. I should have put a hand to my pale brow and crumpled delicately into Xavier's arms. I just didn't have it in me.

"Pardon me," I murmured before fleeing upstairs.

Because not only had we taken tea with a murderer, but it was also becoming a distinct possibility that someone was try-ing to warn me away—or kill me altogether.

That night Colin came to my room. It was scandalous to allow him inside but I didn't care. And his face was so grim, I doubt he would have left anyway. He could be intractable when he chose to be.

"You have to go back to London," he blurted out, his gaze flicking away from my nightdress. "And don't stand there."

I blinked at the abrupt change in topic. "What? Why?" I cast a glance behind me, half afraid there was a ghost looming. There was only a candle flickering.

"The light's behind you. I can see your legs through your gown."

"So?"

"It's distracting." Something about the way he said it,

through his clenched teeth, made me smile. He narrowed his eyes. "Stop that."

I stepped away with exaggerated primness, still grinning. "Did you just come here to tell me not to stand by the candle?"

" 'Course not." His Irish brogue thickened and I knew he was truly upset. "We have to leave. Now."

"Whatever for?"

He stared at me. "Did you miss the part where a chandelier nearly fell on your head, you daft girl?"

"But it didn't. I'm fine."

"For now. We've made someone nervous. That was a bleedin' warning, Violet."

"Which can mean only one thing."

"That you're in terrible danger?"

"No," I replied, sitting on the settee at the end of the bed. "That we're getting close to some kind of answer."

"And the closer you get, the more danger you'll be in," Colin pointed out.

"But we can't stop now. Rowena deserves justice, doesn't she? And what if I'm the only one who can help her?"

"I don't much care about her. I care about *you*."

I felt warm all over when he said that, as if we were sitting in a field in full sunlight. "I can't leave, Colin."

"I reckoned you'd say that." He jerked his hand through his hair. "Mind you don't forget to carry salt. And you remember that punch I taught you?" I nodded. "Don't tuck your thumb in or you'll break it."

"I don't think punching ghosts works terribly well."

"And I don't think a ghost loosened that chandelier. Or pushed the urn over."

"I suppose not." I pulled the spirit board out of the armoire. Elizabeth had left it behind for me to experiment with but I hadn't had a chance. "We could investigate the spirit world while we're at it, though," I suggested. "Just to be thorough."

"What the devil's that?"

"A spirit board," I explained. "Elizabeth and I have already used it to speak to Rowena." I sat on the carpet and placed the planchette in the centre of the board, a lock of my hair falling over my arm. Colin reached out to brush it away, holding it between his fingers for a long, silent moment, as if it were something precious. I slid him a glance out of the corner of my eye. He was very close and very serious. I thought he might kiss me again. He sat back and cleared his throat before I could consider kissing *him*.

"How does it work?" he asked hoarsely, his brogue so thick he sounded as if he were speaking Gaelic.

"You put your fingertips on this piece here and then ask a question. A spirit answers by spelling out words."

His hands brushed mine. His skin was warm, sending tingles up my arm. I concentrated on the board. It was ridiculous to get all swoony just because Colin was sitting next to me in the half darkness.

"Spirits," I whispered. For some reason my throat felt hot. "Spirits, speak to us."

We waited, barely breathing. The planchette stayed still.

"I don't think it's working. We must be doing it arseways."

"Give it a minute," I chastised him. "Spirits, we listen," I announced again. "Spirits, speak! Join us here!"

The planchette trembled, like a butterfly pinned to a board. Colin sucked in a breath, cursing. I raised an eyebrow in his direction, as cheekily as I could.

"Yeah, all right," he muttered.

The planchette didn't point to any letters, however; instead, it spun in place. We snatched our hands away but it continued to whirl, abandoning any attempt to spell out messages. It moved so quickly it lifted into the air, then stopped abruptly and landed with a thud, denting the board.

A cold wind crackled, fluttering the candlelight. Our breaths turned white, mingling. The spirit of an old woman coalesced over the board, the hem of her tattered gown leaving frost on the carpet. She smiled at me, most of her teeth missing. Then she crouched down to peer into Colin's face. She wore a towering wig, the kind that was fashionable a hundred years ago. White rats crawled through the curls and moth-eaten ribbons. Hoar frost clung to Colin's boots.

"Colin, be careful!"

Too late.

The old woman whirled around him, kicking up a cold wind that had my teeth chattering. She crouched behind Colin, then pushed at him until her knobby hands poked out of his chest. He went so pale he was faintly blue. He clutched at his chest though I knew he couldn't see the ghostly hands. He shook violently, fighting the possession. He was strong and clever.

But he was losing.

"Stop it!" I leaped forward. She just clicked her teeth at me. Snow drifted from the ceiling. "Oi!" I shouted, abandoning all of my elocution and diction lessons in a fit of rage. I yanked Colin forward by his shirt and then fished the salt he'd warned me to carry out of my pocket. I dumped some on his head and threw the rest in the old woman's face. He shook some of it on to his hand and licked it. Once he'd swallowed the salt, the old woman screeched and vanished, rats and all.

Colin gasped for air, his chest moving violently as he knelt on the floor. His hair fell into his eyes.

"You should carry salt in your pockets too," I said shakily. He took my hand before I could step back and pressed his lips to the backs of my fingers.

"Thank you," he whispered.

I had the urge to kneel down in front of him so we'd be eye to eye, mouth to mouth.

Before I could move, a sound outside the door broke the moment.

Colin dived under the bed. I whirled, making sure I was blocking the spirit board. The door opened suddenly.

"Violet, what are you doing?" my mother demanded, glancing around suspiciously.

"Practising for the seance," I answered blithely.

"Well, do be quiet," she snapped before marching back to her bedroom. I crossed the carpet to shut the door properly.

Colin poked his head out from under the bed. He was dishevelled, in a faded linen shirt with rolled-up sleeves. Even now, with all the strange new energy between us, he felt like home.

He got to his feet and flipped his hair back. "You're not safe in this house."

He wasn't wrong. I'd narrowly escaped great injury in Lord Jasper's house twice now, and the spirit board did belong to him. Colin was right. Something was untoward. I wanted to ask Elizabeth about it, but I knew she'd never think anything but the best of her uncle.

I wasn't so sure any more.

"I'll be careful," I promised.

CHAPTER 14

The next afternoon, Elizabeth was occupied with her mother, so I went for a walk in the gardens to avoid my own mother. The main seance was the following evening, with more guests travelling to sit with us. The strain made Mother sharper than usual; even Marjorie was hiding from her, pretending to mend the hem of my gown, which I knew for a fact didn't need mending at all. Most of the other guests had gone to the village to shop or were playing games in the billiards room. Even the library was occupied, but it wouldn't have made a very good hiding spot anyway, as Mother would have looked for me there first. The flagstone paths were scattered with rose petals, leading between flower beds and winding into an oak grove. There were ladybirds and honeybees and a waddling hedgehog.

And Mr Travis.

I halted abruptly. He was sitting on a marble bench,

smoking a cheroot and looking morose. I swallowed and turned slowly on my heel, hoping to duck back around the bend in the path before he saw me.

No such luck.

"Miss Willoughby?"

Perhaps I could pretend I hadn't heard him. I didn't turn my head, only kept walking, quickening my pace. I heard him rise from the bench.

"Miss Willoughby!"

I was walking so fast now that it was more of a run. I should probably stay behind and see what information I might get from him about Rowena, but he made me uncomfortable. I would much rather duck back into the house and risk Mother's mood.

I was panting when he caught up with me. He grabbed my shoulder and I squeaked, not expecting such a rude greeting. We were hidden from the house by a screen of thick rose bushes.

"Release me, sir." I tried to shake myself free, glowering. He only moved his grip from my shoulder to my elbow. A small sputter of fear mixed with my indignation. "Mr Travis!"

"I only wish a word, Miss Willoughby." He was intense enough that I squirmed. I wished he wouldn't stare like that.

"What do you want?" I snapped.

"You might have been seriously hurt when that chandelier fell," he remarked darkly. "And the urn."

The comment was polite enough, but somehow it felt like a threat. My hands went cold.

"Don't you think so?" he pressed when I didn't say

anything. His fingers were tight, digging into my skin through the thin silk.

"I really must return to the house."

"You're in danger, Miss Willoughby, don't you see it? What do you know?"

"I'm sure I can't think what you mean."

"Tell me!" he barked. I jerked backwards. My heart stammered under my corset. I was beginning to feel real fear, even with the sunlight and the pretty roses and the house so close. I thought of Rowena's furious face in the pond when I'd brought up the matter of Mr Travis.

"You're not safe here," he insisted, his eyes flaring. He was near enough that I could smell the smoke of his cheroot on his jacket and see the smudges of fatigue under his eyes. He still wouldn't let me go, so I did the only thing I could think of.

I kicked him in the shin as hard as I could.

His hold loosened for a moment when he cursed and instinctively grabbed for his aching leg. I whirled and ran all the way back to the house as if I were being chased by wild dogs.

⸙

That night I waited for Colin in the parlour after everyone had retired to their beds. We had preparations to make for the seance. It felt different this time, to be alone in a dark room with no one to interrupt us. It was ridiculous that I'd brushed my hair carefully and threaded a new ribbon through the neckline of my mended dressing gown. He'd have laughed if he'd known.

I wasn't imagining it; there was definitely something different burning in the air between us. It was the same happy expectation as I had on Christmas morning, knowing there would be an orange to eat and extra pudding. Only better.

Although I did find it rather annoying that my fingers were trembling. I was *not* going to become one of those girls.

Especially since he was late.

I might as well get on with it while I waited. I got down on my knees under the table with my basket. I replaced the paper packet and added a small vial of perfume, tucking it neatly in the cross of the wooden legs. I popped off the stopper and then secured the bottle with a piece of string. I measured the distance to each chair. I had to be able to reach it from anywhere I might be asked to sit. There were no guarantees that I would get the same seat as last time, and one couldn't plan a successful seance without preparing for any eventuality, even down to truly being able to see ghosts.

I was still tucked under the table, my bottom sticking straight out in a rather undignified way, when the door creaked open.

"Violet?"

I jerked up, hit my elbow, and scrambled to catch the chair before it clattered to the floor and woke the other guests. My arm tingled painfully. "Bloody hell," I said, rubbing the bruise. I crawled out and sat on the rug, frowning. Colin's hair was as messy as mine now was and his shirt was untucked. "What on earth happened to you?"

"I had to dig through the henhouse for feathers." He made a face. "Not an entirely pleasant occupation."

I wrinkled my nose in sympathy, romantic daydreams flee-ing from the scent of poultry. "I should think not. Did you get enough?"

"Aye, Marjorie's got a full basket of white feathers and another of red rose petals."

"Good. I've the darning needle in my boot already. At least I won't have to hobble around with the bellows again." I looked up at him. "Do you think she'll stop after this? For a little while?"

His mouth turned down. "What do you think?"

I sighed. "No, of course she won't." The lease on our house expired this summer. If no more money came in, we'd be des-titute. Worse still, mediums were expected to accept gifts, not actual coin, if they didn't wish to be labelled professional. "I hate this, Colin."

"I know."

"You, at least, aren't actually related to her." Maybe these medium gifts were penance for all the lies I'd told.

He shrugged one shoulder, looked away. "It's not so bad, not really."

"Why do you stay?" I asked quietly. "Is it because your mother mentioned me?"

"I knew I shouldn't have told you about that," he muttered.

"What did she say, Colin?"

He didn't answer right away.

"Colin?"

He sighed and raked a hand through his hair. "She spoke of a girl with violet eyes. That's all."

"Do you still miss her?"

"Aye." He came closer.

"Is that why you stay? To honour her memory? Even though my mother is horrid?"

His eyes locked on to mine. "I stay for you, Violet."

I suddenly felt warm all over. "For me?"

He nodded once. "I can't leave you to her. She'd eat you alive." He crouched in front of me. "You should get away from her, Violet. There's better for you out there."

I could smell the rose petals on his hands. "The only way I can get away is if I marry."

"Trethewey," he said grimly.

"Not necessarily," I said, suddenly uncomfortable. "Maybe."

"You don't love him."

"I don't hate him."

He laughed but there was no humour in it. "And you think that's a good enough reason to enter into marriage? You've got it arse backwards."

"But I don't have options, Colin, not like you do," I snapped defensively. "I'm a woman, in case you've forgotten. My options are the stews or the seamstress; Mother always said no wife would hire me as a governess." Though I still harboured the belief that I could make it happen. Somehow. "So that leaves one other option: marriage. And Xavier's a good man." I wasn't sure who I was trying to convince, or why I felt so wretched. All I knew was that the moment was ruined, like good lace unrolled to reveal moth-eaten tears.

"He's hardly a man. He'll never understand you," he said fiercely. "Do you think he'll smile and hold your hand the next time a ghost tries to corner you at supper?"

"He doesn't have to know."

"Then he won't know *you*."

"Don't you think I realise that?" There were tears burning behind my lids. I refused to let them fall. My breath caught as I lifted my chin stubbornly.

He reached down for my hand and pulled me to my feet. I was suddenly standing very close to him. His blue eyes were nearly silver in the gloom of the dark parlour. I could see the tanned glimpse of skin under his collar. His throat moved rhythmically when he swallowed.

And just as I was beginning to wonder if he was going to kiss me he released me abruptly.

"We should get some sleep," he said gruffly.

I nodded mutely. We didn't speak again, parting ways in the hall.

When I reached my room, there were pink rose petals scattered across my pillow. I got under the blankets and lay down, inhaling their delicate scent.

I wasn't sure if they made me feel better or worse.

Mother was drinking sherry out of a teacup painted with fat peonies. Her hair was perfectly swept up, her dress black silk, her gloves black lace. Jet beads dripped from her throat.

I yawned and dropped into one of the chairs, reaching for the teapot.

"Violet," she said. "Good. I need you both to work especially hard. This has to be our best performance yet."

Colin glanced at me, his dark hair tumbling over his forehead. There was something intimate between us now, a secret shared—but one that didn't feel heavy or deceitful. One that didn't have anything to do with my mother or murder.

And I didn't know why, but when our eyes met, I felt like blushing. Instead I stirred more sugar into my tea.

"I can't have you getting missish on me. Violet, are you paying attention?"

"Yes, *Maman*."

I could tell she was nervous. Her fingers trembled slightly and she was fidgeting. She hated fidgeters. Marjorie had long since abandoned us; she fidgeted something awful when Mother was in a mood, and it never ended well. I drank more tea.

"Mother, do you believe in spirits?"

"Don't be daft."

"You don't think some of the others really see and speak to ghosts?"

She glared at me. We weren't ever supposed to speak of fraudulent seances. That was how mistakes were made, how secrets were discovered. It didn't matter how secure or private you thought the conversation might be, there might always be someone else listening; thus there were no conversations at all.

"No, I most certainly do not. Charlatans, the lot of them."

"Oh." Colin and I exchanged looks. I knew better than to ask, but some part of me had hoped she could help me with my newfound, ill-approved talent. Colin shook his head at me, nearly imperceptible. Unlike me, he knew better than to open his big mouth. I drank more tea to keep myself occupied. At this rate, I'd have to slosh my way into the drawing room. Mother scrutinised me for a long moment before nodding her head.

"You look very nice," she said finally. "That dress is becoming on you."

I was wearing a dress with periwinkle and black stripes. I'd sewn silk violets along the neckline to make it more current. She leaned forward and pinched my cheeks.

"Ouch!"

"You need a few roses, a little colour to entice your Mr Trethewey. We can't let all our hard work slip away now."

I'd forgotten all about him.

"I'm very proud of you, darling. He's got deep pockets and a handsome face. You could hardly ask for better."

I squirmed, suddenly uncomfortable. Colin's gaze burned into me but I refused to look over. Mother watched us both. "He'll ask for your hand once we're in London," she continued smugly. "He's already asked to pay us a call, and his mother is all kindness to you. Don't think I haven't noticed."

The sun was setting behind the hills. It was almost time for us to go downstairs.

"Colin, you go on ahead," Mother told him. He stood and executed a very small bow but he aimed it mostly at me.

When I rose to follow, Mother stopped me with a hand on my arm. "Don't be a fool, Violet."

I blinked. "I beg your pardon?"

"He's a good boy but he's no better than he should be. You'd be an idiot to ignore Mr Trethewey and his very respectable family for a penniless orphan."

"I'm not ignoring anybody," I said hotly, jerking my arm away. "And Colin's always done everything you've ever asked of him. How can you talk about him like that?"

"It's the truth," she said with a negligent shrug. "You can love him, Violet, but you can't marry him. What would you eat? Mud? Ash? He has no prospects."

"I don't love Colin." Did I? Surely not.

"Then we have nothing to worry about, do we?"

I shook my head sulkily. I wasn't sure when marrying Colin had even become a possibility, or if it was one I would entertain, but I certainly didn't like the implication that he wasn't good enough. It made me feel decidedly cross and stubborn.

"Can we go now?"

She swept past me towards the doorway.

"Remember," she said, as usual. "No mistakes."

⸎⸎⸎

The drawing room was quite crowded, the guests gossiping and chatting among themselves, sipping glasses of red wine or champagne. The gardens were dark and quiet behind the thick velvet curtains. There was no fire in the grate, but several oil lamps burned and a single candle sat on the mantel, as per my mother's request. Colin was at his post by the door, watching carefully even though he appeared to everyone else to be staring at the wall like any good footman.

Lord Jasper came towards us, his cane thumping on the gleaming hardwood floor. He wore black tonight, as did most of the men, with a starched white shirt. "Mrs Willoughby, we are all looking forward to a demonstration of your rare gifts." He bowed. "And yours, Miss Willoughby, should you be so inclined."

I blushed to the roots of my hair, squirming awkwardly. Mother stared at me through narrowed eyes for a brief moment before smiling graciously at Lord Jasper. "The spirits are eager to join us," she said.

"I am delighted to hear it."

"Quite a crush, tonight," Mother remarked, pleased.

"You are quite a sensation, my dear. Shall we have a seat?"

Mother nodded, taking his arm. "If I could have a quiet moment to open my senses?"

"Of course."

Mother sat in a wide-backed chair at the round mahogany table in the centre of the room. She looked like a queen, merely waiting for the courtiers to bend a knee to her. This quiet moment was part of the show; it showed her off to her best advantage, pale, beautiful and unapproachable. Lord Marshall hovered nearby, his eyes smouldering as he drank from a glass of wine. I didn't like him any more than I had before. Mr

Travis was staring, as always. This time he looked back and forth between Tabitha and me. I turned slightly, not wanting to make eye contact. I was trying to find a way to keep an eye on him without making myself obtrusive when Elizabeth eased away from her mother and spoke quietly at my elbow.

"Do you think Rowena will come?"

I shrugged, even though I knew the answer: most assuredly not. Or, if she did come, my mother wouldn't notice. "How's Tabitha? Mr Travis is watching her, but she really doesn't seem to know him."

"He's in trade, don't forget. She won't speak to him unless absolutely necessary. She only flirts with Xavier to needle you. Besides, she's had a row with Caroline and she isn't speaking to anybody now, not even her uncle."

My stomach tilted nervously. This was worse than our usual small sittings, with the grieving widows and bored peers out for a thrill. There were so many more people here tonight; many had travelled all the way from London for the experience. And they were all watching and waiting for my mother to contact their beloved dead. My mother was pretending, but some of these people really were grieving. I felt awful, like a beetle about to be stepped on.

Conversations shifted and retreated as guests took their seats. Because of the size of the crowd, only a dozen or so had chairs to sit on. The rest stood in a semicircle by the fireplace. I already felt warm and stifled, the air heavy with perfumes and colognes and the sharp sweetness of brandy. There was a chair with a curtain pulled around it for Mother's more spectacular spirit-conversations. It was well known that a medium's gifts were best accessed in private.

Mother still had her eyes closed, breathing deeply. "My daughter will see to the lights."

I made a circle of the room, extinguishing the gaslights. Thick twilight eased slowly into the room. When I reached the last light, I looked up into the face of the man standing near it, our faces the last features glowing in a dark corner.

It was like looking into a mirror.

There was no denying that the man in the black suit, with his dark, curly hair and wide mouth, was a relation. A very close relation. The pause lengthened as we stared, startled, at each other. Voices swelled in fevered whispers, rose and fell, as if we were at the seaside listening to the waves. There was a gasp, a titter.

I wasn't sure what to do.

Mother opened her eyes and turned towards us. Her face went waxy. Her lips trembled. "You." She hardly made a sound, but I could read the movement of her mouth.

"That's not Mr Willoughby," someone murmured with the thrill of gossip. "That's Nigel St Clair, the Earl of Thornwood."

The Earl of Thornwood from Wiltshire. Mother really had been seduced by a lord's son in Wiltshire.

Because this man was clearly my father.

There was simply no arguing with the blue-violet eyes, the shape of his brows, the colour of his hair. I felt as if my every limb was filled with air; I was light, floating, disoriented.

Mother's cultivated and genteel widowhood was crumbling, our entire livelihood was in very real danger of disintegrating. And I could only stand and gape, wondering if my father recognised me, if he realised what was happening. If he remembered my mother even a little bit.

His gaze flicked from Mother to me and back again. I knew the whispers were growing louder, edged with palpable shock, but I couldn't concentrate enough to make out the words.

"Lord Thornwood," Mother said.

"Mar—"

She cut him off with an abrupt turn and clap of her hands. "The spirits will not wait. Violet, *the light*."

I hastily put it out even though I was reluctant to look at anyone else but this man, my *father*.

"Violet, *sit*."

I shook my head to clear it and threw myself into a chair. I knew as well as she did that the only way we might salvage this affair was by truly bewildering the chattering audience with Mother's powers.

The only other option was ruin and disgrace.

CHAPTER 15

We begin with a prayer," Mother murmured. I couldn't look at Elizabeth, who was trying to meet my gaze, or Colin by the door, or Xavier, sitting all concerned opposite me. Tabitha was no doubt in the throes of glee at my imminent downfall. I took a deep breath. I had to focus myself.

The sitters bent their heads for a moment. There was no one else, not a single spirit or ghost. Not even Rowena. We were truly on our own tonight.

"If everyone will take hands? It helps to conduct the flow of energy."

Everyone joined hands. Mother's grip was tight, grinding my finger bones together. The whispering hadn't entirely died down. I had to fight the urge to turn and stare at Lord Thornwood, standing behind us. The back of my neck was all tingles and prickles. What was he doing here? Was he truly who I thought he was? And what did that mean for me, exactly?

"Do you feel that?" someone murmured.

There was a cold breath of air, one I knew had nothing to do with spirits. This one was too rhythmic, too predictable. I wasn't sure where the bellows were or who was manning them, but I recognised the stale air. The table shivered.

"Henry!" A woman gasped, huddling closer to her husband. Henry didn't look any more inclined to bravery.

The shiver turned to a shudder.

"Are the spirits here?"

Three distinct taps.

"Yes," Mother translated. "Three for yes, two for maybe, one for no."

"Grandfather?" a man asked tentatively. "I can smell your cologne."

Three more taps. The young man flushed happily. His eyes were very bright.

"We are indeed blessed here tonight," Mother declared.

The seance was following the same pattern they all did; there were just no ghosts to take part. The metal plate discreetly attached to the bottom of Mother's left shoe was the source of the resounding taps. Whispers again, but this time about ancestors and cold hands on the shoulder. Not about the startling resemblance between Lord Thornwood and me.

Mother's grip tightened painfully on mine. I felt under the table leg with the toe of my boot, slowly inching across the wood until I found the vial I'd secured there. I tilted it so that the liquid pooled on to the carpet, easily absorbed before the end of the night. A waft of heavy perfume, lilac, enveloped us. A woman sniffed delicately.

"Lilac perfume! My mother's favourite!"

No one recalled that twenty years ago there had been quite a craze for lilac perfume. There were few drawing-room sitters of a certain age who didn't have an olfactory memory similar to this one. The woman wept openly. I felt horrid.

"*Maman* always promised she would send me a sign."

My shoulders slumped. I had never wanted to run from a seance as much as I did now. If I could have chewed through my own wrists to tear my hands free, I would have leaped over the table towards the door. Mother often said she provided a service, a comfort to the grieving, no different from any priest, who, after all, couldn't prove the existence of God any more than anyone could prove the existence of ghosts. I couldn't help but feel it was a cruel hoax, but I was caught like a fly in a web. Mother rose gracefully to her feet.

"I will retire to contact them more deeply. Let us sing to welcome them!"

She eased behind the curtain, ostensibly to sit on the stool provided and open herself up to the spirits. I thought of the man at the pond. Perhaps it was for the best that Mother had no real talent for this work.

After a long moment in the singing dark, a pale face emerged in the small parting of the curtains. The eyes were glassy, the expression eerie. Someone squeaked. A glass rattled on a side table when someone else took a surprised step backwards.

"Do you see? Do you see? She's entranced!"

"That isn't her face!"

"The eyes, you know. So different."

Everyone was more than eager to offer up their own brand of certainty. Mother's face did indeed look otherworldly. She kept it frighteningly still before withdrawing. And then the tricky part: for full-spirit materialisation, Mother had to emerge completely from the cabinet, with no one the wiser.

Tricky and yet simpler than you might imagine, if done properly.

The audience was far too busy looking at the window, their attention redirected by Colin, who had subtly pulled the curtains. Marjorie was in the room directly overhead with a basket of distractions.

"It's snowing!"

There was a general outcry of appreciation. Marjorie shook out the bits of shredded feathers Colin had gathered, just enough for a brief and bizarre fall of snow on a fine summer night. By morning, the wind would have carried the feathers away. Any that remained would be removed by Colin, who would spend the dark hours when everyone, including the servants, were abed, cleaning up any remaining evidence.

Earlier, Colin had attached thread to the set of curtains at the other set of windows. Now, he gave it a tug. No one noticed. They were too busy pointing to the magically drifting curtains. Marjorie, knowing the routine, had run to the next set of overhanging windows and was now lowering a specially made wax hand to the edge of the casement. All we saw were pale fingertips scratching at the glass. A flutter of red rose petals dripped like blood.

And then it was Mother's turn.

There was a bloodcurdling shriek and everyone jumped in their seats. Hands fluttered to pale throats, gasps ricocheted through the room.

Alice Owen had arrived.

Alice was always popular as she circled through the room in a white shift, careful not to touch anyone. The shift had been soaked in lavender water and worn damp under Mother's corset. Released, the scent filled the room like another guest. Murmurs and whispers followed in its wake.

"I am Alice," she said, her voice quite altered. She sounded younger, her tone decidedly nasal. She stopped behind an old man's chair. A dignified woman across the table squeaked. "She pinched me!"

She was clearly out of arm's reach from Mother. The pinch came from the small metal darning needle attached to a flexible rod in my boot. It was nothing to slip it out under the table and give the sitters a small poke. It always made them giggle, and I always chose the most disapproving matron or condescending young lord.

"And me!" a young girl exclaimed with a loud chuckle.

I hadn't even touched her.

That happened rather frequently as well.

Mother continued to drift through the room. The sitters seemed well and truly distracted, thoroughly entertained by the promise of scandalous gossip and the shiver of speaking to the dead. I was just as distracted, wondering what Lord Thornwood was thinking and if I would be able to speak to him. Even if I didn't quite know what I was meant to say.

It was my fault.

I wasn't paying attention.

Actually, it was Rowena's fault.

The room tilted, the comfortable chair faded, and I became dead to the whispers of the guests around me. *It was suddenly the middle of the night. I wore a thick wrapper against the chill and there was darkness all around me, even in the corridor just outside the half-opened door. I was in a library, kneeling on the hard stones in front of a fireplace. Only a single ember smouldered, flaring red when I dug through the ash. I pulled at the corner of a folded parchment letter, burned at the edges.*

I couldn't make out the writing but I recognised it. Rowena recognised it. And it sent such a cold lance of fear through her stomach that she had to grab the side of the marble fireplace for support.

Her secret was out.

And she was doomed.

I slammed back into my body when one of the gas lamps suddenly flamed high.

I'd been trapped in Rowena's memory and hadn't seen Caroline move. Colin was across the room and too far away to stop her. She shot me a triumphant glance. The light was soft like honey, touching everything. It dripped over jet beads and diamond hairpins, over starched cravats, over the quivering ferns, and seemed to pool on mother's discarded dress, peeking out from behind the curtain.

Mother herself froze between the sitters and the row of guests standing behind them. Her hair was loose around her shoulders, her throat bare of its necklace. She wore only her linen shift. The light shone through it, revealing her limbs and illuminating every curve.

CHAPTER 16

The silence was as heavy as a stone dropped right into the middle of the room.

But it was all too brief.

It shattered under the weight of several exclamations, startled gasps, and knowing snickers. Lord Jasper sat very still. I couldn't read his expression. Xavier stood abruptly, neck flushed and mouth hanging open. His mother was fanning herself vigorously, making strangled sounds. Elizabeth had tears in her eyes. I couldn't bear to look at Tabitha, but I knew Caroline looked both solemn and pleased with herself. Colin was cursing under his breath. Mother shivered delicately and lifted a trembling hand to her brow.

"Where am I?" she murmured, preparing to swoon. There were some who believed that a medium had no control over her actions when the spirits took her over. I knew for a fact that particular argument wouldn't be enough to save us. Already glares were heating, noses were lifting up with apparent disgust. No one liked to be taken for a fool, especially not the peerage.

As Mother let herself go boneless, Colin marched across to catch her, lifting her up in his arms. It was all very dramatic. And still not nearly enough to save us. I finally collected myself enough to jump out of my chair, snatch Mother's best dress from the floor, and hurry after them. We left a cacophony of voices behind. There was nothing people liked more than a scandal, especially one they'd witnessed themselves. Mother stirred, lifting her head.

"Damnation."

We practically ran up the stairs and down the hallway. Colin didn't set my mother down until we were at the door to our rooms. We poured into them so suddenly it was a wonder we all fitted through the doorway.

"What are we to do?" I whispered.

"Whatever it takes," Mother hissed, whirling to glare at me. I flinched. "Who let that stupid chit light the lamp anyway? Why didn't you stop her?" She let out a howl of rage and tossed a nearby china pot across the room. It smashed into the wall, dripping cold tea down the silk paper to puddle on the carpet. She clenched her teeth. "It can be fixed," she said suddenly. She was still half-undressed but she didn't seem to have noticed. Or she didn't care.

My teeth chattered together even though I wasn't cold. Everything had changed tonight. There was no going back.

"Is Lord Thornwood my—"

She cut me off with a withering look. "Oh, Violet. Not now."

"What do you want to do?" Colin asked. "Shall I fetch Lord Jasper?"

She looked disgusted. "Idiots, the pair of you. We have to leave."

"First thing in the morning?"

"Right now. As soon as the guests have gone to their beds."

"Won't that condemn us further?" I bit my lip. "And how will I get a chance to speak to Lord Thornwood?" If he was my father, as he must be, wouldn't he want to talk to me too? And I had a hundred questions for him already . . . Did I have any siblings? Grandparents?

"Forget him." She grabbed her dress from me. "I won't stay here and have those uptight old windbags look down their noses at me. As if they're better than me. We leave tonight. Get your things."

⚬⚬⚬⚬

We waited until the house was quiet, broken only by the soft hush of the wind at the windows and the ticking clock in the hall. It took some time before the conversations in the parlour died and even longer before we stopped hearing footsteps outside our door. Half the guests were finding reason to walk down this particular hallway, hoping for another titbit of gossip. Someone knocked once tentatively but we held our breath and didn't answer.

Colin had sneaked out and was waiting for us outside, at

the end of the long drive, with the hired carriage. He'd had to walk all the way to the village to find one without alerting the Rosefield grooms. The horses nickered softly, tossing their heads. I glanced behind us when the front door swung shut, half-expecting to see lit candles at the windows, curious faces pressed to the glass, or at least Mr Travis with his habitual late-night pacing. They stayed dark, unblinking. I shivered, wondering what Rowena would do now.

"Violet, do hurry up."

Colin tossed our bags up on to the top. Mother was about to climb the step into the carriage when a figure shot out of the darkness and grabbed her hand fervently. Colin moved to shove it forcibly back when Mother fluttered her eyelashes and smiled demurely. I smothered a groan. Colin fell back to stand behind me, looking just as resigned.

"Lord Marshall," Mother said softly.

"My dear," he said, bringing her ungloved fingers to his lips in a way that made me grimace. He was handsome enough, I supposed, even with grey at his temples. But there was something about the way he moved that I didn't like and didn't trust. He was wealthy though, even wealthier than Lord Jasper, and that was all that mattered to my mother.

"I'm afraid we have been called back to town," she said.

"I understand. They simply do not appreciate the delicacies of your . . . talents."

"Exactly." She tilted her head so that her neck was better displayed in the moonlight, pale and fragile as an orchid's stem. "I shall miss our little talks."

He bowed. "Remember me," he murmured, pressing a card into her palm. "Should you desire a change in circumstance."

"I am flattered."

"Goodnight."

"Goodnight, my lord."

He turned and left, lighting a cigar as he went. He didn't even glance at me. Mother tapped the card over her lips consideringly. Then she disappeared into the carriage.

I wrinkled my nose. "I do *not* like that man."

Colin grunted an agreement before following me into the carriage and shutting the door behind him. The seats were worn and the curtains faded, but at least it was clean and didn't smell like someone's unwashed coat or travel luncheon. Mother didn't speak, only brooded and stared out of the window. I brooded just as fiercely. I hadn't wanted the responsibility of helping Rowena, but now that I had it, I worried about how I was supposed to make any progress back in London. We'd likely never be invited to travel again, and certainly not back to Rosefield. And there was still the mystery of Mr Travis to consider. What if he did something untoward while I was away? Or Peter? I'd never had a chance to witness his temper for myself.

Not to mention the fact that the story of Mother's exposure and ruin would reach London soon enough. And then what would we do? Mother's threat of sewing for long, arduous hours was very real. Worse still, I didn't think I actually sewed well enough to have that option. And what of Colin? Where would he go? Would we be separated?

I was fretting so much that at first I thought it was only the gathering mist, or the stress of the last few days, that was making the shadows into faces. After all, Mother hadn't once turned away from the window and her morose sulking.

The view from my window was decidedly different.

The mist thickened until everywhere I looked there were ghostly faces and pale hands scrabbling at me. Some raced along on equally pale horses; others just hovered on the other side of the glass. There was a lady with curls piled high and a line of blood at her throat like a red satin ribbon; another one in a tattered, moth-eaten wedding gown; a man in a beaver hat; another with a sword he waved about quite uncaring as to which unsuspecting spirit he might cleave in two. They merely fell apart like rain, and then came back together again. We were a ghostly caravan, our single hired carriage and a parade of frantic spirits keeping pace.

My expression must have altered considerably since Colin's eyes bore into mine, willing me to glance away from the hazy spirit-crowds. When I did, his gaze latched on to mine.

"Look at me," he mouthed so as not to draw Mother's attention, but a flash of white had me turning back to the window, which was now fogged with ghostly hands. Colin's boot kicked my ankle. Hard.

"Ow," I mouthed back, rubbing the bruise.

"Only me," he whispered. "Look only at me."

Mother never once took notice of our silent conversation. Colin's eyes turned to silver when the faint light from the driver's lamp caught them. The pupils were black and large, like calm

water at midnight. The carriage rocked softly as we made our way down the bumpy road. The spirits faded away.

I hadn't realised I'd fallen asleep until Colin murmured my name. My cheek was pressed against his shoulder. We pulled up to the station and dragged our trunks behind a copse of cherry trees to wait until morning. We didn't speak, not one of us, but Colin passed me a penny dreadful, creased from being in his pocket. When I opened it to read, a pink rose petal fell out, the same as I'd found on my pillow.

I kept it in my pocket on the train ride the next morning. We arrived in London early, negotiating the foggy London streets in another hired coach. The coal smog was thick, pressing against the narrow houses, against the pubs, against the thin trees. Flower girls stood at the corners with handfuls of violets. The men rolled out their carts, selling muffins, baked potatoes and meat pies. As we passed by Hyde Park and Mayfair, the walkways were lined with maids parading pampered pets, little fluffy white dogs mostly and the odd pug, but a few cats as well, and even one disgruntled monkey.

Our street was still relatively quiet, the curtains drawn tight behind every window. Colin carried our bags in as the horses clopped away. The fog was thicker here, filling up every empty space, every alleyway and crevice. It was hard to breathe. Mother sailed upstairs and locked herself in her bedroom. Colin and I sat in the shadowy parlour and stared at each other. I'd never felt so tired in my entire life.

"What are we going to do now?" I scrubbed my hand over my face. "I can't think what will happen."

We were very aware of the unnatural silence coming from Mother's room.

"It's going to be bad, Vi," Colin said.

"I know."

<hr />

Mother didn't come down for the entire day, not for tea or even for dinner. The plate of beef stew and apple pudding was still outside her door where she'd left it hours before. It was cold, congealed and untouched. I admit I didn't have much of an appetite either, but I forced myself to drink tea and eat some bread and butter with a slice of cheese.

I reread *Northanger Abbey* for the eighth time to pass the hours. When I next looked up, it was to the concerned face of an old woman, thin and transparent as old paper. I yelped and fell off the edge of the bed with a thump. She yelped back in that faint ghostly manner, her eyes widening in alarm.

"Oh!" I snapped peevishly, crawling up on to the feather tick and pulling the quilt over my head. "Go away!"

I'd had quite enough of spirits. How was one expected to think rationally and carry on a normal conversation when one was constantly dealing with this sort of interruption? I didn't know how the other mediums managed and I simply didn't care. I didn't *want* to be a medium.

I sulked until I fell asleep. When I woke from my rest, I wrote Elizabeth a long letter. I couldn't imagine what she was thinking, beyond being thoroughly vexed with me. And then I wrote to my father. I couldn't help myself. I hardly knew how

to start, and if it would even be read. Surely he was as curious as I was?

Dear Lord Thornwood,

It is clear you are my father. I am certain this comes as a surprise to you, as it did me. I wondered if you would call on us or if I might visit? I understood my father to be dead, you see, and I would dearly love to know if I have any brothers or sisters and if I get my love of egg tarts from you? Mother can't abide the taste. I know this is very untoward but surely, in this matter, family might be more important than etiquette?

Sincerely,
Violet

I read it over three times before signing my name. And then I deliberated over signing Violet Willoughby, which felt natural, or Violet St Clair, which wasn't exactly the truth but could have been, had circumstances been different.

I wanted to ask if I might come and stay with him, but I didn't.

———— ⚬⚬⚬ ————

The next morning I was desperate to get out of the house. It wasn't normal for my mother to be so silent when a crisis was brewing. A long walk in the fresh air seemed a prudent escape, but when I opened the front door, there was a shout and then something sailed past my head. A half-rotten cabbage landed with a *splat* on the floor of the crooked hall. I blinked at it, utterly confused. Why was it raining salad?

I turned to see a lady with a pram, two men with long whiskers and a gap-toothed eight-year-old girl. The girl grinned and lobbed another missile, this one apparently a handful of squashed radishes. I slammed the door shut before we had a cold buffet in the front corridor. The shouts grew louder, denied their target. If I had better aim I'd have opened the door and tossed it all right back at them. But with my luck I'd hit the sleeping baby or an innocent old grandmother out for her morning constitutional. And then we'd be dragged through the streets for certain.

Dread uncurled in the pit of my stomach.

"Is that cabbage?" Colin asked, coming out of the dining room. Listening to the raised voices, he reached for the door-knob, frowning. I caught his hand.

"Don't."

"Why not?"

I raised an eyebrow. "You'll get a rotten meat pie in the eye for your trouble, that's why."

"Miss Willoughby?" Marjorie interrupted timidly.

"Yes, Marjie?"

"I thought you should see this."

She handed me the daily newspapers, which were still warm as she'd just finished ironing them to dry the ink. She chewed her lower lip as Colin leaned in to read the scandal sheet over my shoulder.

It has come to my attention, dear Reader, that a certain Mrs W— has been recently exposed as a fraudulent medium. She was discovered in a shocking state of dishabille at an influential country house party. Sources say she fled the scene under cover of darkness, with her disgraced daughter. This is yet another scandal in an increasing blight against the good name of the Spiritualist Society. We must be ever vigilant and on our guard against such trickery. Having been privy to the true talents of our day, this writer, for one, was not taken in by Mrs W—'s decidedly showy tactics.

Mother, of course, chose that moment to come down the stairs for the first time since we'd arrived back home. She was wearing one of my precious new dresses, yellow with white stripes on the underskirt. Even with her trim figure, the dress did not quite fit, so she had left off her stays. Her cleavage was rather startling. She raised her brows at my double-take.

"Well, since I can't go about in half mourning any longer, why shouldn't I have some fun? I've had precious little of it for myself, haven't I?" She came the rest of the way down the steps, movements graceful and steady, speech precise. Still, the scent of rose water wasn't enough to cover the sherry fumes. Her eyes glittered, then narrowed.

"What on earth is going on?" she demanded peevishly when the uproar swelled and pushed through the cracks at the door and window. It sounded a little as if we'd moved to a

cottage by the sea. I tried to fold the newspaper away discreetly but the crinkle gave me away.

"That's today's paper?" She held out her hand as I winced. "Let me see."

"Mother . . ."

She waggled her fingers impatiently. "Now, Violet."

I handed it over slowly, along with a stack of cancelled dinner invitations. Colin and I were frozen as we watched her skim the dark print. Her lips tightened, white lines forming little brackets. When she flung the door open, the light fell over her like a painting of an Amazon warrior. Her hair streamed behind her and rage made her face pale, her cheeks pink. The mob paused for a full moment, baskets of stinking produce temporarily forgotten. The door was smeared with pie crust, mouldy cheese and a single slimy leaf of lettuce trembling in the wind.

"You know nothing!" she yelled at them.

"Liar!" someone shouted, and a tomato landed on the second step, smashing into pulp like a bloodstain. I pushed the door shut with a resounding slam before either side could let loose with another volley. Several more fruits thumped, like the knock of a well-bred visitor.

"Mother, maybe we—" I put a hand on her arm but she shook me off with a snarl. All the other sounds receded, the angry shouts, the carriages passing, the rain of vegetables.

There was only my breath, the push of my blood in my veins and the *crack* of my mother's hand across my face.

Colin swore. My cheek stung, tears scalding my eyes

though I had determined long ago not to let them fall. She pushed past me, whirling towards the parlour, pages wrinkling in her hands as they formed trembling fists. We were frozen, watching her come apart.

"Dried-up old hag," she shouted. "How *dare* she write about me in such a manner." Her anger was punctuated by a thump as something wet was flung against the window, rattling the panes. "Ingrates!" She tossed the paper away with one hand, hurling a candlestick at the wall with the other. The silver left a dent in the wallpaper. "Louts and filthy know-it-alls!"

She threw a porcelain figurine of a shepherdess next, followed by a shell-encrusted lampshade, a teacup and then the entire teapot. Dark liquid rained over the settee, staining the cushions.

"Judge me, will they? Had every bloody thing handed to them, didn't they? Never worked a bloody hour in their lives."

Porcelain and glass glittered on the floor and over the tables. She shrieked and knocked an occasional table on to its side. Colin and I backed away quietly, me cradling my still-throbbing face and a wide-eyed Marjorie huddled in the shadows under the stairs.

CHAPTER 17

I stayed out of her way for the rest of the morning. She stayed in the ruined parlour and drank sherry and threw every breakable she could find at the wall. My face still ached but the redness had faded.

When the knock sounded at the door, we all froze. It was the last sound we'd expected to hear. Surely no one would come calling now that we were social pariahs to be shunned and publicly ridiculed. It was unthinkable—and not to be trusted.

"Marjorie, answer the bloody door." Mother weaved in the parlour doorway, her hair dishevelled, her eyes bleary. Marjorie visibly swallowed before opening the door, clearly reaching the conclusion that the mob was preferable to further agitating my mother. I could hardly blame her. And though I knew Elizabeth must be angry, I was still half-hoping it was the delivery of a letter, sent post-haste and addressed to me.

It wasn't.

Instead, it was Nigel St Clair, Earl of Thornwood.

I smiled hopefully. He must have received my letter and he'd come to call, to meet his daughter. He held an impeccably white handkerchief to his aristocratic nose. Egg dripped slowly down the red paint of the door, behind his head.

"Charming," he muttered stiffly. Nothing else flew through the air though. It was clear he was a gentleman of quality and no one would have dared, enraged mob or not. The bulk of his muscled carriage driver helped.

"I'm here to see . . . Mrs Willoughby, was it? Do let me in before the smell sets into the fabric." He twitched the sleeve of his pressed coat and sailed passed Marjorie, who didn't know what to do. She bobbed a hasty curtsy but he didn't notice. I was sitting on the stairs, trying to decide if there was anything left to salvage in the parlour.

"Nigel," Mother half laughed, half slurred.

"Mary," he said, exasperated, when she stumbled and he had to steady her with a gloved hand on her elbow.

She drew herself up proudly. "It's Celeste."

"I see."

She smiled like any polite hostess. "Would you care for some sherry?"

"No. Thank you."

She shrugged. "Suit yourself."

"You're intoxicated."

"Fancy." She snorted. "I'm not intoxicated, I'm drunk." She was turning to wander back into the shattered parlour in search of her teacup of sherry when I stood up. She caught the movement and turned back, eyes narrowed calculatingly. "Oh, you've come about the girl, haven't you?"

I felt myself flushing. Lord Thornwood cleared his throat.

"I suppose I have." He looked me over carefully and I did the same to him. He was quite tall and rather thin, with those rare violet-blue eyes. His expression was bland, curious and distant all at once.

"Your name, child?"

"Violet, sir."

"And how old are you?"

"Sixteen, sir." I didn't know what the etiquette was for your first conversation with the father who hadn't known you existed and didn't look as if he cared overmuch for the news. So I retreated to thick politeness. I'd wanted him to be pleased to see me. I forced my lower lip not to tremble pathetically. He sighed.

"There's little point in denying the family resemblance, is there?"

"No, sir."

He stared at me for another moment. "I hardly know what to think of this."

And this was all the man who was my father could think to say to me. He didn't seem malicious exactly, just indifferent. When I was little, I'd longed to believe my mother's tales of a wealthy earl. I thought once he found us I would eat cake with pink icing and have my own pony and dolls dressed in French lace. When I got older, I'd assumed my mother made up the story of the titled son from Wiltshire to make herself feel better. I never imagined the man in question would show more interest in the crease in his sleeve than in his own newly discovered daughter.

"You never mentioned it," he said to my mother as she smoothed her hair into some semblance of order.

"Would you have married me then?"

"Of course not." He gaped at her. "You were a housemaid. I had a title to safeguard."

"Yes, your mother thought so too."

"Mother knew?" He blinked, taken aback.

"Of course." She laughed but there was no humour in it, only dryness, like wood about to catch fire. "Women always know these things. She offered me a few hundred pounds to take myself off. Kind, really. Most wouldn't have bothered." She shrugged. "So I came back to London. I'd hardly have made that much polishing your family silverware, would I?"

"Well, you've certainly made a muddle of it, haven't you?" he remarked, not unkindly.

"What would you know about it?" she lashed out. "You've never been hungry or alone, have you?" In her distress her carefully cultivated town accent crumbled under Cockney vowels.

"Mary—"

"I've told you, it's Celeste. Why were you at Rosefield if not to see me?"

"I was invited. Lord Jasper has long been friendly with

my grandfather. I thought it might be amusing." His mouth quirked, tone dry as matchsticks.

"Let's not quarrel, Nigel." Mother pouted prettily, clearly deciding to take another tack. "The important thing is that you have a daughter. Why don't you take her home with you, then?"

He gave a bark of startled laughter. "You can't be serious."

"Why not? She's as much your responsibility as she is mine. More, I'd say. You've never fed her or clothed her, have you? Not a penny."

"I have a wife," he said. "And two boys."

So I did have siblings, after all. I wondered what they were like.

Mother clapped her hands. "Excellent. Violet is wonderful with children. She can take care of them." I could only stare. I'd barely ever even interacted with children before.

"Celeste, you can't expect my wife, a duke's daughter no less, to accept a bastard into her house. Be reasonable."

All the blood drained clear out of me. It didn't matter that I already knew I was a bastard; it was another thing entirely to hear it spoken by your very own father. And so casually, as if it were nothing.

"You have to take her."

I felt weaker still. Neither of my parents wanted me.

"I simply can't. It's out of the question. I shouldn't have come at all." He handed me back the letter I'd written to him. "I'm sorry."

"She's a St Clair!" Mother chased him as he made his way to the front door. "She's one of you—you said so yourself."

He shook his head again.

"How am I supposed to feed her?" she screeched as he went down the walkway to his waiting carriage. She watched him until he was down the congested road and out of sight. Then she came back into the gloomy hall and seemed to deflate. When she said it again, her voice was tiny and broken. "How am I supposed to feed you?"

I sat on the step as the shadows grew longer and longer, until the crowd outside grew bored and went off to find their supper. Marjorie came to light the lamps and sweep out the parlour. Her eye was swollen and bruised, as she'd made the mistake of knocking on Mother's door to ask if she needed anything. Mutely, I helped her gather up all the broken crockery for the dustbin, carted out a splintered chair that required repairing, and rehung one of the curtains. There was a large tea stain that wouldn't scrub out of the paper, nor would it blend sufficiently into the pattern. We covered it with a seascape painting from the hallway. The parlour looked sparse now, empty.

I didn't weep until I was alone in my room, with a single candle and the distant sound of hoofs from the street under the narrow window. And once I'd started, I couldn't seem to stop, even when my eyes ached and were as pink as hollyhock petals. I hardly knew what to do with myself. When I went to bed, I used the cold water on the washstand to clean my face. Looking up, the reflection in the glass was not my own— instead it had blonde hair, white lilies and dark bruises.

"Rowena," I murmured. She faded as quickly as she'd appeared, and I was left looking only at myself. "Wait, come back!"

But no matter how I begged, she wouldn't come back. Another ghost did though, but it was an old man who didn't look my way. He shuffled his feet, walking through the wall.

The thought that he could wander through my room when I was asleep—or worse, dressing—had me scattering salt over the spot where he'd been.

I finally went to bed and lay in the dark, unable to sleep, and turned the events of the week over and over again in my head, as if they were good, rich soil that might sprout an answer or two.

Needless to say, nothing grew.

Caroline had lit the lamp at the seance with deliberate intent. I was hardly a threat to her charge, but it was clear she didn't like me poking around and asking questions about Rowena. Were we looking for a murderess and not a murderer? Or perhaps she was protecting Peter? And what could have induced either of them to take such an action? How on earth was I supposed to prove their guilt and vindicate Rowena's restless spirit?

I groaned and punched at my pillow. There were too many questions circling in my head, none of them willing to let me rest. Why had Rowena chosen me of all people? Lord Jasper knew other mediums, surely, and she might have shown her-self to any one of them.

Poor Rowena.

Because if I was her only hope, she was doomed.

It was past midnight when I gave up trying to sleep. I'd been lying there for hours, listening to carriages rolling down the street and making myself mad with attempting to alternately forget about Rowena and work out what had happened to her. Neither was terribly successful.

I did, however, recall something Elizabeth had said about the funeral.

Determined to do something, even if it was foolhardy and futile, I put on my most serviceable dress and hurried up the stairs to Colin's room in the attic. I knocked and waited impatiently. I knocked again.

"What's the bloody idea?" He swung open the door, grumbling. "Violet?" He was suddenly alert. "What's the matter?"

"Nothing." He wore trousers and nothing else. I tried very hard not to stare at his bare chest. The room behind him was tidy and sparse. I hadn't been up here since we'd stopped slipping spiders into each other's pillowcases.

"I'm sneaking out," I announced in hushed tones.

He didn't waste a moment. "Let me get dressed." He didn't say anything else, just turned away to put on his shirt.

It was then that I knew. Really knew.

No matter what happened, I couldn't marry Xavier. I

couldn't marry a perfectly nice boy who thought I was a perfectly nice girl because he didn't know me at all. I felt certain that Xavier would have entreated me to go back to sleep, but Colin offered to help me straight away, without question. And though Xavier was handsome and well-to-do, he had one major flaw.

He wasn't Colin.

"What is it?" he asked, shutting the door behind him and frowning at me.

I was embarrassed to discover my eyes were watering. "Nothing. Are you ready?"

He raised an eyebrow. "For what exactly?"

"A stroll through a graveyard?"

"You want to frolic in a graveyard?" He tilted his head, suddenly understanding. "The one where Rowena is buried, by any chance?"

I nodded, biting my lip. "Highgate Cemetery. Do you think we can find her grave?"

"Aye, I reckon we can."

We took the back stairs and the servants' door as quietly as we could. We paused in the relative seclusion of a ragged lilac tree. There was a definite smell of rotting vegetables emanating from the vicinity of the front stoop.

"At least the mob's gone home for the night," Colin said under his breath.

"But they'll be back, won't they?"

He nodded, not looking at me. "We'll worry about that tomorrow."

"I have coin enough for a hack to get us there but we might have to walk back." I showed him the pouch tied to my waist before pulling my hood up over my hair to hide my features.

"Where'd you get that?"

"It's the last of the money Lord Jasper gave me. I haven't had a chance to get to the bookshop."

He whistled through his teeth. "Are you sure about this?"

"No." I smiled but there was no humour in it.

Colin waved a hackney down and we climbed in the back. It smelled of stale sweat and spilled gin. The floor was sticky.

"Not exactly the Jasper family coach, is it?" Colin remarked, pulling the window open.

The nearer we got to the fashionable section of town, the more carriages clogged the roads with gilded family crests and armed drivers. Gentlemen helped ladies in silk gowns to the pavement and gaslights blazed in parlour windows. I'd thought Rosefield was gracious and beautiful, but Mayfair glittered with diamonds. There were butlers in starched collars and mansions so immense and lovely, they hardly seemed real. Hyde Park was a green shadow curled protectively around decadent ballrooms and men's clubs. We jostled in the back of the hack for a long time, breathing the smell of horses and coal fog. It was blurring the lights and suddenly we might have been entirely alone in the world. My breath sounded loud in my ears as the carriage halted and the driver called down to us.

"Here you be, lad. Highgate." As I stepped out on to the sidewalk, Colin handed the requisite coins to the driver. He tipped his hat, slipping the money into his jacket pocket.

"Mind the spirits," he chortled, nudging the horses into a walk.

"I assume the Wentworth family has a mausoleum on the west side," I murmured. Highgate Cemetery was split by Swain's Lane, bisecting it into two portions.

"They are rather fashionable," he agreed.

The front gate loomed out of the mist, bordered with black iron and a huge Egyptian-style arch the colour of sand in the wavering glow of gaslights. Colin led us past it, not even pausing.

"Are you ready?" He whispered. "We'll have to climb the railings. The fog should keep us hidden and we can use this tree for leverage."

"Why can't we go through the main gates?" I asked, knotting up my cloak so it wouldn't trip me up.

"They'll have guards, to protect against the Resurrection Men," he reminded me, testing a portion of the fence to make sure it would hold our weight. The Resurrection Men were notorious for digging up graves and selling the body parts to doctors and hospitals for study and practice. It made me think of the first time I'd read *Frankenstein*. I'd hidden under my covers the entire night and hadn't got a single wink of sleep. I wondered briefly if the Resurrection Men were haunted by the spirits of desecrated bodies howling for revenge.

"You're not going to go missish on me, are you?" Colin asked, waiting with his hands clasped together to give me a boost. I scowled, my spine straightening.

"Of course not." I placed the heel of my boot in the cup of

his hands and let him push me up until I could grasp the top of the railings. I hauled myself over as if I were mounting a horse. Which I'd never actually done before.

Needless to say, it was hardly a graceful affair.

I landed with a grunt. Colin vaulted over, landing in a crouch without a single hesitation. It was clear these weren't the first railings he'd ever climbed over. I made a mental note to question him about it later. We crept down a walkway hung with ivy, the centre of my head feeling as if it was being pierced with hot needles. I rubbed it, wincing.

The sound of carriage wheels and horses was faint, seeming more distant than they actually were. Drops of water clung to the wool of my dress and my cloak, the hem dragging in the grass. We were in a soft cocoon. It might have been romantic.

If it wasn't for all the dead bodies.

And the faint scratch of a footstep.

I froze. "Did you hear that?"

Colin tensed as well, listening. After a moment he shook his head. "I don't hear anything."

"Probably my imagination," I said. My brow throbbed. Shapes seemed to coalesce, flitting through the fog. No one was particularly distinct—an eye there, a hand, the shape of a waist in a misty corset. The spirits were making themselves known, but the mist made it hard to see them clearly. That made it worse somehow. "It's crowded in here," I said tightly.

"Will you be all right?" Colin shot me a look of concern.

I nodded grimly. "Yes, let's just find Rowena. The sooner we can do that, the sooner we can get out of here."

Mausoleums sat like ornate boxes and stone angels wept all around us. The stones were hard to read in the thickening fog. It would have been much easier with a lantern, but we could hardly stay hidden that way. I had to trace some of the letters with my fingertips. The names were unfamiliar. We pressed on, following the avenue to the famed Circle of Lebanon, in the centre of which stood a massive cedar tree several hundred years old. In the moist, warm darkness, I could smell the green tingle of it hanging in the fog. The stone circle was pock-marked with doors and yet more names etched into the stone.

"Here's a Wentworth," Colin called quietly. I hurried over to him. It wasn't Rowena but we were at least among her family. She couldn't be far. We checked the other names, squinting in the dark. I was starting to feel decidedly light-headed. I swayed lightly, grabbing a wall for support. There were too many spirits vying for attention, hovering on the edge of my vision. The pressure on my head was making me feel ill. The mouth of a doorway opened beside me.

I was going to have to go in. I hovered in the doorway, a breath of cold damp air swirling around me. Colin came up behind me.

"I should have brought a candle," I said nervously.

"I've matchsticks," he answered quietly, striking one against the stone. The flame was small and feeble but infinitely better than no light at all. And in the little house of death, no one would see it burning. I took a step forward, and another. Colin was a comforting presence at my side, the light flickering madly over his face. It was cool, the ground littered with old leaves. I was glad for the warmth of my cloak.

Rowena Wentworth.

There was her name, engraved in fancy scrollwork, and the dates 1857–1871.

The flame ate at the thin matchstick and it guttered and went out. Colin swore under his breath and lit another one.

"Sorry," he muttered.

"It's all right," I replied, even though my heart had just performed a full pirouette in my chest. I took a handful of salt from my pocket and sprinkled it at our feet.

"Rowena Wentworth!"

She didn't appear.

The matchstick went out again. The darkness felt thick and heavy around us, like a cloak I didn't know how to shrug off. I could hear Colin fumbling for another matchstick. They scattered to the ground.

"Damnation," he muttered.

"Ow!" I yelped suddenly. Colin jumped, jostling me.

"What? What?"

"Did you just pull my hair?"

"No, why would I?"

"Well, someone did!" My palms were damp. I wiped them on my skirt. The air went cold.

"Stay close to me." We were shoulder to shoulder, turning to peer at our surroundings even though we couldn't see. "I can't find the damn matchsticks."

"Maybe we should just leave," I suggested. "We could find a lantern and come back."

"Good idea."

The gate to the mausoleum slammed shut, the clang reverberating through my bones. I yelped, so startled I hit my elbow on the stone wall. Colin cursed and felt for my hand. The air went from cold to frigid until the tip of my nose was numb.

"What the hell was that?" Colin demanded.

I tried to swallow, my throat dry. "A spirit?"

"Can you see him?"

"No, but it's so cold. That often happens." My teeth chattered together. "Though this is extreme." I inched closer to him. "The door's not far. Let's make a run for it."

A hand shoved my shoulder, sending me sprawling. The cold seared through my clothes. I fell hard, bruising my knee. Colin tried to catch me but only managed to trip and fall to the ground with me. The cold wind pressed us uncomfortably against the stones. It was hard to move.

"Stop it!" I yelled to the ghost, scrabbling for the salt I had sprinkled earlier. I flung it into the air. The gate rattled on its hinges.

"Got one," Colin whispered, striking a matchstick. Ordinarily, the warm glow would have been a comfort.

If it hadn't revealed the open shrieking mouth of a man's ghostly face an inch from my own.

I tried to scream so fast I choked. I scrabbled backwards, kicking out even though I knew it was useless. Colin lifted his fists although that was equally useless and he couldn't see who he was fighting anyway. My heart was pounding so hard in my chest, it hurt.

Then the spirit eased back just as abruptly as it had attacked. "Oh, a pretty girl."

"What?" I croaked.

"I do beg your pardon."

"You bloody well should." I hit my chest, trying to ease the pressure.

Colin looked around wildly. "Where is he? Who is it? Show yourself, you bloody coward!"

The old man in Elizabethan hose grinned. His pointed beard and white teeth gave him a rakish air. I sat up, bewildered.

"It's all right, Colin. I think."

"I'm weary of weeping women in veils," the man told me. "So depressing. This is a nice change."

"Which is why you pushed me over?"

He winced. "Terribly sorry about that but you were lurking rather suspiciously. And the only thing worse than a weeping woman is a Spiritualist. They just won't leave us alone, you know. Very rude."

"Oh." I didn't know what to say to that.

"Lord Rupert Wentworth at your service, my lady." He executed a perfect court bow.

"I'm looking for Rowena Wentworth, actually," I said.

"Pity that. Pretty girl too, but she didn't stay and I haven't seen her here since."

"Why's that?"

He shrugged. "Who's to know? We sometimes get lost or bored or refuse to leave our loved ones. I followed my wife around for a decade until she remarried. He was nice enough," he confessed. "But a bit of a milksop. When they died, they went off to wherever it is we go off to. I prefer the view from here."

"He says Rowena's never here," I told Colin. I remembered the night in the parlour when Rowena wouldn't talk to me, only cling to her twin and then fling herself about wailing. "She's protecting Tabitha," I murmured, feeling certain. "She flashed once in the mirror, but she won't leave her sister again. Which means the murderer is still at Rosefield."

Sir Wentworth leaned closer. "How about a kiss?"

I recoiled. "I don't think so."

"Pity." He drifted away.

"Mind the bloke behind the tree," he threw over his shoulder.

I went cold all over. My breath caught.

Colin frowned. "What now?"

I pressed as close as I could against him, breathing my words more than speaking them. "Someone's watching us from the cedar tree."

I felt his muscles tighten. "Hell!"

He blew the match out and we eased back on to the path. Colin tugged my wrist and then we were running between the stones, the fog swirling around us. "Faster," he urged.

"Wait!" A man's voice called from behind us.

We ran faster. My lungs burned. It was difficult to ignore

the hands grabbing at me as we passed by, cold and thin. I was shivering, my teeth chattering violently by the time we reached the iron railings. Colin all but threw me at it. Footsteps pounded behind us. Colin landed next to me on the pavement and we broke into a run again, dodging carriages that seemed to jump out of the fog as we darted across the street and lost ourselves in the maze of London streets. My heart hammered. Now that we were safe, I realised I'd recognised that voice.

Mr Travis.

———

Once we got home I thought I'd lie in bed awake, but the next thing I knew, sunlight was falling across my eyelids and waking me up. I washed my face and wrote Elizabeth another letter, though I had no hope of her answering that one either. When a knock sounded through the house later that afternoon, I considered pretending I hadn't heard it, but morbid curiosity got the better of me. I recognised the carriage waiting on the street. Hearing Mother's lilting tones, I doubled my pace. In my haste I half slid across the wooden floors, nearly bumping into Xavier and sending us both crashing.

"Oh, excuse me," I said. "It's a bit slippery there."

He steadied me, smiling politely. He didn't remove his hat. Mother's expression glinted with a fevered triumph. I knew what she was thinking: here was the man who would save our family and take her daughter off her hands.

"Mr Trethewey," she said, swaying only slightly. "You are most welcome. Do come in."

"Mrs ... ah ... Willoughby." The pause was not remarked upon but it did not go unnoticed. He cleared his throat awkwardly. "Miss Willoughby."

"It ought to be Lady Violet," Mother sulked. I could all but see the fumes of sherry from where I stood. I could only hope Xavier had somehow lost his sense of smell. By the way his nose was twitching, I rather thought not. "Violet is an earl's daughter, you know."

Xavier swallowed, quite at a loss as to how he should reply, if at all. An earl's unrecognised *bastard* daughter hardly received the same consideration as an earl's legitimate daughter. If anything, I probably ought to be calling myself Miss Morgan now.

"Mr Trethewey," I said loudly to cover her next comment, whatever it might be. "Would you care for some tea?" I led him to the parlour. His expression of relief altered to faint bewilderment as he looked around. The parlour looked naked, emptied of most of the decorative knick-knacks which had previously crowded every surface, as fashion dictated. Mother remained in the hallway, calling for Marjorie to bring the tray in an odd, sing-song voice. I tried to ignore her.

"Miss Willoughby—" He ran a finger nervously under his collar. "I've come to see if you're quite all right."

"That's very kind of you."

He was sitting so far away, and so proper. Just a few days ago he had stolen kisses in the dark. Now it felt as if something sat between us, all sharp edges and spikes. He stood abruptly and began to pace. It was quite unlike him to look so flustered. I narrowed my gaze.

"Miss Willoughby." There it was again, the pointed refusal to use my first name.

"Yes?"

"I've come on urgent business."

"I see."

He turned, paced back. "About . . ."

"Yes?" My stomach dropped, even though this was hardly unexpected.

"About our engagement."

"Yes. Shall I tell Mother you'd like to speak to her?" I don't know why I did it. I just wanted to see him squirm. I didn't know how else to hide the disappointment. Even if I knew I couldn't marry him, it would have been nice to know he stood by me regardless. I'd considered him a friend, after all. But I knew perfectly well why he had come.

"No!" he practically shouted. "That is, it's a private matter. Of some delicacy." He swallowed convulsively. "Miss Willoughby, you must see that we cannot marry. It would be impossible."

"Would it?" I was finding perverse pleasure in forcing him to explain every detail.

"My parents won't allow it."

I knew for a fact that his mother must have had the vapours at the thought of our families being joined. There was fame and then there was infamy. "And you?" I asked quietly.

He looked vaguely confused. "I'm sorry?"

"What do *you* think, Xavier?"

"Mother forbids it."

"That's not what I asked, is it?"

"It would never do for me to call off the engagement, if one had indeed been formally made. I am a man of honour, after all. I am willing to let everyone believe that you were the one to cry off."

"How very kind," I answered drily. He didn't even notice the sarcasm.

"I am sorry, Miss Willoughby. Truly."

"And that's it, then?"

"You must understand. We are a respectable family and you are ... well ..."

"A bastard," I supplied with vitriolic sweetness. I stood up sharply. "Good day."

"Miss Willoughby—"

"You may see yourself out," I cut him off. He had to leave before I betrayed myself with a trembling lip or damp cheek. He bowed once. I listened to his footsteps recede, the door shutting softly, the horses walking off.

Mother sailed cheerfully into the room, Marjorie trailing behind her with the tea cart. "Here we are, Mr—" She stopped, frowning. "Where did he go?"

I lifted my chin. "He was called away."

"When will he return?"

"He won't."

She grabbed my arm, her fingers digging into my skin even through my sleeve. "What? You let him go? Idiot girl."

I tried to pull away but she was stronger. "He won't marry a bastard, Mother."

CHAPTER 18

Her eyes were slits.

"So now it's my fault, is it? There's gratitude for you." She slapped me right across the mouth. "You're not to speak to me that way. I am your mother. You don't know what I've suffered. I demand your respect."

I tasted blood on my lip.

"Stupid girl!" she yelled. "We need him. He was our last hope." She slapped me again until I stumbled back against a chair. The legs scraped the floor. "Now we have nothing! Nothing!"

It was a punch this time and pain seared my eye, a bruise already blooming like a black rose. I threw my hands up to protect myself as Marjorie sobbed. One of the other chairs slid into the settee, slamming it against the wall. The table tilted and wobbled, untouched, as if some unseen medium sat there.

The spirits were gathering, and Mother didn't notice their

objections to her treatment of me. The curtains flapped and twisted as if a storm was blowing. Angry faces formed in the mirrors, in the windows, even in the milk jug on the tray.

It seemed like ages before Colin burst through the door and pulled her off me.

"Get off!" he yelled. She scratched at him and blood trickled down the side of his face. His eyes were like tarnished silver coins.

"Fine!" she screeched. "You two deserve each other!"

She flung off his restraining hand and stalked upstairs. Her bedroom door slammed hard enough to rattle the chandelier in the hall. I stayed on the floor, curled into a tight ball. Colin crouched, his breathing hard, his words forced between his clenched teeth.

"Violet, she's gone." He reached out to stroke my hair, so gently I might have imagined it. "You're all right now, she's gone."

Marjorie left and then returned and I still didn't move. She handed Colin a chunk of raw beef wrapped in a towel.

"For the swelling," she whispered before leaving again. The door shut quietly behind her. It was just Colin and me and the sun setting at the window, burning lavender and orange through the gaps in the curtains. He didn't say anything, just handed me the towel and went to light a fire in the grate. The scratch of the matches, the lick of the fire against the wood were a comforting lullaby. I sat up carefully, my face aching, my arms sore. I wrinkled my nose at the red meat.

"I don't know how I feel about having supper on my face."

"It'll help," Colin promised, feeding more wood into the flames. He didn't turn round until I tried to stand up, and then he was at my elbow almost instantly. I tried to smile even though it wasn't terribly convincing.

"I'm all right," I assured him.

He only grunted, but he did step back enough to let me make my own way to the chair nearest the fire. "What set her off this time?" he asked grimly.

I held the raw beefsteak gingerly against my cheek, grimacing. "Xavier came."

"Ah." There was a long beat of silence. "And?"

"And you can't expect a son from a respectable family to marry a bastard, can you?" I tried to ignore the flutter of ghostly movement by the door. Perhaps if I didn't pay them any attention, the spirits would grow bored with me and leave. Already a pair of disembodied eyes watched me from the doorway, and a head hovered through the glass-encased clock on the manlte.

Colin's mouth tightened. "He said that to you?"

"He might as well have. It's what he meant to say between all the polite stammering."

"Eejit."

I tossed the beef wrap aside. "I suppose I'm better off."

He was careful not to meet my gaze. "Did you love him, then?"

"I thought I might be able to. I suppose not, though, as I'm not nearly as upset as I ought to be."

"Good."

"There's no escape for me now though," I murmured.

When I looked up there was a crush of spirits, all watching me intently. I shivered. Colin followed my glance, saw nothing, looked closer, and still saw only furniture and firelight.

"Stop it," I said softly but firmly. They remained and seemed only the more interested.

"Tell Bradley I miss him," came a whisper.

"Can you see us?"

"Where's the old enamelled table that used to sit here? I carved my name on it once, when I was six."

I shut my eyes tightly for a few moments. Colin took my hand, his warm, callused palm against mine. When I opened my eyes again, most of the spirits had faded except for an older man standing at Colin's shoulder, cap in hand.

"Miss, if you don't mind . . ."

I smiled. "Colin, your grandfather was a gardener, wasn't he? Back in Ireland? Bushy eyebrows, big hands?"

Colin blinked at me. "Aye."

I nodded, listening. "When you were five you dug up all of his turnips and ate them. He says you had such a bellyache, he didn't have the heart to punish you."

Colin looked behind him. "Is he here?"

"He was," I said as the old man vanished. "He looks out for you, I think."

"And my mother?"

I shook my head. "I'm sorry. I could only see him."

"Hell of a talent, Vi," he said finally.

"I know." I pushed my hair off my shoulders, wincing when my neck protested.

"Does it hurt?" he asked instantly. "You've got a right shiner starting already."

My eye did feel tender and puffy but at least the sharp throbbing had subsided. My lip tingled painfully.

"You have to get out of here, Violet," he said quietly, grimly.

"Where am I supposed to go? Lord Thornwood won't take me in, and even if he did, do you expect his family would accept me?" I snorted. "I rather doubt it."

"I know she's your mam, but she's no good for you."

"Can we not talk about this?" I asked, mostly because I knew he was right. "I really just want to forget this day ever happened." I leaned my head back. The room was dark now, the sun had long since set completely in the fog. The fire was cheerful and the rest of the house so hushed it might have been deserted. Marjorie and Cook were no doubt in hiding in the back of the kitchen, and Mother always took to her bed after one of her fits, no matter the time. Even the streets outside were quiet.

"Colin?" I was suddenly very aware of his body close beside me, his legs stretched along mine, our boots resting lightly together.

"Hmm?"

"Thank you."

I seized the moment before I could talk myself out of it.

I kissed him because kissing Colin was like being outside during an electrical storm and refusing to go inside where it was safe. He tasted like sugar and smoke. He tasted right. His hand cradled the back of my neck. My cut lip tingled slightly at the pressure but I hardly cared. We kissed as if there was nothing more important, not even air.

Finally, when we pulled apart to rest my already sore lip, we stretched out on the carpet in front of the fire. We drank cold tea, ate all the biscuits and bread and butter sandwiches and talked for hours.

"Perhaps Mother's wrong," I said, watching the flames thoughtfully, chin propped on my hand. "I might make a good governess. I do love to read, after all."

"You're clever enough," Colin assured me. "But your mother's right. No one would hire you. You're too pretty."

"Oh, honestly."

"Wives of earls and dukes don't bring pretty sixteen-year-old girls to live with them, Violet. It'd be daft."

I blew out a breath, ruffling a lock of hair falling over my shoulder. "That's not fair."

He shrugged one shoulder negligently. "It never is." He lay next to me, shoulder brushing mine. "You could be part of the black-letter gentry, like Charles Dickens and the Bell brothers you love so much, and write your own books."

I smiled. "That sounds lovely. I suppose I could also be a teacher in one of those dreadful academies. I'd need to save enough money to advertise first. Or do they advertise?"

"I could find out," he offered. "Are you serious about leaving?"

I touched my aching face. "Yes. But I don't know how." It wouldn't solve my problems to get taken in by some scoundrel in my haste to run away. And even though I was brilliant at picking pockets, it was a risky way to live.

"I'd go with you," Colin said quietly.

"Really?"

"You know I would."

My heart rang like a silver bell in my chest. "If you could do anything, what would you do? Would you go back to Ireland?" The ringing bell tarnished a little at the thought.

"Maybe," he said. "I've no family left there but I miss the green hills. I'd love to show them to you, show you Tara and the Cliffs of Moher. We could live in a thatched cottage and keep sheep."

I grinned at him. "If *you* clean up after them."

"What would be your perfect day then?" he asked, grinning back at me. "If you don't like my sheep."

"Your cottage sounds nice," I allowed. "I'd like to sleep in late and read as many books as I could and drink tea with lemon and eat pineapple slices for breakfast."

"No velvet dresses and diamonds?"

I rolled my eyes, then stopped when the bruise throbbed. "Ouch. And no, of course not. I don't care about that. Only books." I looked at him shyly. "And you."

"That's all right then," he said softly. He ran his fingers very gently under my aching cheekbone. "Does it hurt?"

I nodded. It hurt like the devil and I didn't care one bit. He didn't kiss me and I didn't kiss him. We just stared at each other for a long, delicious moment, the fire crackling beside us. His eyes looked grey in the shifting light, more like a winter lake than a summer sea. His black hair fell into his eyes as usual and I brushed it away.

"What's your perfect day?" I whispered.

"Getting out of London would be a start," he said. "I can't stand the grey air. I want fields and forests and the sky wherever you look. I don't need much, maybe a small garden to grow lettuce and peas and an apple tree. My mam made a brilliant apple pie."

We talked until my eyelids grew heavy but I didn't want to break the moment. I rolled on to my back to rest my head. I opened my mouth wide, moving my jaw.

"What on earth are you doing?" Colin grinned. "You look like a monkey."

"Oh, that's nice. I was trying to see if my face still hurts. And it does, by the way." I arched an eyebrow. "And that's hardly a way to speak to a lady, you know."

"You're Violet." He reached out and fiddled with a satin ribbon that was coming loose off the trim of my dress. "I suppose, you're *not* just Violet any more, are you?"

"I *am*. Being an earl's bastard is hardly coming up in the world, Colin. Nothing's changed, not really."

A small dark grey schnauzer dog pranced towards me. I could almost feel the rough texture of his tongue as he licked my hand, even though I could see right through him.

Well, I supposed *some* things had changed.

I scratched his ears, or the air around them at any rate, and he wagged his tail.

Colin pulled back. "*Now* what are you doing?"

"Playing with the dog."

"Playing with . . ." He paused.

"Spirit dog," I elaborated, as if that explained everything.

He just rolled his eyes. "Of course." I loved him even more for that simple casual reaction. There was no judgement to it, no fear, no disbelief. He trusted me.

"He's rather sweet actually."

"What's his name?"

"How should I know?" I held on to Colin's hand for a moment when the floor tilted at an odd angle. I'd have to get used to this spirit vision eventually. I couldn't get dizzy and fall over every time I saw a ghost. I'd never get anything done. "I don't speak Dog."

The little schnauzer scampered around me.

"Most people have pets others can see."

"Pish. I think I'll call him Mr Rochester." I yawned, despite myself. My lip split painfully. I touched it, wincing.

"You should rest. It's nearly dawn." He took my hand and pulled me to my feet, walking with me up the narrow stairs. "Goodnight, Violet," he murmured when we reached my door. He propped one hand on the doorway, leaning in to kiss me.

"Goodnight," he said again before turning down the other hallway to the back of the house. I wasn't sure how long I stood there watching him go, but the sound of his door closing had my mother's opening shortly after. The ghost of a small girl stood behind her, making faces and sticking out her tongue. Mother saw only me standing there, smiling foolishly.

"Violet. Do you know what time it is?"

"Very late." I turned to go to bed. I tried to avoid my ghostly dog and tripped over my own foot.

"What's the matter with you?"

"I tripped over the dog," I informed her, somewhat haughtily. I was so tired that I felt light-headed and fuzzy. Otherwise I would have known better than to mention it at all.

"Dog? What dog?"

Mr Rochester growled and leaped on to her ankle, sinking his teeth in. She didn't even glance down.

"He's a spirit dog," I told her. Part of me wondered why I didn't keep my mouth shut. The rest of me couldn't muster the energy to care. "*I*, unlike you, can see into the spirit world," I declared hotly, pushing into my room and slamming the door behind me. I crawled into my bed, still dressed, my eye and lip throbbing. Mr Rochester curled up against my side, and we were both asleep within minutes.

CHAPTER 19

I had never noticed before how *sharp* sunlight could be.

It was like little spears and arrows shooting into my bruised eye. I groaned and buried my head under my pillow.

"Marjie," I muttered. "Could you close the curtains?"

The light remained persistent.

"Marjie," I moaned, lifting my head gingerly. Surely I'd just come to bed. It couldn't be time to get up yet.

My mother stood at the side of my bed in a lavender day dress. She was smiling. I didn't trust it one bit.

"Up you get, Violet," she said pleasantly. She pointed to the tray on the table. It held a pot of tea and some kind of juice. "Drink. It will help."

Not a word of apology about what she'd done to me the day before. She must see the bruises. I could certainly feel them. "I just want to sleep."

"Too much to do, I'm afraid. Up you get."

I frowned. "What do we have to do? We're social pariahs. I could sleep all week and no one would notice."

"Not any more, my girl." She pulled the covers away briskly. "Get washed and put on something pretty, perhaps the striped dress. I've just had Mrs Bradley here."

"Mrs Bradley?" I echoed peevishly. "Whatever for? She's the most dedicated of all the gossip-mongers."

"Precisely. We have good news and it needs to travel quickly to all the right ears."

I was having a hard time following her reasoning. Besides, I was more interested in finding out where Mr Rochester had gone. Although there was certainly one good thing about spirit dogs: they didn't leave messes on the carpet.

"Keep up," she said, clapping her hands. "I have lost my gifts, lamentably, in a tragic and abrupt manner; but as a mother I am so very gratified to know it was for a good cause: the awakening of my own daughter's psychical talents."

I shot straight up, headache be damned. "What? What?"

"It's perfect, darling. It will wash the scandal clean away."

"B-but . . . !" I sputtered, horrified. "I don't *want* to be a medium."

Her eyes narrowed. "I'm hardly asking for much. You hate to lie and now you don't have to. You truly have the gift and you're going to use it. You owe me, Violet," she added. "I've fed and clothed you for sixteen years. Now it's time for you to do your part." She clicked her tongue on the roof of her mouth. "Enough of this foolishness, now."

She left me sitting on the rumpled bed, stunned.

<hr />

The day went by in a sort of haze. Mother whisked me out of the house before my stomach had settled or I'd even had a chance to see Colin. Once out, she dragged me back and forth over the busiest streets, looking at bonnets and ribbons, stopping for ices, and once even to browse in a bookshop because she thought she saw someone of quality go inside. By the time my feet ached almost as much as my eye, which was carefully concealed with rice powder, I realised there was no clear purpose to our running around other than to attract attention. Seeing as no one hurled overripe onions at us or crossed the street to avoid our company, the rumours of Mother's talents defecting to her only daughter had already run the general circuit. Every time I tried to hide behind some portly gentleman or some woman's unfortunate hat, Mother pulled me out again, as unrelenting as the tide bringing flotsam to the shore.

We even stopped at Mr Hudson's studio on Holloway Road, where she parted with her precious money to purchase a photograph of me. Mr Hudson was known for using scientific techniques in his photography to show the spirit world.

I sighed with ill-disguised annoyance and relief when we turned a familiar corner, lined with smartly painted terrace houses. We were so close to home now, I would have tripped up an old woman with a cane if she'd stood in the way of the first available chair. In fact, I nearly flattened Marjorie when I burst through our freshly washed front door.

"Tea," I croaked. "For the love of God, Marjie, tea."

Colin wasn't around; he was tending to the errands that actually required running. The parlour had been set to rights, and the few figurines and accents left in the rest of the house had been pillaged to decorate it. I wasn't halfway through my cup when Mother stared pointedly at it.

"Come along, Violet. Don't dawdle."

I cradled my cup possessively. "I haven't finished."

"I'll have Marjorie bring you up a tray. You must change."

I really didn't like the sound of that. "Whatever for?" I asked suspiciously.

"We have guests coming for a sitting. You have to be at your best, dear girl. Everything rides on this."

"What?" I stood up so quickly the tea sloshed over the rim and on to my hem. "You can't be serious."

"Of course I am. It's up to you now to reverse our f ortunes."

"But I don't know anything about being a medium! I didn't even believe in ghosts until last week." Mr Rochester appeared to nudge my ankle comfortingly. His backside was lodged in the settee, only half-materialised.

Mother eyed me curiously. "So you really do have the gift then. That will make everything easier, to be sure."

I rubbed at my face. "Mother, please."

Her mouth hardened. "None of your dramatics now. Save

it for this evening. Go on upstairs and get ready. It won't do to be late—you haven't the following or the presence."

I went upstairs only because I didn't want to be in the same room as her and there was really nowhere else to go to escape. I dragged my feet the entire way, knowing the sullen sound would echo. I still felt dizzy and bone-tired, too much so to have any energy left for a proper rebellion. I would just have to do the best I could for tonight and think of an alternative tomorrow.

I put on my second-best dress. Marjorie ran up to knock on my door, panting and wide-eyed. "Please, miss."

I gave a rather dramatic sigh before scowling crossly. "Oh, very well."

It was worse than I'd feared. The parlour was crowded wall to wall with gossip-mongers, eager for a scandal. Mrs Bradley sat in the rose brocade with her dreadful poodle on her wide lap. Mrs Grey and Miss Wilmington whispered together over tea. The rest were assorted scandal-seekers whose names I didn't know. I looked for Lord Jasper but he wasn't in attendance, which wasn't terribly surprisingly. Lord Marshall was there, however, sitting with one booted foot crossed over his knee and making calf eyes at Mother that I longed to poke right out of his well-bred head.

Colin stood at his usual position by the door, and I knew he could decipher my thoughts exactly. He was the same old Colin—sardonic, perceptive, honest—but somehow it was all different. I felt safe with him, as always, and yet dangerous too. Alive. But I didn't have the leisure to enjoy the feeling. Mother nodded to me as I entered.

"Ladies and gentlemen, my daughter, Violet," she announced. There were murmurs and glasses lifted to curious eyes. I tried not to squirm. I hated being the centre of all that attention. I just wanted to go back up to my room, especially when Mrs Grey sucked in a breath at the bruise flowered over my eye and cheek. The rice powder wasn't thick enough to hold up against my nervous perspiration.

"My word!"

"The gifting of such psychical talents can be quite sudden," Mother explained smoothly. "Often the medium becomes very ill. Poor Violet fainted and struck her eye on the table." She smiled. "Shall we prepare? I know my daughter is eager to read for you all." I'd barely moved from the doorway. My feet itched to take me somewhere else, anywhere else. "I am, of course, sorry that I cannot sit for you as well. It's been a most trying and sudden loss, and my only comfort is that my own talents were sacrificed to improve my daughter's."

What rot.

I didn't know what was worse, her bald-faced lies or the way everyone seemed to lap them up, like an alley cat with a bowl of fresh cream. It was a disgrace all round and I was right in the middle of it. I'd have to find some way to contact the spirit world if I was to salvage any part of this wretched night. It was an effort to produce a smile that didn't resemble the painful grimace of a landed trout. Lord Marshall fawned over Mother's hand, helping her to her seat. He nodded at my approach.

"Miss St—Miss Willoughby—we are equally eager to admire your demonstration."

Colin stiffened. I paused, startled. Miss St Clair. An obvious flattery for my mother's sake. I wasn't entirely sure about the propriety concerning the illegitimate children of the peerage, of which surely there were legions. There were so many lies unravelling and secrets, it was like walking through a murky pond—you never knew if the next step would take you to the steady bottom or give way entirely.

And I really didn't want to do this.

But I could only stand there lost in thought for so long. I sat down without a word. The rest of the gentlemen followed suit, the other ladies having already made themselves comfortable. Mother led everyone through the usual prayers while my mind tumbled over everything Elizabeth and I had read at Rosefield. Surely I'd learned enough there to get through this with at least a small degree of dignity.

We held hands and the lights were lowered, though not nearly as much as we'd lowered them before Mother's unfortunate discovery. There were no tricks planned tonight, no clever plots, though I supposed most of the modifications were still attached to the table. Mother would never leave this all to chance, or to me. Still, I vowed I wouldn't use them. The spirits would just have to cooperate.

I shut my eyes, mostly because I couldn't bear the scrutiny. Although some of these people were truly curious to contact a dead family member, most just wanted to be part of the kind of scandal that ended with Mother in her undergarments. They wanted me to fail because it would make a better story.

Damned if I'd oblige.

"We welcome our beloved dead." Determined, I lifted my eyelids and searched the room. The feather in Mrs Thompson's white curls bounced in a draught. Mr Hunt's whiskers quivered. Lord Marshall sat entirely too near Mother; his knee must surely be pressed against hers. The candle flickered. Someone cleared their throat. The poodle whined, bored.

No spirits.

They'd been hounding me all week; the least they could do was show themselves when they were needed. It was just rude otherwise. "Spirits," I snapped. "I said you are welcome here." Colin coughed once. "As long as you mean us no ill," I amended, remembering the surge of the angry spirit at the Whitestone Manor pond. The guests exchanged knowing glances. *Now*, I thought. *I am in earnest. Show yourselves.*

Mother shifted and I knew she was preparing for a dramatic tilting of the table. Before she could follow through, there was the scent of vinegar and peppermint—a most repulsive combination. And then a man appeared, or most of one, in a faded grey suit and wispy face. A woman sniffed.

"Grandfather," she said.

He looked pleased.

"He always had that dreadful smell."

Now he looked thunderous and vanished, but not before one of the woman's hairpins flew away from her head, landing with a clatter on the table. There was a swell of excited whispers. Mother sat back proudly.

A woman appeared next, floating near the fireplace. She had no aroma and no voice. It occurred to me that this would be a much simpler matter if I could see and hear them at the same time, instead of this blind game where I never knew what to expect. Could one write a strongly worded letter to the deceased requiring their full cooperation? I was willing to try. This was too much of a puzzle, and I was too nervous with such an audience.

"The lady is wearing an old-fashioned dress, with petticoats and a lace shawl," I described. "She wears gloves and her eyes are very dark. There's a locket on a long gold chain."

"Lady Schofield!" Mrs Grey exclaimed. "I've missed her so. We were the best of friends when we were girls."

The spirit nodded. In her hands appeared a bowl of blackberries.

"She is showing me blackberries."

Mrs Grey laughed through her tears.

"We used to gather them every summer by the lake. When we were younger we'd sneak them home and eat them at midnight, staining the pillowcases."

There was another hour of questions and peering into the shadows and trying to make sense of cryptic clues. I was beginning to feel fatigued and a little ill. Mother didn't seem to notice; she and Lord Marshall had their heads bent together.

"Anyone missing the family silver?" he joked with what I thought was forced casualness. "Violet here is doing a brilliant job."

An older woman appeared behind him, only for an instant. She looked disgusted. I liked her instantly, especially when she attempted to smack him on the back of the head. Her voice was still sharp in my ear, even after she faded. I repeated her words. I didn't like Lord Marshall anyway.

"Your wife, Lord Marshall, says that your current mistress is barely seventeen and that she has no intention of letting you spend her family's silver on her."

There was a shocked gasp, a snort of laughter. Lord Marshall looked down his aquiline nose at me. "I beg your pardon?" he said icily.

Mother glared at me viciously before rising. "That will be all for tonight. Violet, you are looking quite pale. You should retire. This work is quite taxing."

I smiled wanly. "Goodnight." I left as Mother apologised profusely to Lord Marshall.

Colin winked at me as I passed.

I winked back.

———— ✧ ————

When I got to my bedroom, I found a letter under my pillow. Colin must have brought it up for me before Mother got to the post. I hadn't noticed it before. I broke the seal. The paper was thick and when I unfolded it another sheet fluttered to the blanket. I recognised the handwriting first.

> *Dear Violet,*
>   *I am still cross that you lied to me but enclosed is a letter I just received from Tabitha. I hope you didn't lie to me about your own talents.*
>   *Elizabeth*

P.S. I am trying to find a solution.
P.P.S. But I'm still cross.

The next letter was considerably longer.

Dear Elizabeth,

I hardly know why I am bothering to write. It's clear from that scandalous display at your godfather's house party that Mrs Willoughby is not a respectable woman. I don't see why her daughter would be any different. I suppose she lied about her gifts too. I ought not to be surprised. I don't believe in that sort of thing anyway. Still, I will admit Violet did give me pause. She knew certain details that had no way of being public knowledge. And that ring . . . I must be mad to be doing this.

The thing is, Elizabeth, I am frightened. Something isn't right here. I can't think what it is, but I am heartily sick of the lies. They fill up this house like water until I feel I might drown too.

Violet said Rowena was scared for me. I'm scared too. Might you come for a visit? Caroline is peevish all the time and Uncle is occupied with some work or other.

Yours,
Tabitha Wentworth

CHAPTER 20

The next morning I ate breakfast alone with a copy of Shakespeare's sonnets. Mother left early to pick up our photographs from Mr Hudson, and Marjorie was hiding in the kitchen. I didn't see Colin until I'd finished the pot of tea and was standing up to leave. He seemed taller somehow, older.

And I suddenly didn't know what to say.

He smiled. "Good morning."

I smiled back. "Good morning."

This was ridiculous. I wasn't going to become one of those girls who was hopelessly tongue-tied and woolly-headed because of a boy. He might be the boy who had kissed me until I was breathless, but he was also the boy who had once sneaked an earthworm into my cucumber salad.

"What did Elizabeth have to say?" he asked, confirming that he had been the one to rescue the letter from Mother's prying eyes. I was grateful for an actual topic of conversation to distract me from his eyes, pale as clouds reflected in a summer lake.

I was getting positively sentimental. It would never do.

"Vi?"

"Sorry." I snapped back to attention. "She sent me one of Tabitha's letters. They're worried." I frowned. "So am I. And I still can't think why Mr Travis was in the graveyard. He's clearly up to no good. What if he . . . ?" I let the thought trail off, clenching my fists. "I don't know what to do about any of it. I can't very well go barging in there."

He stepped closer, reaching out to tuck a loose curl behind my ear. "You'll think of something."

He was near enough that I could smell earth and flowers on his hands, and smoke.

"I'm hardly a detective," I murmured, turning so that we faced each other fully.

"But you are clever," he said. "And Rowena chose you for a reason."

I didn't need to reply as his mouth covered mine, his hands dropping to my waist. My corset seemed suddenly too tight. I kissed him back and we moved, almost as if we were dancing to some music only we could hear, until my back was pressed against the wall. I was glad of the support, my knees suddenly weak. And I was tingling everywhere he touched me, his hands, the press of his legs, his chest against mine.

When the front door opened we leaped apart as if we'd suddenly caught fire.

"Violet," my mother called out cheerfully. I could hear her removing her hat and gloves. Colin and I locked gazes for a long moment.

"Violet," she called again, sharper. "Where the devil is that girl?"

"I'm here," I answered, finally pulling myself away and stepping into the hall. Colin followed me to collect Mother's parcels from the carriage. She looked at us both critically but didn't say anything. I hoped my hair wasn't dishevelled or my lips overly pink.

"The town is positively alight with talk of us," she said finally. "Your demonstration was a rousing success. Everyone is curious to see Lord Thornwood's daughter." She sniffed. "You think they'd remember that I also gave them the best years of my life." She unwrapped one of her parcels. "At least your photograph was worth the coin. You look lovely in it and, more importantly, you're positively glowing with ectoplasm."

That sounded uncomfortable.

"Mr Hudson says it's the best he's ever taken. He's hung a copy in his window."

"There's a photograph of me in his window?"

She nodded smugly. "Think of the exposure."

I could see the rest of my life unfolding before me: sittings, seances, spirit-board readings, all under the sharp eye of my mother as she charged admission for the privilege. It wouldn't matter to her if the work tired me or made my head ache. It wouldn't matter if I didn't want to be the scandalous bastard daughter of an earl put through her paces like a show pony.

"Why are you looking so cross?" she snapped. "Come and see your picture."

I swallowed, half afraid to look.

I was wearing my striped periwinkle dress, standing stiffly and unsmiling. The air around me was hazy, as if the room had been filled with smoke, which it hadn't. A translucent miniature schnauzer was at my feet, tongue lolling happily. Mr Rochester. I smiled to see him. He looked like he was made of moonbeams and dandelion fluff. In the mist behind me were faces, the most prominent of them a girl, her hair streaming water and lily petals.

"Rowena," I murmured, touching the photo.

"Careful, you'll smudge it." Mother snatched it back. "I had a second copy made and had a courier take it to Lord Jasper."

We got a reply the very next morning. I wondered if he'd recognised Rowena, hazy as she was.

Mother read it quickly, already preening. "I knew this would work. Excellent. You see, Lord Jasper has invited you back to Rosefield. He's included a train ticket for you. You'd best impress him quickly," she added darkly, almost venomously. "I shan't support a grown daughter who is lazy." She flounced off, calling to Marjorie for tea and jam tarts.

"What was that about?" Colin muttered.

I raised the letter, beautifully written on thick paper. "She wasn't invited. Just me."

"Good."

I tapped the letter on the palm of my hand. "This is it, then."

"Remember," Mother said, straightening the lace at my collar as the hired hackney waited at the kerbside. "This might be your only chance. Don't squander it away with missish behaviour. Do what you must."

It was hardly an encouraging farewell. She hugged me and then turned away, slamming the door shut behind her before I'd even stepped off the porch. Colin stood in the shadows between our house and the neighbouring one so that he wouldn't be seen. He lifted his hand in a wave.

"Be careful," he mouthed.

I glanced at the front door. "You too."

Lord Jasper sent a Mrs Hartley to accompany me on the train. She nodded at me once and spent the rest of the time with her knitting. She didn't even step out on to the platform when we got there, only nodded one last time and waited to be taken back to London. Lord Jasper's carriage was there to meet me, with a footman to open the door. Elizabeth was inside, frowning.

"Hello," I said quietly as the horses began to walk.

She didn't smile. "Hello."

I chewed my lip. "Elizabeth, you must know how sorry I am."

"You hurt my feelings."

"I know. I hardly had a choice though, did I?"

She sighed, grudgingly. "I suppose not. Uncle Jasper says this isn't your fault."

"Really?" I asked, surprised.

"He says it's just like my mother forcing me to go to all those dreadful society teas. Only with you it was much harder."

My eyes stung. I had hardly expected compassion from that quarter. She grinned suddenly. "Anyway, I'm awful at staying angry." She flung her arms around me. "And it's been so *dull* without you." I hugged her back, feeling as if there had been ice in my belly and it was now melting. She settled back against the velvet cushions. "Besides, you've noble blood now, so I can hardly snub you," she teased.

"Hardly."

"Was it horrible?" she asked me later as we arrived at Rose-field. The roses were glowing against the sky, bees hovering lazily.

"They threw rotten eggs at our house. And cabbage."

"Disgusting! Still, did Lord Thornwood invite you to his house? I hear it's very grand, with marble cherub fountains."

I shook my head. "Earls don't invite their illegitimate daughters for tea, Elizabeth. You know that."

"Well, they bloody well should." She scowled. "When we return, let's sneak some of those rotten eggs into his fountain."

I giggled. "Oh, Elizabeth, I've missed you."

We stepped out of the dark carriage. Elizabeth gasped. "Oh, Violet! Your eye! Whatever happened?"

"Oh, um, nothing." My face powder must have smudged on the hot train. "You know how clumsy I am." The front door opened before she could press me further. "However did you orchestrate this?" I asked to keep her distracted.

"It wasn't me. Lord Jasper got a letter from your mother and sent for you straight away. He wouldn't even let me see it. He's waiting for you in his library." My steps faltered. She tugged my elbow. "Don't be a goose. All is forgiven. In fact, you're quite famous now. Even Sir Wentworth has asked after you."

"Whatever for?"

She shrugged. "Everyone's asking. Since the last seance was so . . . exciting, no one can talk of anything else."

"Splendid." I groaned. A thought curdled my already sour stomach. "The Tretheweys haven't come back too, have they? I thought they'd left the house party."

"They did."

We stopped in front of the heavy oak doors. Elizabeth knocked cheerfully, never having doubted her welcome anywhere in her entire life.

"Come in."

"Wait!" I clutched at her hand. "Come with me."

"Can't." She grimaced. "Mother's likely missed me by now. She'll want to lecture me some more. She's quite convinced you're a bad influence."

I wondered if anyone would mind if I crawled under the carpet and refused to come out. She gave me a little shove and I stumbled into the study. Lord Jasper was seated behind an enormous desk cluttered with papers, an inkwell, a clock and a miniature of his wife. He stood when he saw me, leaning on his silver swan cane.

"Ah, Miss Willoughby, do come in. I suppose it's Miss Morgan though, isn't it?"

"Thank you for inviting me, Lord Jasper," I said properly and politely. There was a long silence. Eventually I dropped into a chair and looked at him miserably through the ringlets at my temples. "I'm sorry," I said. It occurred to me that I was apparently going to spend most of the day apologising. "I didn't know how to tell you. Or even if I should."

He sat down and regarded me solemnly for a long moment, which had me fidgeting. He finally nodded. "I know, Violet. I did think your mother might have the gift, but I was mistaken. It was you all along. I only knew it was someone in your family."

"What?" I blurted out. "How? You're not angry?"

"I'm not pleased," he said drily, "but that is between your mother and me. You're still a girl, Violet. I can hardly hold you responsible for the actions of your elders." I was so relieved, my eyes blurred. I might have felt as if I was getting off rather easily until he speared me with those pale eyes. "But you are not to lie to me again, Violet. I want to be quite clear on that."

I nodded, mouth dry. There was a glitter of power about him that had little to do with the fact that he was a wealthy lord of the realm. "Yes, my lord," I replied quietly.

"Excellent. Shall I have Mrs Harris make a poultice for your eye?"

"I . . . fell," I explained lamely.

"Of course you did. Your mother, I now suspect, does not do well when thwarted."

I gulped. "Um, pardon me, but how do you know that I'm not lying to you as she did?" I rushed to add, "I'm not."

He leaned back in his chair. Through the windows behind him I could see Elizabeth and her mother strolling leisurely through the roses. Elizabeth looked bored.

"My dear girl, you knew about my wife's tea preferences and her reading habits as no one else does, apart from the housekeeper, and I trust her implicitly not to speak of private matters. Besides, you were quite disconcerted with the knowledge, were you not?"

I bit my lip. "Yes."

"Perfectly normal. As was the headache you suffered afterwards, though most are far more gravely ill before the talent comes upon them. And then that photograph, of course."

I hardly knew what to say.

"You are not the first medium to be surprised with sudden talents. But I can teach you how to control them."

"What if I just want them to go away?"

"Do you?"

I thought of Mother, of Rowena and the pond. "I don't know."

"I would advise against ignoring them in any case. Such things seldom fade by lack of attention; instead they tend to grow rather more insistent. Wild, even."

My shoulders slumped. "Oh."

"Not to worry. I have some experience in these matters."

"You do?"

"Yes." He nodded, but his expression was grim, distant. He slid a book across the desk. "You can start by reading this."

I closed my fingers around the leather-bound volume as an idea formed.

"Might I have a small sitting?" I asked. "Something intimate, with the neighbours, perhaps, that I might practise?" It seemed the best way to get Tabitha here and see if Rowena could communicate more useful information to us. I was hardly going to be invited to Whitestone Manor, and Elizabeth was technically still forbidden to visit at all.

"I think that's a wonderful idea," Lord Jasper said. "I'll arrange it."

It then occurred to me that I was going to have to actually sit for people I hardly knew and somehow control my so-called gifts. Not to mention that the same people had been there to witness my mother's rather spectacular downfall.

Not so wonderful at all, actually.

⸙

That night, just as I was about to blow out my candle and try to sleep, there was a furtive knock at the door.

"Violet," Elizabeth whispered. "Vi, are you awake?" I opened the door to find her in her white dressing gown, grinning at me. Her hair was stuffed haphazardly into a lacy cap. "Mother's hardly let me out of her sight today, and I'm dying for a good gossip."

I'd been given the same room I'd had last week, and so we

curled up on the settee in the sitting room. I admired her ability to shut off her anger so quickly. I knew mine would have smouldered, but I could tell by the way she looked at me expectantly that she had already put the whole thing from her mind.

"Come on," she urged. "I want to hear everything that's happened. Did Xavier call on you?"

I grimaced. "Unfortunately, yes."

"Oh no. What happened?"

"His family is too fine to enter into an alliance with Thornwood's bastard daughter, no matter how grand his title."

She sucked in her breath. "I don't like that word." She folded her arms. "There's definitely a bastard in this situation, but it isn't you."

I choked out a laugh.

Her arms were still crossed but she smiled. "Never mind him. We have better things to talk about, surely, than that toad."

I wasn't even angry with Xavier any more. I simply didn't think of him at all. And I had thought to marry him because that's what poor pretty girls do. Wealthy pretty ones too, come to think of it, but with a little less urgency, I assumed.

"Is everyone still in residence?" I asked.

"Yes, mostly. Though Frederic is set to leave the day after next." She sighed wistfully. "No progress on that front, I'm afraid. Tragic, isn't it?"

"And Tabitha?"

"Aside from that letter, I haven't heard a word from her."

"Is she all right, do you think?"

"I think so. We'd have heard otherwise, wouldn't we?"

"I suppose. I went to Highgate."

Elizabeth's eyes widened dramatically. "Was it terribly frightening?"

"A little." I thought of the gates slamming shut. Then I thought of Colin pressed against me. "But not entirely," I hastened to add before I blushed. She'd never let a blush go unexplained. "Though I did see Mr Travis."

She looked confused. "Mr Travis? Not really?"

"Really."

"But . . . why?"

"I wish I knew." I fiddled with the hem of my nightdress. "Rowena wasn't there, I think because she was still here protecting Tabitha. But I can't think of a single reason why Mr Travis would have been there and chased us out if he wasn't involved with her murder in some way."

Elizabeth tilted her head as if she was thinking very hard.

"What is it?" I asked.

"I'm not . . . of course!" She slapped her palm on her knee.

"What?"

"I've just remembered why Mr Travis seemed so familiar." Her eyes widened. "He was at Highgate the day of Rowena's burial."

I went cold all over. "Are you sure? Why didn't you remember before?"

"I only saw him briefly, hovering near the back of the mourners. It's been bothering me since he came here." She swallowed. "Oh, Violet, what can it mean?"

"Nothing good," I replied grimly. "Is he still here?"

"Yes, I think so. He mostly keeps to himself. We only see him at sittings or at that one ball."

"We have to keep an eye on him. We need some kind of proof."

We talked some more but didn't come up with any solutions. I could only hope the seance would be illuminating. If I didn't make an utter fool of myself, of course.

After Elizabeth left I went back to bed, with Mr Rochester curled up at my feet, snoring. It just made sense. I couldn't hear Rowena speak, which would make everything far simpler, but my little ghost of a dog snored like a train under all that misty fur. I woke up a little later to him growling, the rumble of his body tickling my toes.

"Hush," I mumbled, opening my bleary eyes.

My grumble turned to a strangled yelp.

Rowena hovered at the edge of my bed, leaning over me so that when I turned over, we were nose to nose. Water dripped on to the quilt. The white lilies in her hair seemed to glow, as did her eyes, manifesting more fully than the rest of her.

Then she opened her mouth and it was like looking into a dark pond. I was so startled that I screeched and went tumbling off the bed and on to the hard floor, landing in a heap—trapped in the sheets with Mr Rochester barking shrilly. As I fought my way free I blew out a breath, clearing the tangles of hair from my face and pulling my blankets back up in the lingering cold.

Rowena was gone.

CHAPTER 21

The seance was held in the small family parlour this time, the walls done in silvery paper and the curtains a deep blue velvet. Oil lamps burned brightly. Lord Jasper's family was there, along with the Ashfords, Mr Travis, Peter, Tabitha, her uncle and Caroline. Tabitha would not look at me. Mr Travis, on the other hand, wouldn't stop.

"My dear, if you don't mind," Lord Jasper said after one of his sisters sniffed at me disdainfully. "Out of scientific interest, Miss Donovan has suggested you be searched before we begin."

My eyes widened. "Pardon?"

"It is the accepted method in many Spiritualist circles. And you can have nothing to object to, can you, Miss Willoughby?"

Caroline did not smile. Her demeanour was that certain one ingrained in every unhappy governess. Her hair was pulled back so severely it tugged at the corners of her eyes. I wasn't sure what to say or think. Elizabeth scowled on my behalf.

"I have every faith in Miss Willoughby and her abilities," Lord Jasper said smoothly.

I stepped forward, holding out my arms and feeling faintly ridiculous, but I wanted to prove Lord Jasper right. I had nothing to hide about what went on tonight and nothing on my person. Besides, Mother had taught me that mediums never carry evidence that might be discovered. She usually left all the danger of exposure to Colin and me, with the bellows under my skirt. But in the end, she'd been the one caught out in her underwear.

"Why don't you check me over yourself," I asked her pointedly. "That way you can have no doubts."

Caroline looked briefly taken aback. I supposed it was hardly unexpected that such a demand might be made of me. That it was her specifically, however, gave me reason to pause. There was obviously something behind her "scientific interest", and I could not be persuaded otherwise. She was very thorough and not particularly gentle. Peter leered at us over his glass of port the entire time. Tabitha didn't say a word.

"Well?" Lord Jasper asked. "May we continue?"

Caroline nodded stiffly.

"As I thought," he said.

"We still have to bind her," Caroline insisted stubbornly.

"Bind me?" I squeaked. They were going to tie me up? What kind of seance was this? Peter snickered suggestively at me. "You can't be serious."

"Don't be alarmed," Lord Jasper said, which was absurd. I stared at Elizabeth wildly. She stared back just as wildly.

"This kind of testing is all the rage according to the Spiritualist papers," Frederic explained. "I've seen it done myself."

Sir Wentworth rolled his eyes. "Leave the poor chit alone," he said. "This is all a bit of fun anyway. You can hardly take it seriously."

All eyes turned towards me. I was on boggy ground now. If I agreed it was only entertainment, I was damning any future respect and confirming that I was a fraud like my mother. On the other hand, if I wanted to be taken seriously, I was going to have to submit to being restrained. I sighed. I might not particularly want to be a medium, but I didn't want to be accused of lying either.

"Fine," I said reluctantly. "In the name of scientific inquiry."

I was led to a cabinet with a single opening in the front. The sides and back were thick wooden panels carved with leaves and roses and impish gargoyles. There was a short stool inside for me to sit on. Before I could do so, Caroline tied my wrists with red silk thread, even going so far as to seal the knot with a drop of wax from one of the candles. I felt nervous and vulnerable. And, frankly, belligerent.

"Are you quite finished?" I asked her after she'd pulled the excess thread out and looped it to the outside of the cabinet.

"This will ensure that Miss Willoughby stays in the cabinet," she explained to everyone. "Should she move or attempt some trickery, the thread will alert us."

She twitched the curtains in place and I was left in the

darkness most mediums required. The amount of light hadn't seemed to make much difference to my communications with Rowena thus far, but at least this way I was tucked away from any suspicious or mocking glances and Lord Jasper's supremely calm countenance. He had far more confidence in what I was about to attempt than I did. I felt like a fool, trussed up in a cupboard with my bruised face.

There was nowhere to go now and nothing to do but give it a try. I was doing this for Rowena, so she had bloody well better show herself to everyone. Or at the very least I might be able to persuade Mr Rochester to prance around on the table. Or pee on Caroline's perfectly pristine slippers. If only.

I could hear the rustling of everyone taking their seats. There was a murmured prayer and the usual assortment of songs. I could barely hear Tabitha, she was whispering so faintly. Mr Travis was looking around the room almost desperately. I wasn't sure what he was hoping to see.

"Whenever you're ready," Lord Jasper called out.

I had no way of knowing if this would even work. Rowena was capricious, popping up to frighten me at any time of day or night; it seemed monstrously unfair that she might stay away now that I actually needed her. I focused on the spot between my eyebrows. Lord Jasper's book had referred to it as my "third eye". It was simple enough to imagine an eye there, blue as violets, opening slowly, pupil dilating like spilled ink.

"Rowena," I whispered, too softly for the others to hear. "Rowena, make yourself known to them." I blinked several times until the shadows of the sitters at the table wavered slightly through the crack in the curtains. All the light in the parlour seemed to coalesce over the table. No one seemed to notice, though they did seem to feel the blast of cold air. Frost formed on the window panes, delicate as lace.

"Eh?" Sir Wentworth mumbled. "Deuced cold in here, Jasper."

Tabitha stared intently into the shadows. Mr Travis looked hopeful, almost painfully so.

"A trick?" Caroline asked, her voice breaking.

White lilies tumbled down from the dark ceiling, petals scattering like snow. I couldn't help but smirk at the collective gasp. *Ha*, I thought uncharitably. If I'd been ten years old again I'd have stuck my tongue out at Caroline. At sixteen, I ought to be above such behaviour.

I wasn't.

"Rowena," I whispered. It wasn't easy to concentrate as deeply as I needed on that spot on my brow. I was getting the vague pressure of a headache. The room tilted and I was pulled backwards through time, wind knotting my hair, stars blurring.

I landed in Rowena's body. She was holding a letter again, the same one I'd dug through ghostly ashes to retrieve. It wasn't burned now, merely worn at the edges from being handled. I was being transported into a tangled web of memories and somehow I'd have to link them together, like beads on a necklace. For now I could only watch, could only feel emotions that weren't my own, trapped in Rowena's recollections.

She read the letter for what felt like the hundredth time. I knew without conscious deduction that the handwriting belonged to her father and had been sent all the way from India. There was another written on solicitor's headed paper from a London office.

I, Lord Wentworth, Earl of Whitestone and Dainsborough, grant my permission to my eldest daughter, Rowena Wentworth, to marry as she chooses. Her betrothal to Peter Burlington, of the Berkeley estate, has been rescinded and his family has been compensated accordingly, as per my solicitor's instructions, enclosed herein.

Attached was a personal note to Rowena:

Cease and desist, daughter. I have had dozens of your letters, as have all my acquaintances. You've had your way. Be happy now, little one.

Rowena was only fifteen years old. She needed a parent's or guardian's permission to marry. Since her father had already secured her a future husband, she was clearly determined to elope with someone else entirely. It was the only reason neither Tabitha nor her uncle knew about the letter. She kept it hidden inside her pillowcase, with a pile of other letters in a different handwriting. She touched them reverently before hearing a noise in the hall and tucking the coverlet back into place with a sharp tug. It was only Caroline who'd come to tell her Peter was waiting downstairs with a scowl. She'd promised him a tray of tea and lemon biscuits to soothe his temper while he waited for Rowena to finish getting dressed.

The room turned liquid, the colours bleeding and smearing like watercolours. My stomach dropped suddenly, as if I were falling. And then I was back in the same bedchamber, still in Rowena's body, only it was night-time now. *A single candle burned on a chair by the bed. There was a packed suitcase underneath and somehow I knew I'd be leaving soon. Wearing Rowena's favourite nightdress, I reached for the letters, to read them one more time before going to sleep.*

The letters had gone!

And I was back in my body so abruptly, I jerked as if I'd been touched by lightning. I hit my head on the wooden panelling of the cabinet and muffled a curse. The sitters turned their heads towards me, filled with curiosity. Caroline looked smug, as if I'd been caught trying to pull a trick or escape my bindings.

Cross, I snapped an order at Rowena in a quiet undertone.

"Rowena, is your murderer here?"

The lilies shivered as the table rocked back and forth. The flames from the lamps shot taller, dancing madly.

"Show me."

I wasn't entirely sure what to make of the next spirit gift.

A dead trout landed with a marked *splat* on the table. There was the stink of fish. Sir Wentworth wrinkled his nose as it flopped in front of him before shooting across the wooden surface, skidding in a trail of murky pond water and landing in Caroline's lap.

"Get it off me!" she shrieked, leaping back and brushing at her damp skirt.

Apparently this particular spirit gift was corporeal. Elizabeth turned slightly and even in my shadowy cabinet I could tell she was gaping at me. The candlelight continued to coalesce until there was a flash of a young girl's face with blonde hair, quick as a falling star.

"Rowena!" Tabitha called out, stricken. Poppies rained over her head.

Nothing touched Peter, not fish nor flower. He sat, looking bored. Mr Travis was similarly untouched.

My third eye felt like a garden gate, shutting with a snap under a brisk wind. The force of it reverberated through my entire body. There was silence as the frost melted and the table stilled. Fish and lilies and poppies were thick in the air.

Then the quiet broke like a cup dropped on flagstones. It shattered into excited murmurs, shouts and the scraping of chairs shoved backwards.

"Tea is served in the parlour," Lord Jasper announced. "If you'll join me? We'll give Miss Willoughby a chance to rest. Mr Burlington, as you're nearest, if you would unbind her and then join us?"

The guests chattered loudly among themselves as they retired to the more formal dining room for cakes. There was a long, quiet moment.

The last person I wanted to be alone with right now was Peter.

I tested the silk thread at my wrists but it was surprisingly strong and I only managed to irritate my skin. I rose slowly and carefully to my feet. It would be just like me to take a tumble now when I didn't have the use of my hands to break my fall. I was going to have to use my teeth to pull the curtains aside. I was leaning over, baring my teeth, when the thick curtain was yanked aside.

"What on earth are you doing?" Peter drawled. "You look positively feral."

Flushing, I closed my teeth together with an audible snap. I lowered my bound hands. His smile was lazy and yet sharp at the edges. I couldn't help thinking of duelling swords.

"You are quite at my mercy, aren't you?" he asked, clearly pleased with himself. Something about the way he was looking at me made my palms sweat. If there had been room, I'd have stepped back.

"Untie me." I wondered belatedly if appearing less irritated with him would win me quicker results, but I just wanted, quite desperately, to be away from him.

He produced a knife from his pocket. The fact that he'd been holding it the entire time I was trapped between him and the cabinet hardly made me feel more nervous. The blade cut easily through the thread, but his hands closed over mine roughly and he tugged me off balance. I was untied and yet still trapped.

"I don't know what you think you know," he growled, "or what game you are playing, Miss Willoughby, but you would be wise to let it go. You're some earl's bastard and a whore's daughter. No one will believe you."

With a shove that sent me stumbling into the table, he stormed out.

❧

By the time I reached the parlour, Caroline and the Wentworths had gone home, pleading exhaustion. Peter disappeared into the empty ballroom with a bottle of brandy. Lord Jasper nodded at me proudly.

Elizabeth rushed over to the doorway to walk with me to the table. "Oh, Violet, can you believe it?"

"What I can't believe," I grumbled, rubbing my wrists, "is that you left me there, alone, with *Peter*."

She rolled her eyes. "He always finds the pretty girls."

"Somehow, I don't think he had seduction on his mind."

When I told her what had happened, she bristled. "So he must be involved somehow. It's becoming more and more of a mess, isn't it? I hardly know what to think any more. Tabitha looked so dreadful, as if she was going to swoon, that they've gone home." She raised her eyebrows knowingly. "And Caroline smelled like week-old trout."

We grinned at each other.

"Do we really think she could have murdered Rowena?" I asked, sobering. "Doesn't Peter seem a more likely suspect now?" Not that we had evidence of any kind, of course.

Elizabeth shrugged. "She's cross enough."

"But why?" I wondered. "And what about Mr Travis? And is Tabitha in danger? Would Caroline hurt her?"

"Not with her uncle in residence," Elizabeth said, sounding sure. "He's very solicitous of her needs."

I tried not to show my frustration in case the rest of the guests looked at us and wondered what we were whispering about. "We need more information." I paused. "I have an idea. Risky though."

"My favourite kind."

"Peter is in the ballroom, you say?"

"And looks to stay there for quite some time."

We waited until everyone had retired for the night, then we waited a little longer, until we were certain they were all asleep. We crept back downstairs to spy on Peter. He was slumped on the floor, snoring. The bottle at his hand was nearly empty. We crept back upstairs.

"You're certain this is his room?" I whispered.

Elizabeth nodded. "Go on."

"Make sure you keep a sharp eye out," I muttered, easing the door open so it wouldn't creak. "I don't want to be clapped in irons for snooping."

She waved that away. "Uncle Jasper would never do that."

"Peter might."

"Oh. Right."

Peter's guest quarters were palatial, with burgundy paper and a mahogany washstand and armoire. It was dark except for the circle of light shed by my single candle. I went straight to the desk and shuffled through the papers there: a bill from his tailor, a glass of old sherry, an unsigned letter from a lover. Nothing whatsoever to implicate him. I even rifled through his shirts and checked under his cravats. I was half-buried in the armoire when Elizabeth stuck her head in.

"Violet," she whispered. "He's coming."

I pushed myself out so quickly, the cupboard wobbled.

"He's on the stairs," she added, horrified. Peter's steps were unsteady and loud. We didn't have time to get back to our respective rooms. I blew out the candle.

The steps came closer.

I grabbed Elizabeth's hand and yanked her into the opposite room. We huddled, straining to hear. Neither of us dared to breathe, listening for the sound of his door closing.

What we heard instead was snoring.

We both froze.

"Oh no," Elizabeth mouthed. I could see her clearly in the moonlight falling through the windows. There was another snore. We looked over, half-afraid of what we were going to see.

It was only Frederic, sprawled on his back, chest bare. Elizabeth's eyes widened so comically I nearly laughed out loud. She clapped her hand over my mouth to stop me. I had to do the same to muffle her giggles. We stared at each other, nearly choking on nervous laughter.

I nodded my head sternly towards the door. We had to get out of here.

She shook her head and took a step closer to Frederic. I knew that look on her face.

Slipping away before I could stop her, she crept over to the side of his bed. I motioned to her frantically. If she leaned over to kiss him, I would kill her. She did lean over a little, but not enough to actually touch him.

And then he shifted, eyes opening slightly, before closing again on another snore.

Elizabeth hurled herself towards the door and we escaped in a flurry of muffled giggles.

CHAPTER 22

I'd loved Rosefield before, but I loved it even more now. It was a safe haven, surrounded by roses and filled with books. I knew by some instinct that Lord Jasper was trustworthy; I'd been mistaken before to suspect him. I could finally begin to imagine myself as a real person, not simply a pawn in Mother's endless quest for riches and prestige. Everything felt bigger—the room I slept in, the small trunk with my few dresses, the very air. There was finally a measure of space not taken up by her uncertain temper.

And perhaps I wouldn't have chosen the life of a medium, but I couldn't deny that it was thrilling. Everything seemed to be falling into place for me, except for one thing—I missed Colin.

It would be awful to have to leave this place and return to the yellow coal fog of London and the harrowing maze of Mother's moods, but at least Colin would be there. Even as she dragged me about to public halls to make money off my newfound talent, he, at least, would be there. It might be almost bearable. I'd stopped thinking of him as the irritating boy who prowled our house with his big feet and arrogant smirk. Now he was the one I might finally escape with; he was handsome and strong and he understood me. It was an intoxicating combination. I pressed a hand to my warm cheek.

I might have sat there a little longer, immersed in thoughts of Colin, but the press of spirits was in the room. There was that subtle shift in temperature and pressure that I was beginning to recognise, the smell of strong Turkish coffee and the sound of footsteps on the rug. But there was no one else in the library, just me, curled in a leather chair. I squinted, caught a flash of mist in the shape of a dress with silver-netted panniers. As usual, that one glimpse made all the other glimpses easier to see.

And quite suddenly it was rather crowded in the empty library.

The woman with the wide dress had a heart-shaped patch on her cheek covering a smallpox scar. She gave a ribald laugh as she floated to the top of the bookshelf and pulled down a book I felt certain I wasn't allowed to see. She drank coffee from a crystal cup.

Behind her, a young boy with dirt on his face grinned at me.

A cat attacked the motes of dust hanging in a beam of sunlight. I had no idea if he was a real cat or a ghostly cat.

"I thought I might find you here," Lord Jasper said from

the doorway where he'd been watching me swat away invisible people. Perfect.

"It's so peaceful here," I said, hastily lowering my hand. *Even with all the dead people.*

"You know about your third eye now, from the reading I gave you?" He leaned against his cane.

I nodded.

"Picture it now then, and see it closing, as if it were asleep. That way, you'll only see the spirits when you choose to open the eye."

"But what about the ones I want to see?" I was thinking of Mr Rochester. I'd miss his furry, clever little face.

"You can half-shut the eye, as if it were drowsy."

I tried it. Immediately, the shadows receded a little. It felt itchy still, as if a headache loomed, but it was better than the alternative. I beamed at him. "Thank you!"

"It will take some time to master properly, of course."

"Lord Jasper?" I asked when he turned to go.

"Yes, my dear?"

"You have psychical talents too, don't you?"

"I did." He paused and smiled sadly at me over his shoulder. "A long time ago."

—————⟨∞⟩—————

Tea was served in the main parlour for the guests. Lady Lucinda sniffed at me when I dared pass her chair. She turned her head, giving me the cut direct. She clearly didn't approve of my return. Her friends followed her lead, sticking their noses in the air. I went to hide in a chair by the door, behind a cabinet of curiosities.

Everyone else was talking about the farewell ball tonight, which would be even more grand than the one last week. Instead of wishing I could waltz with Colin under the ruby-glassed oil lamps, I was wondering how I was going to solve Rowena's murder if I had to go back to London permanently. She refused to leave Tabitha's side, and Tabitha was keeping to her room, according to Elizabeth.

"You look disgruntled. Have a scone." Elizabeth sat next to me, offering her plate. "Cook puts candied rose petals in them. It's tastier than it sounds."

"We're running out of time," I said, taking the bite she offered me. Her mother glared at us sourly from the other side of the room, rising to her feet.

"Uh-oh." Elizabeth sighed. She crammed the rest of the scone in her mouth in a huge, unladylike bite. "Mother doesn't approve of me eating sweet things," she mumbled though the crumbs.

I felt certain that wasn't the only thing Elizabeth's mother disapproved of.

"Elizabeth," Lady Ashford said, pointedly ignoring me. "Come along."

Elizabeth blinked. "But I haven't drunk my tea."

"All the same. This is not appropriate."

"I've only just finished eating," she grumbled, brushing crumbs off the front of her silk dress.

"You know very well that's not what I mean. Don't cause a scene." She gripped Elizabeth's elbow and hauled her to her feet, despite her admonitions about causing a scene. Nearby chatter paused. I swallowed hard, hoping I wasn't flushing red with anger and mortification. Elizabeth looked like an apoplectic radish.

"Mother!"

"Now, Elizabeth Anne."

She shot me an apologetic glance before letting herself be dragged away. I drank the rest of my tea to give myself something to do while I willed everyone to stop sneaking glances my way. I felt like an animal in one of the cages at the zoological gardens, being gawked at. They wanted me to talk about the dead, wanted me to weep at being snubbed, wanted me to provide as much scandal as my mother had accidentally afforded them.

I just wanted to hide in my room with a book.

But I couldn't do that until I'd solved Rowena's bloody problem.

Mr Travis stood by the buffet table, holding a raspberry tart. His eyes were shadowed again, his thin shoulders stooped.

I might not be an earl's legitimate daughter, I might not have had tutors and governesses and riding lessons, but I had talents of my own that had nothing to do with spirit visions.

And it was time I put them to good use.

I meandered slowly towards the buffet table. I took a plate and piled it with thin slices of ham, cucumber salad and sugar-dusted blackberries that I had no intention of eating. I stopped next to Mr Travis, who turned towards me. I leaned to get a honey-glazed pastry, deliberately out of my reach.

A little more humiliation wouldn't kill me.

I was already accounted a clumsy girl with no breeding; no one would think twice.

I had to remind myself of that before I tipped the plate of food on to Mr Travis. Blackberries bounced off his arm. A slice of ham landed on his shoe. There were gasps and titters. Elizabeth's eyes were so round I had to look away in case I giggled.

"Oh, I'm so sorry!" I exclaimed. The red in my cheeks was perfectly authentic. I grabbed for a napkin and patted his coat. The cream filling in the pastry smeared over his lapel. I fluttered apologetically at him.

He never noticed when I slipped my hands into his coat pockets while I was making the stains worse with my napkin. The first pocket was empty, the second had a folded letter tucked inside. The wax seal gave under my nail.

I stole it.

Just in case. It might be nothing—a bill or a list of supplies for his mother. There was only one way to find out.

I tucked the letter under the flounces of my dress and hurried out of the parlour, still apologising and blushing while a maidservant took Mr Travis's coat for cleaning. He wouldn't find out the pocket was empty for a while yet. And if the letter wasn't important, I could leave it in the drawing room and he'd just think it had fallen out in the commotion.

I would have taken the stairs two at a time if my gown allowed it. Inside my room, I shut the door tightly and climbed on to the bed to unfold the letter. The handwriting was delicate, feminine, and the parchment smelled faintly of lily of the valley.

I tried to read it but was distracted by the boot sticking out from under my bed. It was black and scuffed—and I wasn't entirely sure if it was ghostly or human.

I only knew I wasn't alone.

And that anyone hiding under my bed wouldn't have honourable intentions.

I couldn't remember if I'd seen Peter taking tea with the others.

Edging off the bed slowly, I reached for the iron poker by the fireplace. I held it up against my shoulder like a carpet beater, as if I were about to whack dust from a parlour rug. I crept closer. The foot didn't move.

"That's it," I muttered, swinging the poker down next to the foot. "Get out of my room!" I added a vicious poke.

"Bollocks!" a voice roared from under the feather mattress.

A familiar voice.

Colin scrambled out, smudged with dust and scowling. "What the bleedin' hell are you—oh, Violet. It's you."

"Of course it's me! Who else would it be? What are you doing here?"

"I thought you were one of the maids."

"I meant here in Wiltshire," I said, dropping the poker. My heart dropped back to its normal rhythm. "Scaring me half to death."

He smiled sheepishly. "Sorry." He touched my cheek briefly. "Didn't you miss me a little?"

"Maybe." I narrowed my eyes at him. "Did you miss me?"

"That's why I'm here, innit?"

I admit it. I melted. This new Colin was entirely too charming for his own good. His thumb trailed under my ear and along the back of my neck. Even my knees shivered.

"And I was worried about you."

"Why?"

"Because you're chasing a murderer," he returned drily. "I know you don't need to be mollycoddled but I can't help worrying about you. You get into trouble the way debutantes get into ball gowns."

"I do not. Speaking of trouble, where on earth are you sleeping?"

"I'll find a spot in the stables. No one'll know."

"But . . ." I frowned. It wasn't right. He should have a better bed than a hayloft. Especially since I was eating chocolates and sleeping under brocade bed curtains.

"Don't worry about me." He waved off my concern. "I like horses better than the fancy anyway. Are *you* all right?"

"I'm fine," I assured him, smiling. It was so good to see him. It had been only two days. I shouldn't be missing him yet. "The ladies are snubbing me. Lord Jasper's a little naive, isn't he?" I said. "He thinks he can make everyone accept me. He has no idea what those women would do to me. On a more positive note, I threw a pastry at Mr Travis today."

"You really do have lamentable aim."

I grinned cheekily. "But I can out-pickpocket you any day."

"Let's not be hasty," he snorted. "And is 'pickpocket' even a verb?"

"Do you want to quibble or do you want to read what I found in Travis's pocket?"

"Let me see it."

I held it out of his reach. "*I* haven't even read it yet. You can look over my shoulder."

His smile was crooked. "Bossy."

I unfolded the paper. It was soft from too much handling, as if it had been read every single day, like a favourite poem. But even I hadn't read *The Lady of Shalott* enough to alter the paper it was printed on, and I knew it by heart.

Colin twitched his nose at the perfume. "Why do girls do that?"

"It's a love letter," I explained.

"She must have spilled an entire bottle on it."

"Shhh," I said softly. "Listen," I added and began to read.

Dearest Reece,

I know you think it improper, or at the very least imprudent, for us to write to one another, but I don't care. There are too many rules as it is and they would choke me if I let them. Between corsets and lessons and curtsies and etiquette, I am hardly myself, and that is how they want it. They would prefer we all dress and talk and think (or not think) alike, like paper dolls.

I do not wish to be a paper doll.

Surely you can see that I am stronger than that. I don't give a fig for the scandalbroth or the gossip-mongers. Let us remove to Paris, where no one knows us to care and where they dine on scandal with éclairs every morning.

You will say again that it is impossible but I refuse to believe it. I know with every touch of your hand on mine, with every stolen kiss, that nothing is impossible.

Perhaps love isn't meant to be simple. Perhaps this is merely a test, such as Psyche went through to prove herself to Cupid. Would you have me count lentils, beloved?

And as you claim I have the most to lose, I pray you will let me decide for myself what it is I want and need.

Which is you.

Not silks or lobster soup in crystal bowls or diamonds around my neck.

Just you.

You say again and again that you love me.

Prove it.

I lowered the letter. "He's in love."

"I reckon that explains the mad weeping."

I turned to stare at Colin. "This can't be a coincidence. Rowena showed me a letter at the seance last night. She jilted Peter and wanted to marry someone else."

He stared back. "*Travis?* Rowena Wentworth was in love with that morbid beanpole?"

"Perhaps he wasn't morbid before she died."

He shook his head. "Daft. She's an heiress. I guess he was jealous she was going to marry Peter? Some lover."

I shook my head slowly. "I don't think that's it. Her father gave her his permission," I added, tapping the letter on my thigh. "So he can't be the murderer. At least not for that reason."

"Maybe she tired of him."

"Maybe. Or maybe Peter found out and flew into a rage. Elizabeth said he has a nasty temper."

Colin frowned. "He's a high flyer, no doubt. Going to be an earl and all that. His pride might've driven him mad when he found out."

"How's Caroline involved?" I wondered. "She lit that lamp on purpose. And Rowena threw a dead trout at her last night."

"No wonder she chose you. Between pastries and fish, no one's safe."

A scratch at the door interrupted us. Colin dropped down and rolled under the bed again. One of the maids poked her head in. "Miss?"

I tried not to look as if I was hiding a handsome young lad under the mattress.

"Yes?"

"Lord Jasper sent me up to see if you need help getting ready for the ball." She smiled proudly. "I have a fair hand with a curling iron."

"Oh. Thank you." I needed to get Colin out before I ended up naked in the middle of my bedroom. "I, um, could I have some hot water? To wash my face?"

"Certainly, miss. I'll have the footmen bring up the bathtub, if you like, before all the fine ladies start calling for their own baths."

"That would be wonderful, thanks." I'd never actually been in a full reclining tub before. We had a battered hip bath in the kitchen.

The maid curtsied and closed the door behind her. I let out a breath. Colin crawled back out. "They need to sweep under there," he said, sneezing. "I'll keep an eye on Peter for a while," he added before slipping out of my room.

∞∞∞

By the time I was bathed, coiffed with my hair in long ringlets, stuffed into a ball gown and finally left alone in my chamber, I'd lost the rest of the afternoon. The ball was about to begin and I had no time to find Colin. Lord Jasper was waiting for me and I couldn't be rude, not after everything he'd done for me. I'd have to put in an appearance and hope I could lose myself in the crowd as soon as possible.

The ballroom was even more sumptuously decorated than it was last week, with vases full of orchids and glass lanterns hung on jewelled chains from the painted ceiling. The orchestra was playing something liquid and beautiful, and couples danced in perfect circles. I curtsied to Lord Jasper, then kept my back to the wall, creeping behind the chairs set out for chaperones and wallflowers wishing someone would ask them to dance. I couldn't see Elizabeth anywhere, or Peter, or even Tabitha—and she loved these events.

I sneaked into the corridor, wondering what to do next.

And walked right into Mr Travis.

"Miss Willoughby."

He looked so weary and sad, I instantly felt sorry for him. In the space of one letter he'd turned from sinister to tragic. I felt horrid for stealing something so precious from him. I opened my reticule and pulled out the letter.

"I believe this is yours," I said quietly.

He snatched it away instantly. "Where did you find this?"

"Was it from Rowena?"

He paused in the act of putting it in the inside pocket of his formal coat. "What?"

"It's all right. I won't tell anyone," I assured him, even as I watched for his reaction. He didn't look guilty, just slightly bewildered.

"How did you know?" He grabbed my hand as if I'd made to walk away when I hadn't actually moved. The music from the ballroom poured into the hall. "Can you really see her? I knew you could. Is she here now?" His eyes were a little wild.

"I'm sorry," I said. "She's not here. I can't call her up at will. She's very stubborn."

He smiled his rare smile. "She was exceedingly stubborn. How else would an earl's daughter make provisions to marry a tailor's son with no bloodline to speak of?"

"She loved you."

"She didn't drown," he said grimly.

"I know," I replied equally grimly.

"But I have no proof. Even a year later."

Before I could ask him any questions, a footman stopped in front of me, holding a silver tray. "Miss Willoughby?"

"Yes."

He bowed. "A message for you, miss." He lifted the tray to offer me a folded note with my name scrawled across the front. I took it, tendrils of curiosity and dread unfurling like a poisonous plant inside my belly. I skimmed it briefly, then frowned. "That's odd."

"What is it?"

"It's from Caroline," I said. "She's waiting for me by the hedge at the front."

I rushed down the hall and pushed out of the front doors and past the flickering torches on the lawn on either side of the white gravel drive. I ran to the hedges where Caroline waited, Mr Travis on my heels. Caroline's hair was frizzing out of its strict bun and her eyes were wide with worry.

"What's wrong?" I asked her.

"Please." I could tell she was trying not to cry. "You have to come. It's Tabitha."

CHAPTER 23

"She's been weeping all day and won't speak to anyone. But she finally asked for you and couldn't be persuaded to leave it until morning." She looked determined and ready to haul me bodily away, even though her lips trembled. "It was today, you know."

"What was today?"

"Rowena!" she burst out. "She drowned last year on this day. Didn't you know?"

A shiver went through me. "I didn't know that." I looked at Mr Travis. He nodded.

"You must come with me!" Caroline insisted.

I paused, focusing on my third eye, lifting the lid slowly. Rowena hovered anxiously behind Caroline, throat bruised, expression pleading. She wanted me to follow.

I could think of a hundred things I'd rather do than follow a possible murderess and the ghost of her victim.

Rowena, however, was insistent.

"I don't know what you think I can do," I said as we hurried across the lawns.

"I don't know either, but if she wants you there, I mean to bring you to her."

"Miss Willoughby, wait!" Mr Travis chased after us. "You can't go to Whitestone. It isn't safe."

"I don't have a choice."

We raced over the dark hills until my lungs burned. The pond was still but the white lilies on its banks seemed etched in silver. We didn't speak again until we reached the manor house, and then it was only Caroline panting, "This way." The house was full of shadows, lit only by the odd oil lamp in the wide hallways.

"What does her uncle have to say?" I whispered, following Caroline up the stairs.

"He's been drinking all day."

Up the dark stairs, Tabitha's door was painted with pink roses.

And it was locked.

Caroline frowned, trying the handle again. "Dearest, you must open the door."

Tabitha didn't reply but we could hear muffled sobs.

"Tabitha, please," Caroline begged, clearly concerned. A cold draught skirted around our ankles but I couldn't see Rowena anywhere. I wasn't certain what to think of that. Clearly, as distraught as Tabitha might be, there was a greater danger Rowena was protecting her from, or she'd have been hovering by her twin.

Caroline tried the door again, to no avail. I wondered if it was meant to keep her out specifically. I put a little space between us.

"Why has she locked you out?" I asked.

Caroline was shoving her shoulder against the door. "I told you," she panted, pushing harder. "She's upset."

"Is she afraid of you?"

Caroline paused. "What? Whyever would she be?"

"You tell me."

She was looking at me as if I were mad. "Miss Willoughby, what exactly are you implying?"

I ignored her, speaking through the wooden door. "Tabitha, it's Violet." I knocked softly. No response. "Are you hurt?"

I couldn't very well stand about a dark house all night, especially not next to a woman I had reason to know was hiding something. I remembered what Elizabeth had said about hairpins and locks. I pulled one of the pins from my hair and dropped to my knees. I slid the pin into the lock and pressed my ear to the brass plate securing the handle to the door. I jiggled the pin, listening carefully for a *click*. It took longer than I'd expected, but eventually I heard a satisfying *snick.*

Caroline pushed past me before I could stop her. Tabitha was huddled in the corner, her straggly hair sticking to her damp cheeks. She didn't flinch from her governess. I wasn't sure if that was a good sign or not.

"Tabitha," I said softly. I had no idea what I was expected to do. Tabitha didn't even like me. She was clutching the pearl ring I had found in the pond the day she'd threatened to set the dogs on us.

"I didn't want to believe you," she croaked. She'd clearly been sobbing for hours; her voice was raspy, her eyes swollen. Her pulse was fluttering frantically under the thin china of her skin.

"It's my fault," Caroline wept into her hands.

"I knew it." My temper flared.

Tabitha blinked wretchedly. "Caro, what are you saying?"

"We knew it was wrong, but we couldn't help ourselves."

"Peter?" I asked. "Tabitha, come away."

Caroline nodded miserably. "I love him," she said. "I never meant for it to happen. You don't choose these things."

I gaped at her. "You do choose whether or not you drown some poor girl in a pond, you daft cow."

"What?" She looked confused.

"You and Peter killed Rowena! The trout landed on you!"

She had the gall to look insulted. "I most certainly did not!"

Now I was the one who was confused. "You didn't?"

"No!"

"Then what's your fault exactly?"

"Peter. We had an affair."

Tabitha sat up a little straighter. "You? And *Peter*? And what about the fish?"

At least that explained why Peter had been so rough with

me on the night of the seance. He'd been protecting his lover, no doubt afraid I knew more than I should.

"We knew it was wrong." Caroline sniffled. "He was engaged to Rowena and I'm just a governess. But she broke off the engagement . . . and then she drowned, and I swore to myself I'd take the best care of Tabitha I possibly could."

"I don't understand," I said finally. "If you didn't kill her, who did?"

"Kill her? It was an accident."

"No, it wasn't."

"It's not safe here," Mr Travis said urgently. "We have to leave, all of us. Right now."

Tabitha blinked. "What's he doing here?"

"We have to go," Mr Travis said again. He turned to me. "Rowena threw the dead trout at her uncle. It slid towards Caroline—maybe Rowena was taking a poke at her because of Peter—but it started in front of Sir Wentworth."

Bollocks.

He was right.

Tabitha began weeping again. "She was in love." She rocked backwards and forwards, as if she were still in the cradle, her knees drawn up to her chest, her hands clutched tightly together. I could see where the ring made a dent in her skin. "You seemed so certain," she sobbed at me. "So I went through her things. I hadn't been able to until today. I just couldn't bear it. She was my best friend." She sobbed harder, her words incoherent.

"Tabitha." I leaned over her, shook her shoulder. "Tabitha,

you have to focus." I tried to find the balance between stern and compassionate.

"I went through her hope chest." She hiccupped. She was still pressed against the wooden chest. Rowena's name was painted across the front, with little daisies. "I found love letters." She pushed a bundle of paper towards me. I glanced at Mr Travis. His fingers twitched as if he longed to grab them from her.

"I've been trying to pretend everything is normal, but it's not. Uncle's been drinking more and he won't even consider letting me go to London. I've been cooped up in the country for months. I don't think he'll ever let me get married; he wouldn't even let Frederic and Peter visit. He got so angry. And today he's . . . different." She showed us the ring again. "It was Rowena's favourite."

"I gave it to her," Mr Travis murmured.

"I asked my uncle for it after the funeral. He said she was wearing it when they buried her."

"So he lied to you about it."

"Yes. And when I asked him about it this morning, he got so angry. I've never seen him like that. I didn't know what else to do, so I locked myself in here and had Caroline fetch you. I was so scared he'd . . ." She stopped, gagging on more tears. "And I'm so tired." She blinked at me, smiling foolishly. Caroline and I frowned at each other.

"Is she ill?" I asked.

Caroline shook her head. Tabitha giggled, then burst into tears again. I crouched in front of her. "Tabitha, look at me."

She looked up obediently. Her pupils were constricted, her skin clammy. "She's taken laudanum," I said grimly. I'd seen Mrs Gordon and Miss Hartington in a similar state often enough.

Caroline didn't look shocked. "She takes laudanum for her nerves. Her uncle's been giving it to her for a couple of weeks now, because of her sister. She's distraught. Not surprising, this time of year."

"Or else he's keeping her biddable." I stood up, suddenly unable to be still. I hadn't suspected him at all. He was Rowena's uncle and a lord of the realm. There must be some mistake. Mr Travis must be wrong to suspect him, as I'd been wrong to suspect Mr Travis. I started to pace, stopped to peer out of the window. The gardens were dark and quiet. "It doesn't make sense. Why would he do that?"

"I don't know," Caroline replied, bewildered. "He's always been jovial enough, likes his wine and his cards, has black moods certainly, but nothing unusual for a gentleman. He's overprotective of Tabitha, but that's to be expected. He's already lost one niece, after all, and he is their guardian."

"He wants the money," Mr Travis said quietly. "Rowena wondered if he was the one who found her letter to her father. We were going to elope. I went off to secure us a hackney in town, one that wouldn't be recognised. I shouldn't have left her alone. She wanted to tell Tabitha so that she wouldn't worry. I should have stayed with her."

"He's a second son," I added slowly, "with no land to inherit and money only from the Whitestone estates, which, evidently, are very valuable." I couldn't credit that an uncle would kill his own niece, but I didn't seem to be able to reach any other conclusion, not now. "We have to get out of here." I shook Tabitha lightly but she was limp and distracted. "We have to get the opium out of her. Fetch some water."

Caroline rushed over with the jug of water from the washstand. I held it up to Tabitha's lips. She swallowed a couple of times and then pushed it away peevishly.

"Tabitha, you have to drink more."

"Don't want to."

"You have to. We have to flush the drugs out of your system." I forced her to drink some more, even though half of it dribbled down her chin.

"I don't understand," Caroline said, wringing her hands. "What are you two talking about?"

I glanced at her. "Wentworth murdered Rowena because she was going to elope. He knew she didn't want to marry Peter and would have waited as long as possible to marry, so he wasn't worried about the betrothal. An elopement is another matter."

Tabitha started crying again, so abruptly and wildly I feared she'd make herself more ill. She was green under her pallor.

"She needs to keep drinking," I instructed, handing Caroline the jug and going to the window. I pulled it open, peering out. The ground seemed very far away. "We can't wait for

Tabitha to get better," I said grimly. "We have to go right now, before he realises we know." Mr Travis and I tried to get Tabitha to her feet but she went limp, curling into herself.

"Tabitha!"

No amount of shouting was going to help apparently. I didn't know what else to do. We couldn't very well escape if she was hysterical and drugged.

I slapped her across the face. Caroline shoved me aside. She stroked Tabitha's arm and made soothing noises, all the while glaring at me. Tabitha had at last stopped crying. "Leave her be. This isn't her fault."

"I know it's not her fault," I said with very deliberate patience. "But we have to get out of here. *Now*."

Tabitha pushed her hair off her face. "She's right," she said with a hiccup, shrugging off Caroline's hovering.

I knew her lucidity might only last a moment, so I waved them over to where I was standing.

Caroline's eyes widened. "The window? You can't be serious."

"We can't risk going through the house. He might hear us."

I had to admit it wasn't my favourite idea, but it was the only one I had.

Mr Travis clenched his hands. "I'll keep him distracted."

Caroline looked at him in horror. "He's twice your size. He'll kill you."

"As long as he does it slowly and gives you time to get out of here," he said. "Rowena would want her sister to be safe."

"I'm not sure—" There was no point in finishing my argument; he was already gone.

The breeze fluttered the curtains. I could see I was going to have to go first if I expected Caroline and Tabitha to follow me. But I couldn't climb in my ball gown—it was far too restrictive. I wriggled out of it until I was in my corset, chemise and pantaloons. Caroline stared at me as if I were mad.

I stuck my head out of the window. The stone ledge was narrow and long, running the length of the building. I might be able to follow it to the balcony, hop out over it and then slide down the trellis on the other side.

Or I might just plummet to the flagstones below.

I took a deep breath to steel myself and stuck one leg over the sill, then the other. I pulled myself out, my grip white-knuckled. Another breeze ruffled the treetops, which were too close to eye level for comfort. An owl flew by on silent wings. I envied him. He wasn't about to fall to his death.

"I can do this," I told myself.

"I wouldn't advise it."

Sir Wentworth poked his chubby face out to look at me. In the crook of his arm he held Caroline, in his other hand, a knife. She wilted. Rowena wailed, trying to insert herself between them. The air in the room was frigid. My heart pounded in my ears.

"I suggest you come back inside, Violet, unless you'd like Miss Donovan here to meet a rather messy end."

He'd kill her anyway, eventually. She knew too much. But I wouldn't be the catalyst.

I inched back along the ledge to the window. The walls behind them began to drip with water. No one noticed. When I was within arm's reach, he shoved Caroline and yanked me inside.

"Where's Mr Travis?" I demanded.

"Bleeding on my best rug."

Tabitha looked confused. "My heart's racing."

Her uncle ignored her. "The talented Miss Willoughby," he said to me. Gone was the cheerful, portly man who'd sneaked Elizabeth extra Christmas pudding. There was something disturbing to his smile. "You would have caused me far less trouble if you'd been more like your mother. I did try to warn you."

"You did?" I blinked. "The urn." I understood suddenly. "The chandelier. It was you."

"That blasted Travis boy interfered. I ought to have killed him too, but Jasper kept him busy with lectures and seances. I hope you showed him proper gratitude."

Actually, I'd considered it likely he was a murderer.

"But *you* were the one who saved me from the chandelier."

"Too many damned witnesses. And it kept you from wondering about me, didn't it?"

"And you've been drugging Tabitha," I said, horrified. "Why?"

"She's been getting agitated. Wants to go to London, wants to get married and leave me a pauper. Not a spot of gratitude on the girl. Haven't I taken care of her? And then she asked about that damned ring."

Rowena loomed over her uncle suddenly, until he shivered in the chill.

"You really did kill Rowena."

His gaze snapped on to me. "Clever girl. Too clever by half."

I lifted my chin stubbornly. "She's here now."

He jerked, looking over his shoulder. His eyes narrowed.

"She will always be with you," I added, trying to disconcert him. "She will never leave you alone."

"Shut up!" He kicked out at me, looking grim, wild. Water was beginning to pool on the carpet. "Never mind." His smile was pleasant again and all the worse for it.

"You can't keep us here." My hip caught the edge of the desk, bruising painfully.

"Of course I can. A letter will be sent to Lord Jasper expressing your sincere apologies, but you simply had to return to London and your mother. No one will know you've disappeared; no one will think to look for you until it's far, far too late."

He was wrong.

Colin would know.

I made a dash towards the door, but his hand was a vice around my upper arm. A lamp tumbled to the ground. Caroline squeaked.

"Tsk, Miss Willoughby. I'm only offering you a chance to rest. A little laudanum," he said pleasantly. "Won't hurt a bit. You might even enjoy it." I fought harder. "Drink it, Miss Willoughby. It would be easier on you if you slept. I can't have you carrying tales, and I have to think what to do next."

"No." I pressed my lips fiercely together but he was

stronger than I was. He forced the laudanum into me, pressed his hand over my mouth and nose until I couldn't hold my breath any more. A trickle went down my throat. The taste of the opium tincture was sweet and strong and medicinal. It was familiar. It was the same taste in Rowena's mouth the night she drowned. My knees wobbled like jellied pudding. I took advantage of it and collapsed on to the rug. I rolled my head down, spitting out most of the laudanum so it soaked into the carpet. Enough had made it into my system that I felt floaty and odd, but I wasn't likely to die as Sir Wentworth wanted.

Everything was too bright, too watery. I felt rather cheerful even as my thoughts went foggy, slippery. I struggled to turn my head.

"Don't fight it," Wentworth said. "You'll only do yourself harm."

"Rowena," I mumbled. "She's behind you."

"What are you playing at?" Wentworth roared. But I could see the hairs on his arms lifting. I met his uncertain glare.

"She's everywhere," I whispered.

The surface of the mirror rippled like water, showing Rowena's cold face. Water began to drip from the curtains and run in rivulets across the floor. Sir Wentworth leaped away from it as if it were acid. It felt cool on my cheeks. When one of the pipes cracked loudly inside the walls, more water flooded into the room. I swallowed as much of the water as I could, knowing I'd need to flush the laudanum out.

"What is this?" He was furious, but scared too.

In every window, every gleaming surface—water jug, silver

spoon, silver sequins on a cushion—Rowena's face appeared. Winter filled the room. Where there wasn't cold wind, there was water; cold rain slicked down the wall, puddled at our feet, beat against the windows. The sweet, cloying scent of white lilies was everywhere, touching everything. I wouldn't have been at all surprised if my dress had turned to ice.

Tabitha sat up. "Rowena?" she asked tentatively, hopefully.

Her uncle stumbled back. "This is a trick."

Rowena's hope chest opened and folded letters whipped out, slapping him in the face. The edges cut into his skin, drawing blood. He batted at them frantically. Saliva foamed at the corners of his mouth. Cold wind pushed at him, until he tripped over his own feet in his haste to get out of the room. Rowena drifted through the door, chasing him with a ghostly laugh like shattering glass.

He still managed to turn the key in the lock with a loud *click*, like a pistol.

CHAPTER 24

One year earlier

Rowena was certain her uncle had stolen the letter from inside her pillow-case. She wasn't safe. And neither was Mr Travis. She had to get away, had to warn Tabitha, maybe persuade her to come along. She waited until it was long past midnight before creeping out of her bedroom. She'd have to get her belongings in the carriage and have Reece waiting before she woke Tabitha.

"Rowena, there you are."

Her uncle was waiting for her at the bottom of the stairs, stepping out of the shadows before she even saw him there. He took her wrist, hard enough to bruise. "We need to talk."

He yanked her into his study. "You've been keeping secrets."

Her mouth was dry. "I don't know what you mean."

"I found your father's letter. You mean to elope with a poor tailor's son. I can't think what my brother means by allowing you this madness."

"I..."

He smiled. "There's no need to fret. I only wish you'd come to me about it instead of sneaking around."

"You . . . do?"

"Of course. You're my niece. I only want what's best for you."

"I love him, Uncle Reginald."

"I'm sure you do. You're very young to marry, child."

She tilted her chin mutinously. "It's what we want."

"I see." He handed her a crystal glass of sweet wine. "A toast, then."

She didn't want to drink. She wanted to meet Reece and find a vicar to marry them. But her uncle had always looked after her and Tabitha; it would be rude to turn away a gesture of reconciliation, even if her nerves suddenly felt like embroidery floss, tangled and frayed.

She drank the horrible, cloying wine. It clung to her tongue like syrup. She made a face.

Her uncle smiled. His bulk had always been cheerful. Now it was menacing. "Shall we take a turn around the garden? You look a little pale."

She blinked, perplexed. "What?"

"Come, we'll go now." He took her arm tightly, manoeuvring her out through the door leading outside. The moon was a pale curve of light, nearly blue through the haze of clouds. She stared at it for a moment. It was so pretty.

She blinked again, lifted a hand to her head. "What's happening to me?"

The crickets sounded like little violins in the hedges. They made her giggle.

"Let's walk, shall we?" Her uncle was all hard politeness as he dragged her out beyond the yew hedges and the stand of birch trees. The lawns gave way to green fields. Rain pattered softly over them. The water was silvery, falling oddly, as if it were moving through molasses instead of air. Then the raindrops felt sharp, like needles. She recoiled.

"What have you done to me? Is it poison?"

"Certainly not, that would be far too messy. It's only laudanum, my dear. You were overset."

She froze, tried to stop from feeling as if the ground were undulating under her feet. "I didn't take any laudanum." She was weaving back and forth and couldn't seem to stop herself. Over the drenched hills, the pond glimmered. "Did I?" She knew she should be terrified but she felt only floaty, sleepy. "The wine."

He still hadn't released her arm. She felt the bruises lifting to the surface of her skin already. She might have struggled but it seemed like an awful lot of effort.

He gripped her chin, peered into her eyes. "Pupils are changing," he said. "Good. Not long now."

"What are you going to do?"

"I'm afraid you're about to have a tragic accident." He shook his head sadly. "I wish you'd had better manners, Rowena. I hate to do this."

She stumbled. Her tongue felt thick in her mouth. "But I'm your niece."

"All the more regrettable." He hauled her to her feet when she would have collapsed. "You thought you'd leave me destitute, did you? Thought you could elope without me knowing about it?"

The euphoria was fading. She felt only exhausted and strange, as if she had little control over her own limbs. She struggled weakly. "Uncle Reginald," she begged thinly. "Please."

"You did this to yourself," he said sternly. "If you think I'm going to let you marry some tradesman and take this all away from me, you're stupid."

Reece. The thought of his serious face made her struggle like a scalded cat with a mouthful of pepper. She fought so violently her uncle cursed, unable to restrain her. His hands came around her throat. She clawed at him, choking. He applied more pressure, strangling her slowly until her vision went black.

When she fainted, he shifted her unwieldy weight, carrying her to the edge of the pond. The water was soft and dark as he slid her unresponsive body under its surface.

She opened her eyes only once, barely, before the water claimed her.

CHAPTER 25

I lifted my head groggily. Nausea rolled in my stomach and my mouth felt like a frog pond. I groaned, my head aching abysmally when I tried to sit up.

"Violet!" Caroline exclaimed. "Oh, thank God, I thought he'd killed you."

"He meant to." The room spun a little. I held my head between my hands to anchor everything to its proper place. "I hate that man."

Rowena floated briefly over me. She lifted her hand off my forehead. Her eyes burned. She'd used the effects of the laudanum to show me what her uncle had done to her, what she feared he would do to Tabitha.

I fumbled for the glass of water on the nightstand and forced myself to drain it. "Has he been back?"

Caroline shook her head. "He's mad."

I nodded, then wished I hadn't when both my head and

stomach protested. "We need help." I managed to push myself to my feet even though I felt about as steady as a newborn colt. I wobbled. "But first I need a chamber pot." Caroline pointed to the painted silk screen in the corner and I shuffled towards it.

"I can't leave Tabitha," Caroline said again when I emerged, bladder empty and feeling marginally less like I was made entirely of spider webs. "And she's even worse off than you."

"Then I'll have to go," I said. "Help me block the door. This time, I mean to get out."

We pushed the heavy armoire in front of the door, then added the desk and settee for good measure. I felt as if I'd moved the whole of Stonehenge by the time we had finished. I felt dreadful. But Wentworth wouldn't get in again to use either Tabitha or Caroline against me. I sincerely hoped Mr Travis wasn't dead. Sweat dampened my chemise. I had to force myself to keep moving, and it was the hardest thing I'd ever done. I offered up a silent apology to Mrs Gordon and her sister, wondering if they'd felt this ill after each of our visits. Then I drained a cup of cold tea left on the cart for fortification.

Caroline bit her lip, watching me swing out on to the ledge again. I gripped the stone so tightly that I could feel my palms cramping.

"Violet, you don't look well enough. Perhaps you should wait."

"Can't," I grunted, cheek mashed to the wall as I tried to stand up without falling backwards. The stone was cold. My left foot slipped. I swallowed a scream, clutching at the wall.

Caroline gasped. "Be careful."

I didn't reply, concentrating fully on shuffling along the last few feet to the balcony balustrade. Whitestone Manor was dark below me, but across the hills I could see the lights flickering at Rosefield and hear the music drifting out of the open windows. It seemed impossibly far, with the pond gleaming in the centre.

I mustn't think about that. There was only right now, only the railing of the balcony under my hand, only my knee bending as I pulled myself over, only the ragged tightness of my breath as I collapsed for a moment, waiting for my head to stop spinning.

I'd made it this far, I'd make it further still.

There was a trellis on the other side of the balcony. I leaned on it briefly to test its strength before abandoning the security of the balcony. The roses tickled my nose and the thorns pricked into my skin. I lowered myself slowly, so slowly, my arm muscles quivering with the effort it took to hold up my body. I'd never been so deliriously happy to feel the ground beneath my feet. I glanced up, nodding at Caroline. She nodded back, pale as the moon at the sill.

I crouched behind the yew hedges, catching my breath. Behind the glass of the main parlour, an oil lamp burned. Wentworth's shadow moved across the papered walls. He was going back upstairs.

I couldn't let that happen. He needed Tabitha alive and reclusive so she wouldn't marry, but now Caroline knew too much. He'd kill her. Especially when he realised I'd escaped.

"Rowena," I whispered. "You're the reason I'm in this bloody mess in the first place. Help me, damn you."

The first raindrop hit me in the eye. I wasn't entirely sure what to make of it.

As a sign, it was murky at best.

More rain fell, soaking into my hair, dragging down the hem of my skirts. But the cool damp on my neck had a bracing effect on me as well, chasing away the lingering traces of the laudanum haze.

I knew what I needed to do.

Even if I really, really, really didn't want to do it.

I straightened under the spears of lightning hurling out of the sky. I approached the window and stood there, hands pressed against the glass. I waited until Wentworth saw me there, waited until he'd reached the doors, before I began to run in earnest, leading him away from Tabitha and Caroline and into the dark shadows of the fields.

I slipped through the muddy grass as rain pelted us from every direction. He followed me, his shirt stained with wine, his hair sticking up every which way.

"Come back here," he shouted. "You've cursed me, you little witch. She won't leave me alone!"

I flew over the hills, my lungs burning. I stumbled but forced myself to keep running. I nearly wept with relief when I saw Rowena hovering over the pond's pebbled surface. Thunder growled around us. The wind shredded the lilies. Wentworth grabbed the lace fluttering on the hem of my pantalettes and I tumbled, landing hard. I was winded but still managed to kick out at him.

"Get off me!" I kicked harder, missed. The rain fell slower, pausing as it gathered and froze over the pond. Ice crackled over the water.

Wentworth spat out a mouthful of lily petals. "What the devil?"

There was pressure on my chest and then a searing flash of cold on my hands. Everything was rain and lilies.

I knew the exact moment he saw her floating towards him. He blanched, even in the darkness of the sudden storm. "No, no."

She came closer, pale as frog bellies and lily petals. She reached out to touch him and he flinched. Her hand went through him. Frustration sparked though her. She glided through the tall grass, paused above me before reclining as if she meant to lie down and sleep.

Using me as her bed.

My hands tingled, as if I'd held them in ice too long. I felt faraway, and my hand lifted and formed a fist of its own accord. I tried to scowl but my face wouldn't cooperate. I tried to unclench my fingers, but they seemed to belong to someone else. My hair floated in the air around me, as if I were underwater,

"Uncle Reginald." It wasn't my voice coming out of my mouth. My throat hurt.

"No." He went the colour of curdled milk.

I smiled. Or rather, Rowena used my face to smile. I fought the catharsis, feeling trapped and frightened. She was in my head, my bones, my blood.

"This is where you killed me." She said it almost sweetly. "Do you remember?"

"Not possible." He rubbed his eyes.

She turned my head and my hair, still drifting and matted with blood on one side. "You strangled me and watched me sink below the water." Bruises turned purple on my wrists. I felt them on my throat. I wished she'd been this vocal a little earlier. "All because you wanted Whitestone."

"I deserve Whitestone." His teeth clattered together. Frost bloomed like creeping ivy over the grass, the flowers; even the crickets were now suddenly silent.

I was cast adrift in my own body. This was taking too long. I had nothing to steady me, to keep me tethered. *Don't let go*, Rowena said sharply in her own voice, in the floating darkness inside my head. I got to my feet. A confession here in the middle of a field wouldn't do any of us any good. I stumbled. Rowena would have drifted gracefully, but my movements felt clunky and jerky, as if we were fighting for the strings of a marionette.

She floated out of my body and back in, enticing Wentworth to follow. I tried not to throw up on my own feet. I forced myself to move, used the trees to pull myself towards the Rosefield gardens. The cold wind was nearly unbearable.

"You're not real, not real," Wentworth mumbled even as he followed after me.

I ran faster.

The weeds gave way to manicured lawns and I nearly wept with relief. Not far now. I could smell the roses, see the glow of lamplight spilling out on to the terrace. The music was soft, happy.

Wentworth crashed through the hedges, swearing. I ran past a murmuring couple, startling them out of an embrace. The doors were open, letting in fresh air to cool the dancers.

I fell into the ballroom. The guests froze, turning to stare. I knew I must look a fright, wet as a drowned rat and covered in mud, in my underwear. I was shaking from the effects of the storm and the laudanum and Rowena's possession. The strains of a pretty waltz faltered, then stopped. I closed my eyes for a moment and when I opened them again, Colin was propping me up.

"What the devil?" he asked, looking terrified. I blinked at the shiny buttons on his coat. He'd stolen a footman's uniform to get around the party and watch Peter who, as it turned out, didn't need watching.

"Wentworth?" Lord Jasper came forward as the other man burst through the doors only seconds after me. The light hit the silver swan of Lord Jasper's cane. Wentworth looked as wild as I felt, all white eyes and tangled hair. He gave an odd, strangled laugh.

"Murderer," I croaked loudly in that odd voice not my own. Everyone glanced at Wentworth, who straightened, anger giving him a bolstering jolt of courage. He hardly seemed to notice where we were, or else he was past caring.

"Had no choice, did I? Wanted to blackmail us. Your fault." He sneered down at me. "Planning to elope with my tailor's son, of all people. Absurd! Think Reece Travis would have loved you after he'd got hold of your inheritance?"

"I loved him." I was shivering violently, barely able to stand up. Colin steadied me. "And you murdered me for it."

"I couldn't let you squander the last of the family money like my worthless brother," he raged. "No one else gives a damn about this family—not him, not you. I took care of you and how were you going to repay me? By taking the last of the Wentworth land and giving it to a poor tailor. What would have become of me?" When Tabitha wanted her debut, he felt the same fears. If she married, he'd be destitute. But he knew two twin girls dying accidentally might raise questions, so he refused to take her to London and secretly fed her laudanum to keep her pliable.

"I wouldn't have made you leave Whitestone."

He shook his head, stared harder at me. "This can't be real," he slurred, as if his lips were numb. "This is a dream, just a dream." He whirled, shouted at the orchestra. "Play, damn you! This is a ball, isn't it?"

The hushed silence was pockmarked with gasps and frantic mutterings. No one moved. Rowena was staying too long, nestling into my bones. I was beginning to wonder where she ended and I began. Her memories and my memories intertwined too closely together.

"She's cold." Colin rubbed my hands between his. "Look at her eyes."

Jasper cursed. I gathered from that my eyes looked odd. "Spirit," he said, leaning close to me. "Leave this girl."

I shook my head, or Rowena did, I couldn't be sure.

"Leave her! I command it!"

Rowena ignored them. Someone shrieked.

"That's not her face!" I heard that same person slide weakly to the ground.

Colin took salt out of his pocket and forced it under my tongue. "Leave her be!"

Rowena recoiled from the taste of the salt.

"More," I murmured.

Colin emptied his pocket. I swallowed thickly, mouth puckering. Rowena screamed. It was working but she was fighting it, desperate, wailing in my head. I shuddered, trying to escape the sound.

"Not until he confesses properly. They need to hear him say it." Half the words were in my voice, half in Rowena's. I could feel the pond water closing over my head and I struggled violently, gasping for air. No, Rowena's head. I was in the ballroom. *The ballroom.* I hadn't drowned. I clung to the scent of beeswax candles and oil lamps and the potted orange trees.

Colin released me gently to the floor and then leaped up, ploughing his fist into Wentworth's face. Blood dripped from his nose.

Rowena fell a little bit in love with Colin at that moment.

I recognised the feeling, even through the chaos.

"Confess, damn it!" Colin shouted. I crawled forward to where Wentworth had fallen.

I touched his arm, and white frostbite travelled up to his shoulder. "Say it!"

He moaned, spat blood. The frost nibbled at his chin, spread over his cheek. He shivered so violently, blood spattered over the floor. "I murdered my niece." Shards of ice fell from his lips, which were blue as bruises. Ice clumped in his eyelashes. "Make it stop! Make it stop!"

There were shocked gasps. Someone dropped a flute of champagne. The rain found its way indoors, pooling over the floors. Jasper leaned on his cane, his face hard and not entirely surprised.

Pain throbbed in my head. And then Rowena vanished so quickly, I crumpled at Lord Jasper's feet while the dancers gaped at us, still frozen in their best ball gowns. Before I passed out from exhaustion, I heard Lord Jasper's sister gasp.

"And in her underthings, no less!" Murder was less scandalous than my corset and pantalettes. She sniffed. "Like mother, like daughter."

EPILOGUE

Is she dead?"

"I don't think so. Poke her."

"You poke her!"

I didn't recognise the voices. I groaned, trying to open my eyes. The candlelight seemed impossibly bright. And the faces gathered around me weren't any more familiar than their voices had been.

"I'm not dead," I croaked at the ghosts. My throat felt like it was full of sand. Mr Rochester whined and licked my hand. A young girl gave me a gap-toothed smile. "I don't think."

The man who'd spoken first looked vaguely like a pirate. He grinned wickedly at me. I could see right through his teeth to the ceiling above him.

"There you are, lass."

"Not another ghost." My head felt like it was on fire.

He threw back his head and laughed. "Don't worry. I know exactly who killed me and I deserved it."

"She's awake!" It was Colin's voice this time, flooded with relief as he rushed towards me. "Are you hurt? Can you sit? Violet?"

The pirate winked at me. "Love, lassie. Good for you." He fell apart like smoke. The matronly woman on my other side sniffed disapprovingly at Colin. "He oughtn't be holding you like that," she complained before fading away as well. "'Tisn't seemly."

I couldn't see Rowena anywhere. I probed my memories gently, as if they were an aching tooth in my head. Some of the events were fuzzy, but at least I knew which events had happened to me and which had happened to Rowena. I was finally alone inside my head.

"Thank God," I said. I clutched my head when Colin hauled me up. "Ouch!"

"Sorry, sorry."

I'd never seen him so worried and frantic. He looked years younger and years older at the same time. His hair was dishevelled, as if he'd been shoving his hand through it. His shirt was dry and I was in a proper nightdress, which meant I'd been unconscious for a good length of time.

"Where am I?" I couldn't be sure what lay behind the glow of the candles.

"In your sitting room," Lord Jasper said mildly from a chair by the hearth. "You are quite a resourceful girl, aren't you?"

"Rowena?"

He smiled gently at me. "Gone. One would imagine she is finally at peace, thanks to you."

I sighed, relieved. "Good."

"I owe you an apology, Violet."

I blinked. "Whatever for?"

"I invited you and your mother here for my own purposes. I'd hoped a medium in the presence of the same people at the same time Rowena died might bring some of the facts to light. I had no idea."

"You knew Rowena's drowning wasn't an accident."

"I suspected not."

"What of Tabitha?" I asked. "Is she all right?"

"I'm here," she croaked from the room my mother had used on our first visit. Colin helped me shuffle over to the doorway and I collapsed against it. She was lying under a pile of blankets, looking wretched.

"I had her brought here as soon as I could," Lord Jasper explained quietly. "The doctor's been and gone. You're both to rest."

"You look dreadful," she whispered at me. I thought she might be trying to smile. I tried to smile back. I felt limp as a wilted leaf.

"You too."

"Violet?"

"Yes?"

"Thank you."

I nodded, then clutched at my head. Colin practically carried me to the empty sofa. "Might I have some water?" I drank greedily when he brought me a glass, then lay back against my pillow, exhausted. "What of Mr Travis?"

"He's recuperating at home. He had a nasty gash on his head and his leg is broken. He'll likely have a limp but he'll survive."

"And Wentworth?" I would have spat his name if I'd had the energy.

"Newgate Prison," Lord Jasper told me. "The constable's already taken him away. He won't be tried, since he's a peer, but I suspect he'll be deported. In fact, I plan to make certain of it."

"Good." I yawned. "I really don't like him," I muttered groggily. I glanced at Colin. "Thank you for punching him."

"My pleasure," he said grimly.

I struggled to peel open my third eye, which felt crusted over with sleep. Mr Rochester sat up from where he'd apparently been curled up on my lap. He looked straight at me and barked happily. I had to smile.

Tabitha watched me hopefully. "Rowena?"

I shook my head. "Gone," I whispered.

She nodded, biting her lip.

"Finally at peace." Lord Jasper touched her shoulder. "I've sent word to your father. You will, of course, stay here with us until he can be located."

"Thank you." She fiddled with her ring.

"I want you both to rest now," he added, taking Caroline and Colin with him.

<hr />

After another day of rest I woke ravenous. I ate a mountain of food and felt well enough to get dressed. Tabitha still kept to her bed though she looked as though she was improving. Elizabeth sneaked into our adjoining parlour before the breakfast tray was even cleared. She wasn't properly dressed, just swaddled in a voluminous robe.

"Oh, Violet, you're better!" she exclaimed, rushing to hug me. I hugged her back.

"I'm much better," I assured her. "I thought you'd left already."

"We're the last of the guests and we're off today. That's why I sneaked over here. Mother forbade me to talk to you." She pouted. "Which seems a fine how-do-you-do since you discovered a murderer and brought him to justice. To your own peril, I might add."

"But I did it in my underwear."

She sighed with a small grin. "Yes, that doesn't help."

I shrugged. "I'm just glad it's over."

"No sign of Rowena?"

"Not since the ball."

"That's good, isn't it?"

"I think so."

She hugged me again. "I'd best go before she comes looking for me. I'll write to you."

It occurred to me that I wasn't entirely sure where she should address her envelopes. The lease on our town house had expired and we didn't have enough money to renew it. I wasn't sure I could do enough readings to fix that particular problem. My head hurt just to think about it.

I decided to go for a walk now that I was finally out of bed. I found Colin around the back of the stables, leaning against a tree, shirtsleeves rolled up. I picked my way through the dandelions towards him. He pushed away from the oak, grinning.

"Violet."

"I was worried you'd gone back to London." I couldn't help the wide, silly smile on my face.

"As if I would leave without you," he said as if I was daft. He reached for my hand. His palm was warm and callused and comforting, even as pleasant tingles danced in my belly. "Where are you off to, then?"

"I'm going to visit Mr Travis."

"I'll come too."

We walked the hedge-lined road down to the village. Colin picked blackberries and wrapped them up in a handkerchief for later. The sun was warm on my shoulders. We stopped once so I could steal a few apples from a tree at the edge of an orchard. I gave one to Colin, remembering what he'd said about his mother's apple pie. He placed it very carefully on the low stone wall before closing his hands around my shoulders and hauling me up against him. I felt a small bundle in the top pocket of his coat. His kiss was long and slow and wicked. We stopped when a cart rumbled down the road towards us.

The village was small, with pretty cottages and a main street lined with shops. We found the painted sign for Travis and Sons Tailors and went inside, where one of Reece's brothers pointed us upstairs. Reece's very pregnant sister-in-law answered the door and led us into the bedroom.

Reece lay on a narrow bed by a window, a table cluttered with medicines beside him. There were bruises on his face, a bandage wrapped around his head and another bandage binding his leg.

"Miss Willoughby." He smiled. "I'm glad to see you're well."

"I've brought you a gift," I said gently, handing him a ribbon-wrapped pile of letters. The smell of lily-of-the-valley perfume thickened the air. "I persuaded Tabitha to give them to you." His eyes were suspiciously bright. I looked away to allow him to compose himself. Colin stood just behind me, his shoulder brushing mine.

"Thank you." Reece's hands trembled slightly when he reached for the packet. "I only kept the one," he explained. "I sent them back to her when I tried to leave her. She kept them and planned an elopement instead. I never could deny her anything." He clutched them tightly as if he meant to never let them go.

We left him so he could read them in private and headed back to Rosefield.

"I'm really going to miss it here," I told Colin. He just wound his fingers around mine, and we went up the tree-lined lane and through the forest of roses to the front door. Lord Jasper was in the foyer, finishing a consultation with Mrs Harris about dinner. A footman bowed to me, handing me a letter. I nearly groaned as I reached for it. I'd had my fill of letters lately.

This one was no better.

"Mother has left the town house," I told Colin quietly, "and has accepted Lord Marshall's protection." My mother had set herself up as a mistress. I grimaced and kept reading. "Marshall moved her into new lodgings. And as daughters are a liability to a paramour's work, I am not welcome." Colin's hand clenched at his side. "She says she was on her own at sixteen and I can be too, seeing as I stole the Spiritualist reputation she had worked so hard to maintain."

"Bollocks," Colin muttered. "Never mind, you're well rid of her."

I took a deep breath. "What shall we do now? Advertise for a position? Keep sheep?" I tried to smile.

"You'll stay here." Lord Jasper thumped his cane insistently. "You clearly need more training," he insisted. "You can't be letting spirits take up residence in your head like that, my girl."

I smiled, nervous and hopeful and grateful. "But what about Colin?" I didn't want to be greedy, but I wasn't going to abandon him. "I can't just leave him to fend for himself." I squeezed his hand.

"Never mind me," he said.

"His grandfather was a gardener," I offered helpfully.

Lord Jasper shrugged. "What's one more? We have extensive gardens. I reckon Godfrey could use the help."

"Thank you, sir," Colin replied. It wasn't ideal, but it would afford us some time to make plans of our own. And besides, he hated London.

"I can work too," I assured Lord Jasper.

He just shook his head. "You'll be working hard enough learning how to use your gifts properly." Being a medium under Lord Jasper's tutelage seemed far less disconcerting than doing so under Mother's control. "You should get some rest now," he added. "You're still recovering."

Colin walked up the stairs with me, incongruous in his plain clothes against the fine paintings and gilded banister. He was more beautiful than any antique carvings of Jasper's knightly ancestors.

"Do you mind very much?" I asked. "Being a gardener, I mean?"

"It's a sight better than being your mother's lackey," he said, brushing my hair off my face. "I don't mind hard work, never have."

I kissed him lightly and used the moment to slip the package out of the inside of his pocket. It was a white kerchief folded into a square. "What's this?"

He pretended to look put out. "Did you just pick my pocket?"

"Yes."

"Good thing it's for you then."

"It is? Really?" I'd only been teasing him when I went

through his pockets. I unwrapped it, touched. It was a small brooch made of tin, in the shape of a rose. "Oh, Colin, it's lovely. Thank you!"

"I thought the rose would remind you of this place. I suppose you don't need it now." He pinned it to my blouse, just under my collarbone. "I love you, Violet. Could you love a gardener who can't afford real silver, now that you're an earl's daughter living in a fine house?"

I leaned forward so that my lips were so close to his they brushed lightly when I spoke. "I love *you*, Colin Lennox."

His grin was crooked and wicked.

"Then we'll be just fine."

The Drake Chronicles

Two best friends
Seven handsome brothers
Hundreds of ruthless vampires

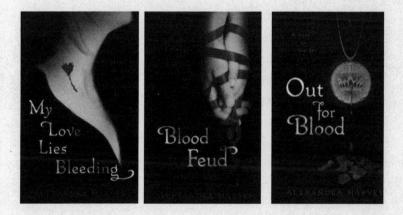

Enjoy the whole story